Psyborg

By A.J. Trimble

To God,
who kept me going through all the struggles while
writing this book and not give up on it.

Chapter 1: Just an Average Guy?

John Boyd wasn't one to expect much. After all, he knew early on he probably wouldn't do much with his life.

Even at twenty, he hadn't found a lot that stood out about him. His family was quite average. He was an only child born into a middle-class income. Even the school he went to wasn't extraordinary in any kind of way. Well, there was that one thing...

He'd managed to get a black belt in karate at the age of twelve, taking only eight months to go from white to black. Boyd knew how impressive his fighting abilities were, and had even tried to capitalize on them, applying for multiple jobs that would allow him to use his expertise. The only issue was that people didn't take "a kid's karate experience" as a true skill. He'd found a company hiring for security and decided to give it one more go, going in for an interview. It seemed like things didn't go so well once he brought up his skills, however.

"You call a black belt in karate as a kid experience for this job? That's hardly enough to qualify for this position. Sorry, bud. This interview is over," the manager said. Boyd nodded as he left the office.

***

I knew it. No one wants some kid who did karate for jobs like this, Boyd thought. It wasn't in security, but at least he had a job. As a kid, one of his favorite stores was a small retail shop called "Pang's Eats," which supplied a diversity of food from different cultures. He loved the Japanese section, especially since one of his favorite foods at that age was mochi. Though he'd usually bought it from a regular store, he was shocked by what he had been missing out on once he tried some from Pang's Eats. The store owner, Pang, had explained to him at that age that the foods sold in American stores were usually Americanized versions. Things like "mochi" in stores would usually not have the authentic taste the real foods did. This fascinated Boyd, and drew him closer to cultural foods, and the shop, even more.

When he told Pang he was looking for work, Pang offered him a job on the spot, and from seventeen, Boyd worked at the shop. He'd started as a cashier, but his hard-working attitude led him to being promoted to co-manager within a couple years. He made a modest income, but thought it would be a good job to stay at until retirement. Sure, he'd have some fun with friends and hobbies, but he didn't need anything else in life. Boyd was perfectly fine living this perfectly average life.

***

"You mind closing for me tonight?" Boyd asked. Nift was a co-worker of his, someone he had bonded with during his time at the shop. Though his real name was Bob, he went by "Nift" due to how nifty he was around the place. Boyd liked having him close the shop often, especially tonight, since it was Friday, and he wanted to binge some Netflix this weekend.

"Sure, can do, though before you leave, I meant to ask you. How'd the interview go?" Nift asked.

"Not good. As soon as they heard about my experience, they ended the interview."

"I'm sorry to hear that. You know, it's okay if you can't find work in that field. You've got a great job here; you don't need to stress yourself with another one."

"I know, I'd just hoped I would at least find someone who valued that skill. You're right, though, I'm perfectly fine staying here. Anyway, see you Monday."

"Right back at ya, Boyd," Nift said as Boyd left the shop, making the small bell chime. As he walked to his apartment, a mile away from the shop, he thought, *this job is enough for me, right?*

Soon after, his head began aching a bit. *I can't let this stress get to me*, he thought, shaking his head and increasing his pace. He started to wobble, which continued until he could no longer stand, and his face slammed into the sidewalk cement as he blacked out.

He woke up a few minutes later and immediately had a vision. He noticed that it was the city he lived in, Atlanta. It didn't look too good, though. He saw buildings falling onto the ground, with chaos ensuing everywhere. People ran all around him, some being crushed by the falling buildings, and some being blown up by lasers pouring down from the sky. He looked up and saw a giant ship. It came down, destroying an area around it as it landed, with dust engulfing the place. A few seconds later, the dust cleared, and the ship opened a hatch, revealing a gray figure in a sleeveless black jumpsuit. The figure was bald, and quite tall from what Boyd could tell. He couldn't make out his face clearly.

"You humans will pay for what you've done to us!" the figure yelled.

Chapter 2: Visions?

Boyd shook his head as soon as the vision ended. *What just...happened?* he thought, confused. *Am I letting my stress get to me this much? I might need to see a doctor.* He quickly made it back to his apartment, housed in a modestly sized building on the bottom floor. He rubbed his sore nose as he unlocked the door, walked in, shut it, and jumped into bed without a second thought. *Sleep. Yeah, that's all I need....*

***

Morning came, and as soon as he woke up, Boyd had another vision. This time, the world wasn't ending, but instead he was in one of his favorite places to eat, Grand Chicken. He was sitting at a small table with two chairs, located by a window. Across from him sat Max, his best friend since third grade.

"So this vision you had...do you think something like that could actually happen?" Max asked.

"Max, let's not kid ourselves here, that couldn't possibly happen...right?"

"Well, I've heard about cases like yours, but what evidence do they have to back it up? None. Something as extreme as being able to see into the future is just not possible," Max said as the vision ended. Boyd rose out of bed, looking around. He was in his apartment, and it was morning. *That wasn't real!?* he thought, getting out of bed. *But it felt more real than any other dream I've ever had....*

He remembered today was his meeting with Max at Grand Chicken and checked the time: 11 a.m. Luckily, he hadn't slept in too late. He was to meet with him at noon, so he had time. He decided to wait to schedule a doctor's appointment for a few days and get input from his friends and family first. He'd start with Max and see what he thought. He went to his small kitchen and poured some BowlApples, "America's favorite apple-flavored, bowl-shaped cereal!" Bowls within a bowl, essentially. He dressed in a cotton shirt with jeans, his favorite kind of clothes. Then he brushed his teeth, grabbed his wallet, and headed out the door.

Like many city folk, Boyd took an Uber to get to farther destinations within Atlanta. Fifteen minutes later, he arrived with a bit of time to spare. He went into Grand Chicken, ordered food for two, then went to sit down.

Wait...is this the same seat I sat at in my vision? he thought, closely observing the spot. It was the same type of table, with the same chairs, and even the same location by the window. Boyd wasn't sure what to think as Max came through the door and went to sit down with him.

6

"Hey, Boyd, how's it going?" Max asked.

"It's going all right," he said. "Hey, you mind if I tell you about something strange that happened to me last night?"

"Go ahead."

"Okay, so last night, I was walking home from work as usual, right? Well, on my way to the building, I got a headache suddenly, and next thing I know, I'm out cold. When I woke up, I had this vision of the city being invaded by some kind of aliens. It was chaos everywhere, with buildings falling and lasers all over the place. There was also a ship that landed and an alien who said, 'You humans will pay for what you've done.'"

"Huh, okay. So this vision you had...do you think something like that could actually happen?"

"Max, let's not kid ourselves here, that couldn't possibly happen...right?"

"Well, I've heard about cases like yours, but what evidence do they have to back it up? None. Something as extreme as being able to see into the future is just not possible."

Boyd understood at this point his other vision was playing out right in front of his eyes, but he wasn't sure what to say next. *Maybe I should just....*

"Well, Max, what if I told you I also had one this morning? And that that one was of this conversation we're having right now."

"I'd call you crazy if you weren't joking. Are you kidding me?"

"Uh, no, I'm not."

"Well then, you're definitely out of your mind. The world isn't ending anytime soon, Boyd, and either you're messing with me, or you're taking your dreams way too seriously."

Boyd decided to drop it there as the chicken sandwiches arrived, and they both scarfed them down.

***

Boyd had finally gotten around to finding a Netflix series to binge. The weirdest new trending show on the platform was a series called *Armstrong*, in which a tribe believed in cutting their own arms off, but after much struggle with conflict with other tribes, allowed a baby to be born with arms, a baby called Armstrong, the main character of the show.

Why do people like this? The premise is so strange, too strange, he thought, turning it off before the first episode had finished. Even something this weird couldn't get Boyd's mind off the visions. He knew after his meeting with Max that they were real, and that he could see into the future, but who would believe him? *No one. But I have to at least try.*

Chapter 3: Does No One Believe in Visions?

Boyd sat in thought Sunday night. He'd spent that day mainly watching more Netflix and pondering what these visions could mean. *They must be real, how else would I have seen that conversation with Max before it happened?*

He wasn't sure what to do. He knew the invasion was likely real and was going to happen. Still, what was the point of telling anybody if no one believed him? Would it really be worth losing his reputation over this? If it meant a single person believed him and was able to prepare for the inevitable? Boyd knew the right answer was yes, but wondered how the visions worked.

Come on, give me a vision! he thought, but nothing came. *Looks like it'll have to come to me naturally.* He dozed off.

***

Another vision came to Boyd the next morning.

"Do you *really* think I'm supposed to believe that, Boyd?" Mr. Pang asked. In this one, he was in Pang's office. He was an average-sized, middle-aged guy of Asian descent, wearing his usual black suit, with a white shirt and red tie. Usually he was a kind person, but clearly something was up.

"Mr. Pang, please—"

"Boyd, I can't have you talking like this around here. If you won't stop, I'll have to ask you to take a few days off and go see a doctor. Honestly, though, you *should* go see a doctor if you truly believe in this stuff. Do you understand?"

"Yes, Mr. Pang," he said in his vision, sighing. *Is it worth pushing someone who isn't willing to hear me out?*

It then ended, with Boyd quickly springing out of the bed. *Another one? And I can hear my thoughts from them, too?* He also noticed that the visions had become much less dream-like, feeling more vivid and real.

I guess I'm getting it from Mr. Pang, then. Let's get this over with, he thought, getting ready and leaving his apartment for the shop. Not long after he started his shift, Mr. Pang called him into his office. *Oh no, what's about to happen?* he thought as he went into Mr. Pang's office and sat down.

"Hello, Boyd, I called you here to let you know that I'm going to be giving you a raise soon. Business has been booming lately, and you've been a big help with that, with your hard-working attitude and how polite you are to your co-workers, so I wanted you to have one," Mr. Pang said, grinning.

"Wait, seriously?" *That's what I was called into his office for!?*

"Yes, you've earned it, Boyd."

Boyd sighed, relieved. "Thank you."

"You're welcome, but why the sigh?"

"Oh, nothing that important."

"Boyd, you know you can tell me anything. I've known you for nearly half your life, after all. I think you can rest safe knowing I won't tell anyone."

"Are you sure?"

"Well, you're making it sound pretty juicy, so go on, lay it on me."

"All right...well, recently I've been having these...visions. Basically, I was able to see a conversation with one of my friends before it happened later that day. I even saw one with you, Mr. Pang."

Pang chuckled a bit. "Now come on, Boyd, if you don't want to tell me, that's fine, but don't avoid it with stuff like this."

"I'm not avoiding it. What I'm telling you is the truth. I also had a vision of some alien species invading the city, which is most concerning to me, since it obviously hasn't occurred yet. It could soon, though."

"You serious?"

"Yes, I am."

"Do you *really* think I'm supposed to believe that, Boyd?"

"Mr. Pang, please—"

"Boyd, I can't have you talking like this around here. If you won't stop, I'll have to ask you to take a few days off and go see a doctor. Honestly, though, you *should* go see a doctor if you truly believe in this stuff. Do you understand?"

He sighed, "Yes, Mr. Pang."

"Good. You're dismissed now," Mr. Pang said. Boyd stood up and walked out of the office. *Is it worth pushing someone who isn't willing to hear me out?*

Things didn't get better from there. When trying to tell Nift about his visions, he shrugged him off, saying "Good one, Boyd. I *wish* you could do that."

When he called his parents, his mom chuckled, and his dad laughed. "That's a good one, Johnny boy...or should I say Johnny *Boyd*?"

Boyd wasn't sure what to do. He was tired of the constant rejection. At this point, there was only one thing he could think of.

Boyd, think about this rationally for a moment. You're going to be seen as crazy for this. He fought with the idea he had, but he wanted to at least get the message out there. *Remember, if just one person does something because of me, it'll be worth it.* So he went to the store and purchased a megaphone, something that would be very helpful for what he was about to do.

***

"Listen up, everyone! Listen up!" Boyd yelled into the megaphone as he patrolled the sidewalks. In a bustling city like his, plenty of people were on the streets, even later in the day. "I have had visions! An alien invasion is due for this city at any time! Please, do whatever you need to protect yourself and evacuate! Tell your friends and loved ones as well!" He said the same lines a few more times, then went to another block and did the same thing. Most people just shook their heads and kept walking—just another nut in the city. Soon enough, though, reactions began to erupt.

"Stop yelling, you're out of your mind!"

"No one cares about your crazy lies!"

"I'm calling the cops on you if you don't stop!"

It wasn't long before he was put to a stop by a local police officer.

"Hey, kid, quit the yelling!" the officer said as he approached Boyd. He promptly stopped as the officer put his arm on his shoulder.

"Listen, kid, you can't go around doing stuff like this. You can get into a lot of trouble if you disturb the public peace. Now, look, if you stop it now, I'll let you off with a warning. Deal?"

Boyd nodded and said, "Okay."

He chucked the megaphone into the nearest trash can after that disaster and slouched his shoulders. *What can I possibly do now?* he thought, out of ideas. Then he remembered the slogan of one of his favorite stores.

When you're down, go to Gamers Crown! Excited, he headed toward the direction of the store. He thought it'd be a good idea to get his mind off this vision situation, seeing as he had no clue when the invasion would happen. It could be a long time for all he knew. Plus, he'd been wanting to expand his video game collection, so it was the perfect time to visit.

He entered the familiar, giant store, which housed two floors of gaming goodness. Shelves on the walls were lined with the latest offerings of games, continuing down to older and older selections all the way back to the 1970's. Boyd glanced over at the worker at the reception counter, and realized he was new. *Maybe he would believe my visions. After all, he's probably a nerd*, he thought, walking up to the counter.

"How's it going...Joei?" he asked, looking at the worker's name tag.

"Going all right. It's my second day here, and so far the job seems decent enough," Joei said. He was a white guy about Boyd's age. He was skinnier, though, and a bit taller, too. He had very messy hair, as opposed to Boyd's more refined style, and it was very curly and very orange. He wore the employee red shirt with black pants.

"Good to hear. My name's Boyd, and I've got something I think you'd want to hear."

Joei raised an eyebrow. "Maybe you do. Why don't you tell me what you're thinking?"

"Okay, so the premise is that a few days ago, while walking home from work, I blacked out on the sidewalk. When I woke up, I had this...vision. It was about these grayish-skinned aliens invading the city. Lasers were—"

"Hold on, did you say 'grayish-skinned aliens'? Tell me more about them."

"Um, all right, I only saw one, but he had this black jumpsuit on, with no sleeves. He was bald for some reason, and also quite tall. He said, 'You humans will pay for what you've done to us!'"

Joei stood there for a moment, in thought, before saying, "Boyd, I believe you're the warrior I've been told about by my grandfather. You're lucky you caught me right at closing time, so let me lock up real quick, and we'll head to my place. I think I've got some valuable information for you."

Boyd stood there for a few seconds in awe. *Is this guy serious!?*

15

Chapter 4: Saving the World with What?

Joei lived several blocks from the store, so it took them a bit to get there. Joei started walking down an alley.

"Do you live in a dumpster or something?" Boyd asked hesitantly.

"No, down here," Joei said, waving at him. Sure enough, on the side of the building to their right was a door, which Joei unlocked and went through. After going down a flight of stairs, Boyd was met with a room that was akin to a garage in size. Near the stairs were multiple workbenches, strewn with tools and metal parts. At the back of the room was a bed, with a toilet and sink near it. There were also stacks of chairs, and even a few tables on the other side of the room. The area was dimly lit by some fluorescent lighting on the ceiling.

"Okay, Joei, can you explain what you were talking about? Why have you brought me here?"

"Let me explain. As I said back at Gamer's Crown, I believe you could be the guy my grandfather mentioned to me."

"Okay…but what did he tell you, exactly?"

"Essentially, he had a vision similar to the one you mentioned having, saying aliens would come to invade this planet. He also believed someone would be there to stop them, and considering you had a vision like that, maybe you're the warrior he was talking about."

"*Me*? A *warrior*? There's no way I could do that, that alien looked huge!"

"Well, do you have any offensive skills?"

"I mean, kind of, I got a black belt in karate when I was twelve."

"I'd consider that to be some pretty good fighting experience, Boyd, and a great starting point to becoming Earth's defender."

"Okay, but these aliens don't seem like something a mere human could handle. How would I get around that hurdle?"

"With these," Joei said, grabbing some metal gloves off the table and showing them to Boyd.

"What…are those?"

"Well, as you can see, they're metal gloves, but they're more than that. Each of these have two small air propulsions on them, which detect a quick or strong movement a person makes, which activates them, releasing a small but powerful burst of air that propels the punch in the direction it's moving. They allow it to be *much* stronger than it normally would be. According to my calculations, they should be able to release double the power your average boxer can pull off, and that's before considering the power of the hit without the propulsions. They were inspired by my dad's inventions, which sadly went too far and ended up killing him."

"Oh, wow, I'm sorry to hear that, Joei."

"It's okay, it's been years since it happened. He had been testing out metal gloves, similar to these, that could fire off laser shots. Unfortunately, during one of the tests, one of them backfired, shooting into his body and killing him within seconds. What really hurts, though, is that aside from close family, nobody cared about his death. After all, everyone thought he was just a lunatic, but truthfully, he was a genius that was far ahead of his time. He was able to take the technology of our current time and make it into something that you wouldn't see for at least several decades with normal technological development. Sure, a lot of his stuff wasn't the safest, and people thought he went too far for that, but it never was a real issue. Not until he died from his own creation, of course." Joei walked over to a shelf and tossed Boyd a magazine. Boyd read the front. It was a *Time* magazine, with what appeared to be Joei's dad on the front. It read, "World's Most Insane Mad Scientist" in a giant font.

"What an awful thing to slap on a cover."

"Yeah, I know. One thing I should mention though, is that my dad didn't like building weapons for the fun of it, and it wasn't technology built to assist in human wars, either. He built those weapons for the inevitable alien invasion. Originally, I thought maybe I was the one who'd have to be up to that task. Sure, I don't have much fighting experience, but with these metal gloves and my self-defense knowledge, I figured I'd have to take up that job. Now, after hearing about your vision, I see that you're definitely the warrior, Boyd. What's worse, the fact that you had a vision about it means it's probably happening soon."

"How soon?"

"I don't know. All I know is that I don't think we have long. Boyd, I need to know: Are you willing to take up the task of being Earth's warrior against this invasion, and fight until the very end?"

"J-Joei, that's a lot of responsibility to put on a guy like me. I'm just an average guy, after all. How could an average joe like me ever do such a thing?"

"Are you so ordinary, though? You have fighting experience, firstly, but you also had a vision that was similar to my grandfather's. It feels like it was meant for you to be the warrior of this planet. Can you at least try out these metal gloves on the punching bag over there?" Joei asked, pointing to a black one hanging beside the stacked chairs. Boyd simply stared at the gloves for a moment.

19

Those gloves are pretty nice looking, he thought.

"Fine, I'll give them a go. That doesn't mean I'm for sure helping you with this, though," Boyd said, taking the gloves and putting them on. He walked over to the bag and readied a punch. He went for it, and halfway through, the propulsions went off, sending his fist straight through it. His arm slipped out as he fell flat on his face. "Well, that didn't go so well, did it?"

"I'd say the contrary. You're not used to punching with that kind of power, and I was never able to break through that bag with my punches. If you decide to become Earth's warrior and train with these, you'll learn on your own how to control them. Truthfully, I have no clue how to control them myself, but maybe an experienced fighter like you can. Please consider this...it could mean the difference between Earth being saved and it being destroyed. How about I give you a day to make up your mind, and you can tell me what you decided tomorrow evening at Gamer's Crown?"

Boyd thought for several seconds about this. "I can do that. Same time as before?"

"Yes, that'd work well. Then I could close the store, and we'd be able to get straight to training you."

"Okie dokie, I'll let you know what my decision is tomorrow, then."

"Sounds good. I'll see you then."

"Yeah, you too," Boyd said, walking up the stairs and leaving. *There's no way a normal guy like me could ever do something that amazing, right? Is a black belt in karate really enough to fight off aliens? Could I truly be the warrior?*

Chapter 5: Can I Save the World?

Boyd had thought hard over his decision, contemplating it multiple times. *Is this the right choice?* It didn't matter now, though, because after hours of agonizing, he had made up his mind. That day after work, he headed to Gamer's Crown to share his decision with Joei.

Okay, but is this really what I want to do? Yes! Now go tell him! he thought to himself, heading to the cashier counter.

"Okay, Joei, I've decided: I'll be your warrior and do whatever it takes to take these aliens down!"

"Woohoo! I knew you'd do it! My man! Let's head to my place." Joei closed and led Boyd back to his home.

***

"The first thing you need to land is your weight distribution. As you probably figured out the hard way, the force the gloves give off moves you forward, and if you can't control it, it makes you fall, too. You need to figure out how to balance yourself when they go off so that you don't fall every time you use them. Personally, I have no clue how to do that, as I'm not skilled enough in combat, but maybe you can," Joei said, grabbing a different set of gloves.

"Of course, I'd rather you not train with the actual ones yet, because that could result in them being damaged, so I made these up last night in case you decided, you know, yes. They weigh twenty-five pounds combined, so they should be perfect for you to train with. Try them out."

Joei handed them to Boyd, who observed them. They were regular boxing gloves with weights shoved into them. He put them on and took a swing, which caused him to fall on his face.

"As I figured, you're not used to punching with that kind of weight. I'd recommend trying to go slow at first and working up to faster punches once you figure out how to handle that kind of strength," Joei said. Boyd nodded, and tried slower punches, which seemed to work. Things didn't go anywhere for a while, with the issue of balance still being a problem. After half an hour of punching, he was becoming discouraged.

Anytime I try to go faster, I nearly fall.

"Joei, are you sure this is the way to go? I feel like I'm not making any progress."

"This isn't about working up to a larger force. It's about getting there and figuring out how to handle it once you release it. That's the key to getting this to work."

Suddenly, Boyd got an idea. *Will that actually work, though...?* There was only one way to find out. He gave a strong punch, and let the force guide his body. Although he nearly fell in the process, he managed to keep himself upright, having moved a bit from his original spot.

"Well done, Boyd. You have figured out what I could not. After seeing that, I think I'll let you try out the real deal," Joei said, handing the real gloves to him. He took off the ones he had on, dropped them to the floor beside him, and quickly put on the others. He concentrated for a few seconds and then went for it, letting the energy move him. He nearly fell, having to jump to keep him from falling, but he managed to land on his feet. "Well, you make this look effortless, considering the actual ones are way stronger than those practice gloves."

"Oh, really? I *definitely* didn't notice that."

"Seriously? I tried both out; the actual gloves are far harder to control."

"Man, you really don't understand sarcasm? It was a joke, Joei; I nearly fell trying to use the real ones."

"Ah, understood. I patched up the punching bag after you tore through it yesterday, so now you can train with it again. Just make sure not to jab it too hard, or you'll find yourself in the same situation as yesterday."

"Noted," Boyd said, walking over to the bag to begin training.

***

After only an hour with the gloves, Boyd had become quite comfortable using them, being able to make the bag roll in circles around the chain with his gloved punches.

"All right, I think I've had enough for now. These gloves really do work well," Boyd said, handing them back to Joei.

"Your mastery over them has improved significantly from when we started. I think in just a few days' time, we could be seeing the rise of the Earth's warrior."

"That's a big title. Let's wait until I actually do something of significance before I'm called that, okay?"

"You clearly are skilled enough for it, so I'd say it's fitting."

"Am I, though? For so many years, I've been the 'normal' guy, someone who couldn't get a job with the one thing that might have made him special, and now I'm expected to do *this?* It's a lot, Joei, and even now I feel unsure about it all." Boyd's head went low as he put his hand to his face. Joei stepped over to him and put his hand on his shoulder.

"I may not know you too well, but what I do know is that you're far from ordinary. What you've shown here today is proof that you're the person who can do this. Your skill, combined with my technology, will be able to put a stop to whatever those aliens have in store for us, so don't sell yourself short."

Boyd lifted his head and gave a small smile.

"Thanks, Joei. There's actually a couple of questions I wanted to ask you," he said, pulling up a chair from the stack of them and sitting down.

"Okay, what're you thinking?"

"Well, I was thinking, since you're so smart and have these technological creations you've made, why don't you have a proper lab? Why do you live in this warehouse-looking place underneath a building?"

"I told you about my father, Boyd. It's unfortunately because of him that I couldn't achieve a proper education and get into the university I wanted to. Anytime I tried to apply, they'd soon figure out I was the son of Hoover Parett, the 'nutty scientist' who ended up killing himself with his own contraptions. Thinking I was just like him, they'd reject me. I managed to find low-paying jobs like the one at Gamer's Crown, where no one cared about my reputation, and I found this old storage area that I could rent for cheap and use as my home. It's not luxurious by any means, but it gets the job done."

"Yeah, but you deserve better, Joei. If everything goes well, and we save Earth, I wanna help you get a better place to work on your inventions and stuff."

"Well, that's very kind of you, but you don't have to do that."

"A smart guy like you deserves it." He stood up, ready to head home. "Have a good night, Joei."

"To you as well, Boyd," Joei said as Boyd went up the stairs.

As he opened the door that led to the alley, he noticed something tall run by out of the corner of his eye. It appeared to be inhuman, so he went down the alley and peeped at the sidewalk where it had gone, and saw a very tall figure, taller than any human he'd ever seen. The figure was wearing a black hoodie and black pants. It then turned around stared at Boyd.

The same face as the alien from my vision! He quickly swung back in the alley and put his back against the building. He couldn't believe what he had seen. *Was that my mind playing tricks?* he thought. As he turned to look again, the tall alien now towered over him. Boyd stood there, frozen in shock.

"Did you really think I wouldn't see you here?" it said.

Chapter 6: The Aliens Are Coming! Time to Fight!

"**Well**, now that you've seen my face, I can't let you go free," the alien said in a raspy tone.

"Get away from me, alien, or I'll have no choice but to fight you," Boyd said. *What am I doing!?*

"'Alien' is a subjective term, is it not? I could call you an alien, but does that mean you *are* one? Plus, what can a human like you do against me?"

The alien then went for a right hook. Boyd barely had any time to dodge and was struck in the side, slamming into the brick wall.

W-wow, this guy could've killed me if I'd gotten hit directly!

"This is your last chance. Come without defiance, or die," he said.

"I'm not going anywhere with you!" Boyd yelled, going in for a hit. The creature easily dodged and went for his face. Boyd only had enough time to cover his face as the alien drove him into the ground. He looked at his hands and saw blood.

Man, this guy nearly broke my nose even with my hands in front of it! Boyd thought, knowing this was serious business. Since he didn't have his gloves, he tried using his karate abilities instead, taking a stance and going for a punch. This time, the alien stood still until he got near, and he put his hand in front of Boyd's swinging fist. The impact didn't move him.

"Well, looks like you're all talk. You humans truly *are* pathetic!" he said, going for another hit. Boyd managed to narrowly dodge by doing a backflip, putting distance between them. "Let's make this one my last, shall we?"

The alien ran toward him while readying a punch.

I gotta get to the lab, Boyd thought as he ran to Joei's door. The alien jumped right in front of him before he could get there.

"Don't try to run from me. Nobody can help you now."

Boyd felt hopeless, until his gaze shifted to the alien's legs, seeing the gloves between them on the ground.

Thank you, Joei! he thought as he dove at them, managing to grab them and shove them on. The alien attempted to strike him, but Boyd stopped him with a gloved punch to the jaw, dropping him to the ground.

"My jaw! You'll pay for that, you brat!" he said as he scrambled to his feet and pounced toward Boyd. Though he was still quicker, he couldn't do anything about Boyd's stronger punches. As he neared him, Boyd decided to end it, putting both of his fists together side-by-side and punching the alien's gut. Squishing noises could be heard as Boyd's punches landed, and moments later, the alien went flying across the alleyway, landing near the edge. Boyd waited a few seconds before determining he had been knocked out.

"Is he out?" Joei asked, peeking through his door.

"Yes, he is. Thanks for the gloves. How did you know I was in trouble?" Boyd asked, out of breath.

"Well, it was kind of hard not to hear the fighting noises from inside my lab, so I knew something was going on, and decided to place them right in front of my door, hoping you'd see them."

"Ah, okay. What do we do with this guy now, though?"

"Let's tie him up in my lab and try to get some info out of him," Joei said, running downstairs to get some rope.

***

Joei had decided to play it safe and tie multiple layers of rope around the alien and sit him in one of the fold-up chairs. They could get a better look at him now. He certainly looked different from a human, having a flatter nose with longer nostrils. His skin tone was also gray, just like in Boyd's vision. Every part of his body was also longer, including his fingers. His hair was black, and was so short that they had to feel his head to see if he was bald.

30

"I'm not saying anything!" the alien yelled. Boyd knocked him down, taking the chair with him.

"We sub-humans are taught to never give in when it comes to the annihilation of our species!"

"Sub-humans, eh? Aren't you guys the ones who are trying to annihilate us?" Boyd asked.

"Our kind has been oppressed, so we're simply taking our due and destroying those who try to fight us."

"All right then, tell us why you're invading Earth," Joei said.

"How do you know about that? Plus, why should I tell you? You're the ones who originally rejected our kind and despised us."

"Because if you don't, I'll pummel you until you can't stand anymore. Now, elaborate," Boyd said, readying his fist.

"All right. You *really* wanna know why we hate you guys so much? It's because—"

The wall where Joei's stairs were located exploded, sending the three flying to the other side of the giant room. Boyd looked up and saw nothing but chaos outside. People were running everywhere, with lasers pouring down from the sky destroying everything.

"Haha! My kind has finally arrived! You'll never be able to beat them all!" the sub-human said, laughing maniacally. Boyd only stared at the mayhem.

I'm...I'm not ready for this yet!

Chapter 7: I'm not ready! Can I Get an Upgrade, Please?!

The sub-human managed to break free of the chair and run toward the opening in the building, quickly disappearing. Boyd and Joei climbed up the stairs, which were somehow still intact, and they saw the invasion in its terrifying glory.

Multiple buildings had already fallen, and bodies could be seen everywhere. They walked toward the sidewalk and saw crowds of people running in every direction. They also saw a ship slow its descent in an area where multiple buildings once stood, now turned to rubble. The entrance to the ship opened, falling into place as a ramp. A sub-human walked down to the bottom of the ramp, yelling, "You humans will pay for what you've done to us!"

"This is the first vision I had, Joei! It's here!" Boyd said.

"Yeah, but you aren't ready for this yet! You've barely had any training, and although you're getting better, you'll need to improve further in order to defeat them!" Joei cried.

"You're right, let's go!"

They started running, trying to find any building where they might be safe. It wasn't long before he started having doubts.

You've made this decision to be Earth's warrior and you're running? Serve up justice, save humanity! Boyd thought. *Even if I haven't trained long enough, I have to at least try.*

With that, he put his gloves back on, turned around, and started running in the other direction.

"Boyd, what are you doing? Come back!"

"I have to serve my part as a warrior, even if I haven't had enough training," Boyd said, slamming his fist into the nearest sub-human. Other ones noticed, though, and soon a dozen of them surrounded Boyd.

Now what am I gonna do? Boyd thought. Desperate, he threw a punch at the two sub-humans in front of him, knocking them down. He took the opportunity to run toward Joei, who had caught up with him.

"I admire your courage, Boyd, but you're not strong enough to take on multiple sub-humans like that yet!"

"I see that now, and I'm sorry. Let's focus on getting away from these guys for now, okay?"

Joei nodded as the two ran from the group. They turned a corner and saw large piles of debris everywhere, deciding to hide in one of the piles. The sub-humans took a quick glance before leaving the area. Once they were gone, Joei and Boyd climbed out of the pile and took a look around.

"Where can we settle for now?" Joei asked.

***

After an hour of walking past destroyed buildings and mangled bodies, they managed to come across a grocery store that was mostly intact, but abandoned. When they got inside, they noticed the power was somehow still on, but the place was quite messy, with food and other items being strewn across the ground. They sat down at the cashier aisles and talked.

"Boyd, do you have any idea how poor your decision back there was? You could have gotten killed, and it would have all been over!" Joei said, unable to keep his composure.

"I felt like I had to do something! People were dying all around us, and it felt wrong to just run away. Is that what 'Earth's Warrior' would do?"

Joei took a deep breath, regaining his composure. "You have no chance as you are now, and you realized that after getting into a conflict with more than one of them. A single sub-human is one thing, but you're gonna have to fight off a bunch in order to save humanity, and that's not something you're up for yet."

35

"You're right, and like I said before, I'm sorry about that. I have to ask, though, if you don't think how I am now is gonna cut it, then what will?"

"Well, after seeing how fast those sub-humans are, I realized a pair of gloves wasn't going to do the job. It appears my grandfather wasn't just talking about pure strength when it came to them."

"What do you mean?"

"I neglected to tell you this, but my grandfather had a bit of knowledge on the aliens—the sub-humans—which he acquired through his visions. Things such as the fact that they're ten times stronger than your average human. I figured he meant in fighting strength, but it seems I failed to account for the fact that he could've also meant speed. Those sub-humans back there were gaining on us fast, so I'm sure that's what he meant. Because of this, I've made the decision to build you a pair of propulsion boots to go with your gloves."

"That's great to hear, Joei, though how would those work?"

"Basically, instead of giving an extra 'punch' to your punches, you'd be getting an extra 'kick' from your kicks. They could also help you run faster, which would be very beneficial against the sub-humans, who are clearly faster than your average human."

"Gotcha. What do you want me to do until then?"

"Stay low and train here. If you get taken and killed, humanity is doomed. I'll make sure to be careful, as I'll need to go outside to gather materials to build the boots. With so many buildings in pieces, I'm sure I can find what I need."

Boyd did as Joei said, staying low and continuing to train himself to become even better with the gloves. He also dug into some of the snack aisles as well whenever he got hungry. He'd managed to find a video game console in the break room, which he'd play whenever he finished training for the day. He'd tried to get in contact with his friends and family, and although he reached his family, who told him they had evacuated the area, he'd heard nothing from Nift, Max, or Mr. Pang.

I hope y'all are okay, Boyd thought.

Despite Joei coming in and out of the building to check up on Boyd, he'd never seen him with the boots.

He must be saving them somewhere so that if we're found here, they don't get ahold of them, Boyd thought.

A few days later, Joei returned from one of his many trips outside the grocery store and showed Boyd something on his phone.

"The situation's gotten worse, Boyd. Look at this," Joei said, playing the newscast.

"The invasion in Atlanta has only become worse, with thousands confirmed missing as of today, as well as much of the city going to ruins. Although none are confirmed dead, it is presumed that many of the thousands missing are deceased, as multiple viral clips from social media showed buildings falling, lasers being shot down from the sky by the ship, and foreign invaders coming after the humans. Local news channels have had a very difficult time making it near the city, as it's been confirmed that getting too close could result in the attempted intruder being shot down by the foreign invader's ship. We saw this with the incident Channel Five had when they attempted to fly a helicopter into the city and were shot down. President Clark has said today that he is working on sending military forces to the city to stop the foreign invaders from progressing and has already issued a quarantine for the city. Residents in neighboring areas are being told to evacuate to avoid any trouble with the foreign invaders," the newswoman said.

"You weren't kidding, that's awful," Boyd said.

"Yeah, I know. Have you heard from any friends or family of yours?"

"My family is okay, but I have no clue about my friends. What about you?"

"All I had was my dad. My mom died when I was little. The good news is that I've been making progress on the propulsion boots, helped by the fact that a few survivors I met led me to some materials I was able to use. I can't tell you where they are for now, only that I'll bring them back here as soon as I'm done with them. If the sub-humans find us before then, we'll have to move to the spot the boots are located at."

"Is there a reason you're hiding them?"

"Yes. To them, those boots are weapons, and they'd take the first chance they got to destroy them if they knew of their existence. We can't risk that if we get found here."

"What changes when they're in a different spot?"

"I've put them in a mostly inactive area. The only time there's movement in that place is when I'm working on them, so they're much less likely to find them there."

"Right. I guess I'll have to focus on getting better with my gloves for now, then."

Being nighttime, the two headed to bed.

***

A week later, a sub-human managed to find them, and they were on the run again. The ambush had happened right before Joei was getting ready to leave, so they were able to run away together.

"I don't think we're gonna be able to hide from them this time, and they're catching up quick!" Joei said.

"I know. I think I've got an idea, though. Can you trust me?" Boyd asked.

"Sure, just tell me quickly!"

"All right, get on my back."

"What—" Joei said before being lifted onto Boyd's back.

Please work, Boyd thought as he crouched down onto the ground and punched it with his gloves, cracking the concrete and causing them to jump into the air. The impact sent them flying into the building on their right, crashing through a window and being thrown into an office room.

"Don't make a sound," Boyd whispered. Joei nodded as he got up and crouched. The two laid low for a few minutes, listening for any signs of the sub-humans. Surprisingly, there was nothing to be heard. "Wait, did we actually lose them?"

Joei peeked through the window they had crashed through.

"Apparently so; I don't see them anywhere." The two let out a sigh of relief as they stood up.

"I could have done that easily with the boots. Can I finally see where they're at?"

"You're not wrong. I'll go ahead and take you there."

After half an hour of walking around the open land where buildings once stood, they came across the warehouse where the boots were.

"So this is where you've been working on the boots." Boyd stated.

"Yes, the building isn't too far from the grocery store we were staying at, so I chose it as the workplace for the boots, since the sub-humans haven't found it yet. Now that we're here, I can finally show them to you," Joei said as they entered the warehouse. The place seemed to be long-abandoned, with cobwebs and bugs having taken over. In one of the office rooms was a desk, from which Joei opened a drawer and took out a pair of metal boots. "With these, you'll be properly equipped to deal with the sub-humans." Boyd's eyes widened at the sight of them.

Chapter 8: Training Time! Propeller Propulsion!

"**Wow**, I'm impressed with what you came up with in such a short amount of time. How do I use them?" Boyd asked.

"What you're gonna do is put them on and try to take a step in them hard enough to activate them. They'll be difficult to use at first, but the goal is to get you to be able to walk and run faster with these on. They'll give your kicks additional strength as well, of course," Joei said. Boyd put them on and tried taking a step, which caused the propulsions to activate. Unfortunately, they didn't deactivate, so Boyd fell flat on his face as he spun around in circles. Joei ran over to deactivate the boot.

"I take it they're not finished?" Boyd asked.

"They're basically done, but I hadn't tested them properly, so I couldn't gauge any issues that could arise in a real situation. Give me a bit to fix that up, and they should be good to go. Also, I haven't asked in a while, but have you had any visions recently?"

"No, and honestly, I haven't been focusing on them. I've been working on training more to prepare myself against the sub-humans. It makes me wonder if that's why I haven't been having visions recently...."

"Well, I'm gonna work on the boots, and you can continue training for the rest of the day. If you'd like to, you can beat up on some of the defunct equipment in this ware-house."

Boyd nodded as he left the office to go look for some junk to demolish with his gloves.

***

The next morning, Boyd woke up and was greeted by his first vision in a while, with a horde of sub-humans surrounding him in this one, walking closer and closer to him as they made it harder for him to escape. One took the initiative and pounced at him. The last thing he noticed before the vision ended was the familiarity of the location: The very warehouse they were staying in.

Joei needs to hear about this! Boyd thought as he ran to find Joei. He was sitting in the office, working on the boots.

"Joei, you're not going to believe this, but I—"

"Morning, Boyd. You mind trying these boots on for me again? I think I worked out the technical glitches in them that you were having issues with yesterday," Joei said as he handed the boots to him. He didn't hesitate and slipped them on. He tried the same thing as yesterday, and the issue was solved; he was able to walk around in them quicker than he normally could, and now without falling over.

"All right, now that we've confirmed those are fixed, what were you saying?" Joei asked.

"Okay, so basically, I had my first vision in a while. I saw these sub-humans walking closer and closer to me, forming a circle I couldn't get out of. The only other thing I remember is that it took place in this warehouse."

"Well, that's not good. That means we can't stay here much longer. I've been wondering if you can hone your visions to the point where you can see your opponent's next move. You'd become a much better fighter with an ability like that. That's for the future, though; I'd like you to focus on getting used to the boots first."

Boyd agreed, and went to the largest machine in the warehouse, some sort of oven. He took several kicks at it, sending metal pieces flying around the warehouse. After half a dozen hits, the oven was little more than scrap metal. Joei applauded, saying, "Your fighting abilities never cease to impress me, Boyd. You've barely used the boots at all and yet you've already figured out how to use them. Great job."

"Thanks, but you know I've had a lot of practice with my gloves. It was natural that the skills from that were gonna carry over to my boots. Still, I wanna develop some cool signature moves for myself, like this one," Boyd said as he jumped onto the ground, landing on his hands. He held himself up with his hands as he kicked the air, causing his entire body to spin a-round with his legs out.

"It's like a propeller, so I think I'll call it 'Propeller Propulsion.' It can knock out multiple enemies at a time, and more importantly, enemies all around me. I feel creative moves like this will help me get better at fighting with them."

"Anything to improve your combat skills is a plus. You may not have much more time to train here, though. While looking for food early this morning, I saw some sub-humans near the warehouse. It'll only be a matter of time before they find us, so I wanted you to be prepared if they break down the door and go after us."

"Well, you saw my skills. I bet I can fight off any sub-human that comes at us," Boyd said as he kicked the air, causing him to jump and fall flat on his face.

"Go train some more, why don't you?" Joei smirked.

***

A few days later, as Boyd slept and Joei was preparing to go scavenging for food, he saw a gray face peep through one of the windows from the corner of his eye. As he glanced toward it, the face quickly disappeared.

"Boyd, wake up! We gotta get out of here. The sub-humans have found us!" Joei yelled, running to his friend. Boyd awoke, dazed.

"What'd you say...?"

"Sub-humans, Boyd! We gotta go!"

45

Boyd nodded, slapped himself fully awake, and put his gloves and boots on. They ran to the door, but a group of sub-humans was already there to greet them.

"You thought you could foil our plans? Get 'em, boys!" one of them said as they quickly surrounded them. They started walking closer and closer, making the circle smaller.

You know what to do, Boyd, he thought as he readied himself. As soon as one of the sub-humans pounced at him, he slammed his foot into its head, sending it to the ground. He landed on his hands as he yelled, "Joei, get down! Propeller Propulsion!" and kicked the entirety of the sub-humans in the circle, sending them all to their backs and knocking them out. He jumped off the center one and landed on his feet.

"Impressive, Boyd. Now come on, before they get up!" Joei said, bursting through the exit. Boyd followed, and they ran off into the outskirts of the city.

Chapter 9: The Plan to Stop the Invasion. Let's Take Down the Sub-humans!

For the second time, both Boyd and Joei evaded capture. They soon found themselves in the outermost parts of the city, where even this far out buildings had been laid to waste. The two continued to walk farther out, getting close to the suburbs.

"Do you think the suburbs are okay?" Boyd asked.

"I'm not sure, but the fact that buildings this far out are destroyed has me feeling not great about them. We'll have to go check them out ourselves. What's also odd is that while scavenging for food, I've noticed the ship that once lay near the center of the city is gone now, meaning it could be anywhere by now."

"That's not good. How do we figure out where it is?"

"We'll need to find a house that has a working TV in it to check the news. I'd check my phone, but the service is terrible out here, and we need to find resources anyway, so it would be quite beneficial to find one."

There was still one thing they had to get past. After a quarantine had been placed onto Atlanta, groups of troops were placed across the border of the city. They'd already dealt with worse, so they knew it would be easy to handle. Once they reached the border, Joei hopped on Boyd's back as they jumped across the group with Boyd's boots, making a quick getaway.

Though it took a few hours, they managed to find an empty home. It was a modest, one-story home with rustic, brown-wood siding and a black-tiled roof. A carport was attached to the left of the home, where a small red car was housed. The two entered through the front door and noticed the mess inside. Everything was strewn about, furniture flipped over, and food all over the kitchen attached to the living room.

"All right, you go check out the other rooms for a TV, and I'll go through the mess in the living room," Joei said. Boyd nodded as he took a quick glance into the kitchen, not finding a TV in it. He went to the hallway beside the kitchen and started looking in the bedroom at the end of the hallway. After only a few seconds, he saw the giant TV on the ground.

"Joei! I found one!"

"Already ahead of you, Boyd. I just found one myself here. Help me out."

Boyd ran back into the living room and helped Joei lift the TV onto the dresser. They then plugged it in and turned it on. It was already tuned into the news channel.

"We have an update on the alien invasion from Atlanta, as law enforcement is now investigating a ship that's landed in Time Square. It touched down only fifteen minutes ago, and the area is being evacuated as we speak. Officials are saying that the ship is the same as the one that landed in Atlanta just a few weeks ago, as viral clips confirm," the male news reporter said. Joei shut the TV off.

"That's exactly the information we needed. We have our plan now: Get to New York City as quickly as we can. Boyd, start looking for car keys."

"What? Joei, you're kidding."

"What other choice do we have? Not only have these people probably been gone for a while and aren't coming back anytime soon, but we have no shot of getting there on time without the car. Now please, help me find the keys."

"I suppose you make a fair point, but don't we need some food as well?"

"Of course! You can do that instead while I look for the keys," Joei said as Boyd started rummaging through the cupboards for food. He found a few cans of beans and soup, as well as packs of chips and crackers lying around the kitchen deck. The fridge was scarce, but had a few packs of Lunchables in it, plus some sliced cheese. Once he found a jar of peanut butter, he decided they had enough food.

"Any luck with finding the keys?" Boyd asked.

"Unfortunately not; I think we'll need to use an alternative solution."

"That being?"

"Follow me," Joei said, leading him to the red car. "Can you smash the driver's window for me?"

"I guess...."

Boyd stepped toward the window and punched right through the glass. With the click of a button inside the car, the door opened, and Joei hopped inside, pulling out a few tools as he went through the internal wiring of the car. After only a minute, he managed to successfully start the car.

"Hop in, Boyd. We're going to New York."

Chapter 10: Road Trip! Let's Go Save the World!

Boyd still felt guilty for stealing someone's car, but he knew there wasn't any other choice if he wanted to get to New York on time. "How long is it gonna take to get there?"

"The phone is saying thirteen hours from here, so I'd be getting settled in for the night if I were you, Boyd, since we'll be trying to get some final training in at midnight to fully prepare you for New York," Joei said. Boyd gazed at his own phone and realized it was five thirty in the evening already. He reclined his seat and settled in as sleep slowly came to him.

***

Boyd was startled as he felt himself being shaken by Joei. It was midnight. He got out of the car and put his gloves on. He noticed they'd stopped in a grassy field in what appeared to be the middle of nowhere.

"Where are we, exactly?" Boyd asked.

"We're in North Carolina currently, close to Virginia. Anyway, I want to try and train your visions so you can see your opponent's next move. I'm going to come at you with my punches, and you need to rely solely on your visions to dodge them. If you don't see a vision, don't dodge," Joei said as he prepared to make his first punch. Boyd concentrated as Joei went for it. No vision. He continued concentrating on forcing a vision, but as the punches continued coming, nothing happened.

What else am I supposed to do? he thought to himself as the punches kept hammering him.

"I'm surprised, Joei. Your punches are harder than I expected from someone like you."

"You can thank a self-defense class I took for that. My punches are optimally made to transfer as much power as possible through them."

"I guess that would explain how toothpick arms like yours can pack a punch like that," he teased. Joei's punches got stronger after that remark, and Boyd made more of an effort to make a vision happen as he continued taking hits. Suddenly, a vision overcame him as he saw Joei throw an uppercut. He went to dodge but got slammed in the chin, being knocked back onto the grass.

"That was a pretty bad dodge. Why'd you do that?" Joei asked.

"I saw a vision of you going for an uppercut, so I dodged accordingly. I guess it was in the more distant future, though."

"So maybe higher stakes can force visions...let's keep going; hopefully we can improve your vision skills to see your opponent's next move instead of a distant one," Joei said as they went back to training.

Over an hour later, Boyd hadn't gotten any better, and he was becoming discouraged.

"I don't think I'm going to improve in such little time. Maybe we should call it quits for tonight," he said, sitting on the grass.

"How about we go for another hour? I believe you can get this down."

Boyd reluctantly agreed as they continued. Sure e-nough, half an hour later, a vision came, and he saw Joei throw a sucker punch at him, and he dodged as such. It ended, and he saw Joei attempt a sucker punch and dodged it.

"W-wow, you were right! I guess I really can get the hang of this!" he said.

"Indeed you can. Do you happen to remember what you felt that may have made you have that vision?"

Boyd thought about it for a moment before saying, "No, I don't really know how it happened. All I know is that I saw the vision and it happened to be your next attack."

"Good thing we've got another thirty minutes before we have to start driving again. Let's see if we can figure out what causes you to have these specific visions," Joei said, throwing a punch at him as the two started training yet again.

Right at the end of the remaining thirty minutes, Boyd saw a vision of Joei going for a right hook, and he avoided it.

"Right at the end of our training! Did you notice anything that might have triggered it?" Joei asked.

"Nope, it came to me so suddenly without warning. The only faint thing I can think of is adrenaline."

"That's a start to figuring it out. For now, let's get back on the road."

The two then walked back to the car.

"How much longer do we have, anyway?" Boyd asked.

"We still have eight hours to go, so I would try to get as much sleep as possible so you're ready for tomorrow. Who knows what fight awaits us in New York."

They got into the car and started driving again. Boyd reclined the seat as he went to sleep for the second time that night.

Chapter 11: Road Trip End! The Race to the Spaceship!

Boyd opened his eyes, and realized it was already morning.

"I'm glad you're awake, Boyd. We've now approached the outskirts of New York City," Joei said. "I want you to stay on guard now that you're up, because I imagine we'll see sub-humans swarming the area as soon as we get into the city."

"You think it's already abandoned?"

"It's likely. These sub-humans have proven to be a true threat, and because humanity saw them invade one city, they would have been quick to evacuate this one as well to limit casualties. Would you mind checking your phone so we can get an idea of the current situation?"

"Yeah, sure," Boyd said, grabbing his phone and looking for the latest news video on the situation.

"An investigation by local police officers after a space-ship landed in Times Square yesterday ended in tragedy. Residents were asked by the local police force to evacuate the area.

Soon after, an official request was given to all citizens of New York City to evacuate. The investigation in question caused the casualties of at least ten officers on site. As of this morning, most people have been evacuated out of the city, with only certain areas with larger populations still not being fully evacuated," the newswoman said on the video.

"How long ago was that?" Joei asked.

"A couple hours. I'm sure it's gotten worse since then if they've asked everyone to evacuate. Any updates on a plan to infiltrate their spaceship?"

"Just the basics. We can't plan anything detailed since we have no clue what the layout of the spaceship is like. All I know for sure is that you need to save as much of your strength as you can. Don't focus on weaker opponents, just run straight into the ship and see if you can find their leader. Once you take that leader down, this whole invasion should stop for the most part."

"Sounds simple enough to me," Boyd said, continuing to stay on guard.

***

As they entered the city, Boyd was shocked at what he saw. Things had become even more wrecked than what he saw in the news report. Many buildings had collapsed completely, and any buildings that hadn't were either barely standing, or in pieces.

"Those sub-humans will pay," Boyd said under his breath. It wasn't long before they ran into trouble. He could see sub-humans lurking in the crevices of the destroyed buildings, ready to attack.

"You see the sub-humans, right?" Joei asked.

Boyd nodded.

"Good, get ready to run toward the ship."

As Boyd put on his gloves and boots, a sub-human attacked the driver's side of their car.

"Get out and run, Boyd!"

"I'm not letting you get hurt!" Boyd yelled as he threw an uppercut at the sub-human, causing him to go flying. Joei realized he wasn't driving, and tried to stop the car as it crashed into one of the destroyed buildings. The left side was mostly intact, though the front of the car and the right side had taken the brunt of the damage and was crushed.

"Joei, quick! Hop on my back!" he yelled as he jumped out of the car.

"Boyd, I...I think I broke my ankle," Joei said weakly, grasping at his lower leg. Boyd lifted Joei's pant leg and noticed that his ankle was becoming swollen.

"I think you're right, but we can't focus on that right now. We gotta get to the ship!"

He lifted Joei up onto his back and started running in the direction they'd been driving. "Which way?"

"Turn at the next road going right," Joei said. Boyd noticed multiple sub-humans running behind him, so he booked it as fast as he could. After he turned, more were waiting for him.

"Hold on tight, Joei!"

He jabbed one of the sub-humans in the nose, bringing them to the ground. Boyd took the other one by the neck and pushed him into the one on the ground.

"All right, keep going straight, and we should be there in a few minutes," Joei said, holding the pain in. Although they had escaped the horde that was waiting for them at the turn, the combined groups were becoming too fast to outrun. He didn't know what to do.

"Boyd, you need to push hard into the ground to go faster."

"But if I do that, I'll fall."

"What other choice do we have? We gotta get away, come on!"

Boyd took a deep breath as he slammed his foot into the ground, causing the propulsions to fire even harder. He nearly fell when he did this, but he quickly adjusted, and within a few seconds, he started losing the horde.

"Great job. Remember, try to avoid all the sub-human soldiers, and find their leader. You need to save all your energy for the leader so we can stop this."

"I got it, Joei. Their leader is going down."

Soon after, they approached the spaceship. The entire area was cleared around the ship, with only some debris here and there. Most of it had turned into small pieces of rocky concrete. They also noticed a sub-human taller than the rest standing in front of the ship. *The one from my first vision!*

Sure enough, as they got closer, Boyd saw that it was the same tall sub-human wearing a black, sleeveless jumpsuit.

"Hey! I don't know who you guys are, but I think you missed the memo. We've taken over this place, so you'd better scram before I get you," the sub-human said, grinning.

"Well, actually, I'm here to take you guys down," Boyd said. The sub-human had a good laugh for several seconds at that.

"So, you're a tough guy, eh? Surely you've noticed by now that our kind is much stronger than some regular human."

"Yup. So far, I've fared fine, though, so I don't think you should be too much of an issue."

"Lemme make one thing clear: I, Yugbar, am the commander of this ship, second in command to my captain. As a result, I've had to rigorously train my body under stronger conditions than your average sub-human soldier. My fighting skills are much greater than those of one of our soldier's, so don't think that you're gonna take me down." Yugbar threw a quick jab. Boyd couldn't dodge in time and was slammed several feet away, knocking the wind out of both Joei and himself. Yugbar began to approach them. Joei stood up in front of Boyd.

"You're gonna have to get past me if you want to hurt him!" Joei said as he spread his arms wide open while facing Yugbar.

"Heh, it seems neither one of you understands the weight of the situation," Yugbar said as he slammed his fist into Joei's chest, sending him flying several yards away. After he landed, he didn't get up.

"Joei!"

Chapter 12: Now It's On!
Boyd Vs. Yugbar!

Boyd quickly ran over to Joei as soon as he hit the ground.

"Shouldn't you focus on yourself first?" Yugbar said as he jumped in front of Boyd. The two traded a singular blow, which neither budged from. "You're stronger than you look; I'll give you that. Too bad that was only a casual punch for me."

Yugbar went for another hit as Boyd did the same, this time jumping for more power. Boyd was sent to his back.

"Now you see, even with that fancy equipment of yours, you can't defeat a commander of the Sub-human Army."

Boyd stood up as Yugbar ran over and punched him in the gut, spitting out blood as he was sent flying onto his back meters away.

I need to save my energy for their leader; how do I take this guy out quickly? Boyd wondered. Then he got an idea.

"I'm getting bored, let's finish this," Yugbar said as Boyd began jumping repeatedly, getting higher with each jump. He managed to avoid a right hook from Yugbar because of it. "You let on more than I thought you did. See if you can dodge this!"

Yugbar jumped toward Boyd as he did the same, clashing fist with fist.

"Is that the best you got? My punches match yours now," Boyd said.

"Nah, I guess I'll have to go all out, against a human of all things!"

Yugbar's smile widened, and his pupils shrank. He began stretching as Boyd continued jumping higher and higher. After stretching, he squatted onto the ground, legs shaking as he got ready to pounce.

"Here's a quick fact: Us sub-humans are able to build up energy into our joints and release it all at once. It's usually only a small amount, but if you train it up, it can become a lot more potent."

Yugbar jumped through the air and was rushing at him. Boyd jumped toward him with both fists as he attempted to clash with him, but Yugbar had become too quick and trapped him in a seemingly endless barrage of fists, hitting him all over his body.

"Don't you see? You're finished!" Yugbar said as he cackled. He continued jumping and pummeling him until Boyd clashed with him again, with Boyd being sent to the ground again. Boyd quickly crouched onto the ground as he got a new idea. He placed his hands on the ground and pushed off with both gloves and boots, sending him high into the sky. He traded a blow with Yugbar and bounced right back up, matching a right hook with him. He used the opportunity to punch the air around him, going up, then down. He started kicking too as this motion became faster and faster, all in midair.

"Stop messing around! I'm not holding back anymore!"

Yugbar launched himself at Boyd. Boyd went in for a double kick as Yugbar caught it.

"You're done, kid."

"Check again."

Yugbar quickly noticed Boyd had grabbed onto his legs with his own. Boyd then began kicking the air up and down, up and down, punching to make the motion faster. The motion became faster each time as Yugbar tried releasing himself, to no avail. Once fast enough, Boyd went down as he let go. Yugbar, now dizzy, was sent flying to the other side of the ship, hitting the ground with a sickening crunch. Boyd landed on his back, exhausted. He then remembered Joei and ran over to check on him. Luckily, he still had a pulse, though he also had a large bump on his forehead now and was unconscious.

"Let's hide you so no one can find you," Boyd said, gathering some nearby debris that wasn't too big and covering Joei in it. He ripped off one of his pant legs, tying it around his broken ankle.

"Stay safe, Joei."

Boyd turned around and headed toward the ship, unsure of what awaited him.

Chapter 13: It's Like a Labyrinth! Entering the Ship!

The moment Boyd entered the ship, he realized just how many sub-humans occupied it. He could see that the entrance consisted of a hall with multiple doors to other rooms, and down the hall, a few hundred feet in front of Boyd, was a center room of sorts. Unfortunately, multiple sub-humans walking down the hallway saw him, and only stared for a few moments before walking slowly toward him.

"What have we got here, eh?" one spouted.

"A human got onto the ship?" asked another.

"He probably snuck on somehow. We'll clean up the mess Yugbar missed!"

At that point, they started running toward Boyd. He jumped at one and managed to knock him down with a single attack. He then kicked one to his left, another to his right. More continued to come, but Boyd wasn't interested in fighting more.

"Sorry guys, but you're too weak for me," Boyd said, maneuvering around the sub-humans by jumping and punching through a few of them. Several continued to come after him, so Boyd ran and turned into a room that ended up being another hallway. He found the supply room and hid among the cleaning supplies. The sub-humans, of course, saw the hallway that Boyd had gone down, so it was only a matter of time before they checked the room he was in.

What to do, what to do? Boyd thought, desperately trying to look around for some way to escape this mess. He looked up at the ceiling.

***

"Where'd he go?" a sub-human asked another. A group of them were going down the hallway.

"Check every room."

Each sub-human went to a separate room to check if Boyd was hiding there. Room by room, he wasn't found, and then one opened the door to the room he'd been in. The sub-human trashed the room looking for him, but he wasn't there.

"He's not down this hallway. Someone call security and have them deal with this guy. He's not an average human."

Boyd, sweating profusely, was relieved they were gone. The vents he had managed to climb up into were unlikely to hold him for long, but now he had another issue with the security guards. Whether they were as strong as Yugbar or not was a genuine concern, so Boyd knew the pressure was on.

***

"Captain! Captain!" a sub-human yelled.

"This had better be good. I'm trying to relax after invading this city," the captain said. Unlike the other sub-human soldiers, he had a bit of gray hair on his head, though it was still quite short. He was a bit taller and wore a black military vest on top of a gray shirt, something the other sub-humans didn't wear. He also wore heavy-duty pants with black shoes.

"It is! A human has infiltrated the ship! He's somehow defeated multiple soldiers!" The sub-human reported to him. The captain's eyebrows rose.

"You're joking, right?"

"They're currently being treated, and a few reported the situation, so security guards are on the lookout for him."

The captain went to the security camera screens and gazed at the one for the doctor's office, and sure enough, multiple soldiers were being seen to.

"You weren't kidding. Let me know if he's found so I can get back to relaxing," he commanded.

"Okay, Captain."

***

What to do, what to do? Boyd thought, worried about when he was going to encounter a security guard. He knew he couldn't crawl around in a vent, because he could barely fit into the vents in the first place. All Boyd could do at this point was find the captain's quarters and defeat him, which is exactly what he intended to do.

Boyd turned around the corner and saw a bunch of sub-human security guards. By the time Boyd tried to turn around to head the other direction, it was too late.

"We found him! We'll request backup if we need it!" One of the security guards said into the communicator. Three started running toward Boyd with their bare hands. The only guard-like thing about their appearance was their futuristic caps, which resembled baseball caps, with a small communicator built into the brim. Boyd ran at one and roundhouse kicked him in the head, causing the guard to flinch. The guard recovered a moment later and quickly attempted to grab Boyd. Boyd flipped and stood upright again.

"You guys are certainly more of a pain than regular sub-humans, what with your quick recovery and all," Boyd said.

"Well, we are guards, so what did you expect?"

They then came at Boyd. He attempted to dodge but was grabbed at the ankle by the same guard.

"Not so tough anymore, are you?" the guard exclaimed. Boyd was now dangling upside down by the ankle. Luckily, the guard was only holding him by one of the propulsion boots, so Boyd wiggled out of it and grabbed onto the guard's neck. He flipped the guard onto his chest, knocking him out. He then took the boot from his hands and slipped it back on.

"Anyone else wanna play with the Psyborg?" Boyd taunted the other guards, now shocked.

"We need backup! I repeat, we need backup!" One of the guards yelled into his communicator. Boyd retreated, guards now running after him. With backup coming, he knew he couldn't stay in one place. He ran for around ten minutes, more guards joining the chase, until about a dozen of them were after him.

Gotta find the captain's quarters soon so I don't waste much more energy, Boyd thought. He saw a double doorway not long after and dived straight toward it. The doors refused to open.

"Those aren't doors you wanna go through, buddy," one of the guards shouted toward Boyd.

"And why not?" Boyd asked.

"Cuz it's the captain's qu—"

Another guard placed a hand over his mouth.

"You just gave away the captain's location!"

"You just did as well!" the rest of the guards, including the one who was silenced, said in unison.

"Whatever, those doors are made of iron. I doubt he could possibly—what!?"

Boyd managed to dent the iron doors and was prying them open with his hands.

68

"Get him!" one of the guards commanded, but it was too late. Boyd had already pried the doors open. To the left of the room was a windshield that spanned that entire side of the deck. Above it were dozens of small screens displaying security camera footage. The control panel was below the windshield, spanning the entirety of the edge on the left side. In the center of the room was a black chair, where a sub-human larger than most was sitting. He swiveled his chair to face Boyd.

"Well, who do we have here? The sub-human-beating human? A shame really. Your journey ends here," the sub-human said, revealing himself to be the captain.

Chapter 14: An Uphill Battle! Showdown Against the Captain!

"**What** makes you think I'll lose?" Boyd asked the captain.

"Well, let's just say I saw what you did out there to my commander, throwing him behind our ship. I haven't seen him get up since, so who knows if he's still alive. Your strength may be impressive for a human's, but you've hardly begun to see the true potential of a sub-human's power!" the captain answered, getting out of his chair and raising his hands up.

"That so? Guess that gives me an opportunity to become stronger, then!"

"I don't think you understand your situation. If you were struggling against Yugbar, you won't stand a chance against me. I consider myself three times stronger than him."

"Well, then, I'll use my battle against you to become stronger."

The captain walked toward Boyd.

"One punch from me will at least severely injure you, if not kill you. I'm not going easy on you just because you're human; I saw what you can do against Yugbar. If you turn back now, I'll spare you."

The other sub-humans in the room laughed, thinking Boyd would leave.

"Oh, thank you so much! I'm so sorry about all this. I'll just go ahead and leave," Boyd said. With that, he turned to head out the door. Boyd spit onto his metal glove finger and flicked it toward the captain, hitting his left cheek. Every sub-human in the room gasped. Boyd turned around.

The captain wiped his cheek off.

"So, that's how you're gonna play it. You're dead," the captain said, cracking his knuckles and lunging toward Boyd. He had no time to dodge and could only avoid a direct hit, being struck in the side and sent flying across the control room, slamming into the metal wall and falling on his back.

"Your reflexes aren't bad, for a human's, of course, but that wasn't even my most powerful punch, so I know you're finished."

"I'm not done yet," Boyd said, getting back up and jumping toward him with both fists. The captain avoided the attack and struck him in the back, sending him toward one of the security TVs, smashing the screen into pieces. Boyd fell onto the control panel and rolled onto the floor. Now on his back, he tried to get up.

"Oh no, you don't."

The captain came toward him and punched him in the gut, sending him flying at the wall. Now in a sitting position, Boyd was at a loss for words.

Think, Boyd, think! What can I use to possibly defeat him? Boyd contemplated. He thought about options in the little time he had before the captain came to attack him again. Then an idea came to him, something he hadn't done in a long time...

"Come on, Boyd, you're so close! Your black belt is waiting for you tomorrow if you master those moves," a voice told Boyd. It was his karate instructor, Mr. Shin. Boyd, twelve, was practicing the moves he needed to learn.

"I know! I can't wait to finally be a master," Boyd said. "Can I teach classes once I've gotten my black belt?"

"I'm afraid you'd need to meet a certain age require-ment, plus undergo training for teaching karate. Just because you can do it doesn't mean you can teach it," Mr. Shin chuckled.

"Well, at least I can be a karate master!"

The final move Boyd had to learn was incredibly difficult to master, involving a jump using only the toes, then following up by punching the opponent, and finally doing a roundhouse kick in the neck, specifically where the vagus nerve is located. Boyd struggled with the first part, as doing a jump using only your toes was very difficult.

"It helps if you position your toes right before you leap so you can do the move without messing up," Mr. Shin suggested. Within a minute of taking the advice, Boyd had figured out how to do the move and pulled it off. His instructor gave a bit of applause.

"Outstanding as always, Boyd. I expect some great results tomorrow," Mr. Shin commended.

It's been so long since I last did it, though. Would it actually work against him? Boyd wondered, snapping out of the memory. *I have no other choice. I'm a goner if I can't get past him, so I'll have to pull out all the stops.* Boyd decided. He stood up.

"You've still got some fight left in you, eh? Guess I'll have to beat some discouragement into you," the captain said, stomping over to where Boyd was with a wide grin on his face. Boyd started spinning around. His boots caused him to speed up rapidly, and after a few seconds, he attempted the move.

"Propulsion Knockout!" he yelled, managing to catch the captain off guard. He punched him in the nose, then quickly followed it up with a roundhouse kick in the neck. Boyd landed on the ground right behind him. The captain started wobbling, but after a few seconds, he self-righted, and turned around to face Boyd.

"Well, well, you're smarter than you look. Trying to knock me out, I see, and you almost succeeded, too. Unfortunately for you, we sub-humans don't succumb as easily as regular humans do!"

He grabbed Boyd by the waist. He attempted to wiggle out of the grip, but was unable to.

"Your name?"

"My name's Boyd, and I won't stop until I've taken you down!"

"How fun. I'm amazed you nearly defeated me; however, I, Captain Zaizo, will be finishing you off now."

With a simple finger flick in the neck, Boyd was out.

Chapter 15: It's Over! Captured by the Sub-humans!

Boyd opened his eyes and saw that he was chained to a wall. He looked around and realized he had been captured. He was in a small cage, not that it mattered, since he couldn't move around. He saw there were other cages, though no one currently occupied any that he could see. They were only made of bars, so he could see what the rest of the room looked like. The entire room was full of dozens of cages, though he only saw a few from a far distance.

A few minutes later, Captain Zaizo entered the room to talk to Boyd.

"I see you're finally up. You were quite the nuisance on this ship, weren't you?" Captain Zaizo said.

"Yeah. What's your point?" Boyd asked.

"My point is that I'd rather not kill you if I don't have to."

"Why on Earth not?"

"Well, there's only one way that I'll allow you to live, and I suggest you comply with it. How would joining the side of the sub-humans sound to you? I could make you vice-captain of this ship with your strength, and you'd be treated as an equal among us, too."

"Sounds ridiculous to someone like me who wants to save this world. I'd be abandoning my own kind if I joined up with you, so I'll refuse that offer."

The captain smirked at the response. "I was afraid you'd say that, so I got a certain someone to help you make the right decision."

He grabbed something from behind his back. That something was Joei, being held by the collar of his shirt, and he was wiggling, trying to break free of Zaizo's grip.

"Let me go!" Joei yelled.

Zaizo opened the gate to Boyd's cell and let him out. He then made a proposal.

"Here's how things are gonna go. If you don't join me, I'll have both you and your friend here killed today. If you do join me, however, I can have all this reversed. Your friend here will also be freed and welcomed into sub-human society."

"You know what to say, Boyd! Right?" Joei asked. Boyd stared at Joei for a few seconds, then nodded.

"I refuse. Plus, my friend would die for the sake of humanity, right Joei?"

"You'd be correct."

The captain clenched his fist.

"So, you guys are serious about this, then? Guess I'll just kill you here and now, Boyd. Your friend will join you soon after."

He then proceeded to throw his fist at Boyd.

No, no, no! was all Boyd could think of before getting a vision moments before the punch landed. Zaizo would throw it directly at his head. Boyd barely managed to move his head out of the way, causing the captain to smash his fist into the bars. The captain flinched from the pain for a second, giving Boyd enough time to grab the gloves and punch the captain, causing him to drop Joei. Boyd grabbed the boots from the captain and used them to take him and Joei away from the cage.

"That was an amazing dodge you did just now. Here's your gloves and boots," Joei said.

"Thanks, Joei. You stay back now. I'll finish what I started here," Boyd replied. Joei limped back several feet away from the two figures. All that was left now was a duel.

"Well, this isn't how I wanted things to go, but you won't be any issue. Now that I've seen you fight once, you can't do a thing against me," Captain Zaizo said.

"Oh, please, you haven't seen all my tricks."

My visions aren't reliable, but they're the only way I can win this, Boyd thought.

"I guess it's time to tango, then," the captain said, immediately running at him with a left hook. Boyd thought hard, and attempted to force a vision, but instead he was smashed into a nearby cage. He tried again, and was sent across the room and smashed into a wall.

"Boyd, if you're trying to see into the future, please stop! Just try to dodge normally," Joei yelled.

"I'm sorry, Joei, but...I'm gonna die for sure if I don't try to. At least if I try to see into the future I have a—"

He saw a vision of Captain Zaizo throwing a right hook at the side of his head. He just managed to dodge it when it happened.

"So, you weren't kidding me then when you said you had some tricks left. Guess you'll be facing my wrath at full power then," the captain said, jumping forward with both fists. Boyd attempted to do the same and traded a blow; however, the captain's overwhelming power sent Boyd flying back when they clashed. "Don't think you can power your way through this like you did with Yugbar. Remember, I'm quite a bit stronger than him."

"Even if I can't, I'm gonna try until I can't anymore!" Boyd said, continuing to try and concentrate to avoid attacks using his visions. Since it was only working some of the time, Boyd continued to get pummeled, only dodging occasionally. Soon, Boyd began to wobble.

"You're still standing, eh? Looks like you're finally beginning to waver. This next attack will be my last, since you'll probably die if it hits head on. Sayonara, Boyd."

The captain cranked his right arm for one last punch, then squatted to charge his legs up. He sprang forward, fist in lead, toward Boyd.

At that moment, Boyd closed his eyes and a voice echoed in his head.

Concentrate, Boyd. Control your breathing and focus solely on what you are trying to do. If you do that, you are much more likely to succeed in your moves, the calming voice said. It was Mr. Shin. Boyd took a breath in, and a clear vision came of the captain. He was aiming for Boyd's heart. The vision ended, and Boyd narrowly dodged, then hit Captain Zaizo right in the neck. The captain stumbled, but remained conscious.

"What did I tell you about trying that? I've trained myself to not be easily affected by such moves. I'm putting everything I got into my next attack," Zaizo said, cranking both his arms this time for a dual punch. He sprang forward again, and Boyd avoided it, this time trading a blow with the captain. This continued several times; however, the captain's attacks were too much for Boyd to counter, so he would always get pushed back.

"You've certainly improved your combat skills in such a short amount of time, but it's all for naught if you can't counterattack!"

Boyd was unsure what to do until he got another idea. The two traded a few more blows, then Boyd saw an opening and went for the captain's neck. With his arms tightly around his neck, he squeezed so Zaizo couldn't breathe.

"You little—ack!" It was beginning to work. Zaizo was beginning to gasp for air, but then he grabbed Boyd by the neck, choking him.

"It appears the tables have turned. I think I'll crush your windpipe."

Once more an idea that he wasn't sure would work sprang into Boyd's head. He took a finger and jammed it into the captain's neck, causing him to drop Boyd, stumble for a few seconds, and then finally fall onto his back. Boyd went over to check if he was out, and when he did, the captain didn't move. It was over.

"Quick, Boyd! I'll get a chair, but you need to start ripping the cage bars off and bend them around his body so he can't escape!" Joei yelled, running out of the room to find a chair. Boyd used his gloves to rip the bars off, then bent them around the captain.

***

The captain slowly opened his eyes and was immediately greeted by Boyd, who was staring at him.

"You've got some questions to answer for us, captain," Boyd said.

Chapter 16: It's Finally Discovered! The Truth Behind the Sub-humans!

"Tell us about the sub-humans, Captain Zaizo," Boyd demanded.

"Why do you care? You guys are the ones who want to kill us, after all."

"You guys were the ones who invaded Earth, destroyed cities, and killed many people," Joei said.

"You guys deserve it for what you did to us."

Boyd took a step closer to Zaizo, now clenching his right fist with his gloves equipped.

"Start from the beginning. What did we humans do to you sub-humans?" Boyd asked.

The captain began a story.

"I guess you guys are humans, so you wouldn't know. About fifty years ago, a dozen regular humans were all colleagues who worked together as a result of going to the same high-level university. These dozen people were all geniuses, people who were smarter than most gifted people who do exceptionally well in school. They all aspired to go into different careers that would innovate their respective areas of work. Some wanted to go into engineering, others wanted to invent. One of them, my father, wanted to go into medicine and try to cure viruses and diseases that were normally deemed incurable. The problem was, because of their intelligence, their ideas were often deemed as too far out. They were called lunatics. Whenever they'd try to come up with an idea, they'd be denied any way to make it happen because it was 'insane and too far ahead of its time.' They weren't wrong. These dozen people had IQs comparable to or higher than that of Einstein himself. It went farther than just being shamed, though. They kept pushing their ideas and received little to no support for them. Eventually, they were barred from receiving an education of any kind due to their ideas and their unwillingness to keep them to themselves. They were kicked out of the university they had been attending. Not long after, society shunned them, and they were left homeless. These dozen were angry about their situation, and planned to try and steal a rocket ship from NASA. Their plan was to fly to Mars and start a new society where they could be free to pursue their ideas. One among this dozen, however, didn't agree with the idea. His name was Hoover Parett, and he called the plan ridiculous, saying that it wasn't the right way to deal with the situation."

"Did you say Hoover Parett?" Joei asked.

"Yeah, so?"

"That was my dad's name, and he had a very similar experience to what you're describing."

"So you're the son of the traitor, eh? You're worse than the regular humans just for that, though it doesn't matter at this point. Anyway, the other eleven weren't happy to hear what Hoover had to say and tried to convince him otherwise. He was unreasonable and wouldn't be swayed, so the eleven left him behind. With their combined intelligence, they were able to hijack a NASA base and managed to steal a rocket without anyone noticing until launch time. Nine months later, they arrived on their desired planet: Mars. During those nine months, they prepared in order to endure the cold conditions of Mars, and once they got there, they got to work on their civilization. As four of them among the group were female, they managed to create a society slowly but surely. Their higher intellect allowed them to create a society comparable to Earth's in little time, and within a couple decades, they had already surpassed Earth's technology. On top of that, the inhabitants were able to adapt to the cold weather. Their time on Mars made them less human. The decreased gravitational pull caused them to become taller and slenderer, and their noses flatter to take in the cold air more easily. Due to Mars being farther from the Sun, our skin became paler and grayer. These changes made us less human, therefore we are no longer real humans, but instead sub-humans. All of us are required to work out intensely to not become weak. That is why we are much stronger than regular humans, and our slender, muscular builds make us taller and faster than regular humans."

"Some great information you've given us, captain, but why the invasion on Earth?" Boyd asked.

"Simple. You humans rejected us, so we're going to make you regret ever messing with us in the first place by showcasing our advanced technology and forcefully integrating our society into yours."

"That's a poor excuse to murder so many people, so it's a good thing we'll be heading to your planet and putting a stop to all of this," Joei said.

"Didn't you hear me? Sub-humans are much more powerful than regular humans. Your average sub-human is around ten times stronger and faster than a regular human, and I'm not the strongest one there is. That title goes to our ruler, and you, Boyd, couldn't even match my power. Just try going to Mars, because the moment you step foot there, you're finished."

"I have one of the smartest humans on my side. If I need improvements, he can give them to me," Boyd said, knocking him out. Joei was looking out of the prison room, and glanced back at him.

"Boyd, we have a problem!" Joei yelled.

Chapter 17: The Sub-human Problem! Boyd Vs. A Hundred Sub-humans!

"**All right,** how many?" Boyd asked, already running toward Joei.

"It appears there's about a hundred of them out there right now."

Boyd looked into the hallway and saw the sub-humans a few yards away from them. There appeared to be a variety of security guards and regulars. Boyd could already count a few dozen in the front of the giant group.

"You weren't kidding. Even if they're weak, this is gonna be difficult," Boyd said. "What's the plan?"

"The plan for what? Defeating them?"

"No, the plan for actually stopping the invasion."

"Well, first we need to deal with these sub-humans, then I'll input coordinates to Mars. We'll then fly over there and try to stop them."

"You know how insane that sounds, right?"

"Yes, but we have no other choice. Now go!"

With that, Boyd ran toward the crowd of sub-humans and yelled, "I've already defeated your captain, so give up! I'm taking over."

He grabbed two by their necks and slammed them down on their backs. He then picked both up by their heads and swung them around, knocking multiple sub-humans off their feet. Ten down, Boyd was already beginning to tire due to his fight with the captain not long ago, as well as from his injuries.

"Tiring already? You're dead meat for us!" A sub-human yelled at Boyd, running toward him. He punched him in the side of the face, and he fell. With eighty-nine of them surrounding him, Boyd was becoming overwhelmed by the numbers.

"Get back! You'll just be defeated if you try to attack me," Boyd said.

"Why should we? Not only are you visibly worn out, but there are still several dozen of us left. We're taking back this ship!"

The large group of them gave a war cry and charged toward Boyd. All he could do at this point was continue attacking. He punched through sub-humans, and used Propeller Propulsion when it was needed. Eventually, however, they overwhelmed him. Boyd couldn't handle it any longer. With his mind rapidly becoming more and more stressed, they engulfed his body.

"No...more!" Boyd yelled. With that, the ground beneath him turned a pinkish tint. This tint spread across in a ripple formation. It made every sub-human it passed by bounce into the air and fall onto their backs, until all of them had fallen.

What...was that? Boyd wondered. He saw that all of them were now on their backs and were beginning to get up now.

"What...did you do?" One of them asked.

"I told you already: I'm going to take you all down, no matter how it happens."

Boyd had no clue what he had done, but it was a matter to deal with later. For now, he had the advantage, and he wasn't going to let it pass by him. He quickly jumped on top of a few of them and stomped into their stomachs, making each one cry out in pain. A dozen sub-humans later, and he was down to about half the amount that he started with.

"You're obviously tiring. If you surrender now, we'll make your death painless and instant."

A sub-human then lunged toward Boyd. He swiped with his right arm and punched the sub-human's face. With forty-nine of them left, Boyd was at a loss at how to beat the rest without passing out.

He decided he had to find an equipment room. He unfortunately had to run away, which was embarrassing, considering he was much stronger than them. With their number advantage, however, he had no choice. Boyd looked for any signs that would imply an equipment room, but after a couple minutes was not having any luck.

I must find that equipment room now. I can't stay conscious much longer, he thought. After another minute, he saw a sign with a tool symbol on it. With forty-nine sub-humans running behind him, he went through the door to what seemed to be the equipment room and slammed it shut. He locked it and gave himself a few seconds to find any kind of explosive. He found a single small grenade and then went to the back of the room and waited. After only a few seconds, they broke through.

"Don't move, or I'll throw it," Boyd said, holding up the small grenade in his hand. They all froze, except for one at the front of the group.

"Don't listen to him, boys; he's just bluffing. He's on his last leg and trying to threaten us so we go away. He won't actually set it off."

"I'm braver than you think."

Boyd ran toward the group and punched three of them down, then activated the grenade with a timer of two seconds. He dropped it in the middle of the group and then ran away from the room. The grenade went off right as Boyd escaped the group, and the room exploded, sending multiple sub-humans flying across the hallway. The trouble gave him enough time to turn a corner and make an escape. He managed to find the control room relatively quickly this time, and Joei was standing there, messing around with the controls.

"Hey, Boyd, did you manage to take them all out?" Joei asked.

"No, there's still about forty left."

"Well, we need to get the door shut before they get here."

"They didn't see where I went, so we should have some time."

"All right, well I need you to slam the doors shut so they aren't able to get through for a little while if they decide to come here."

"I'm on it."

Boyd managed to pry the doors shut with his gloves on and sat down in the captain's chair.

"So, what are you doing right now?" Boyd asked.

"I'm trying to find the coordinates for Mars on this thing, but the interface is very different from any I've ever seen on Earth. I think I've found them, though, so we should be ready to go soon."

A few minutes later, the forty sub-humans found the control room, and began banging on the door. Boyd ran over to the doors and tried to keep them shut, but he knew that any second, they were going to get through.

Whatever I did before, maybe I can use it again, Boyd thought, thinking about the same power that caused them to bounce into the air. He concentrated his mind onto the power, hoping that it would activate. A few seconds later, the sub-humans broke down the door and started running into the room. Joei ran to the far side of the room and hoped he wouldn't get attacked immediately.

It's over, I can't fight anymore, Boyd thought, lying on the ground as the sub-humans ran into the room.

Suddenly, a sub-human came from the back of the group and started mowing them down. The sub-human slammed his fist into the heads of each one he came across. Within a minute, all forty of them were down, and he reached his hand out to Boyd.

Boyd, barely able to lift his arm, asked, "Who are you?"

"I'm Taizen, son of the captain of this ship, Zaizo. Don't worry, though, I heard about your ideals and know you aren't what everyone else seems to think you are."

Boyd stared at him, confused.

Chapter 18: A New Ally! Mars, Home of the Sub-humans!

"So wait, you're not gonna hurt us?" Boyd asked.

"No. Honestly, I was already a skeptic of the actions of my people with this attack, not to mention the motivation behind it, but seeing your dedication and hearing your goals have made me want to support you guys. So, are you gonna take my hand or not?"

"Oh, uh, sure," Boyd said, raising his right arm out and grabbing Taizen's. Once he was up, he walked toward Joei.

"He seems like he's on our side, Joei. Should we trust him?"

"Well, he helped us beat up the sub-humans that came after us, so I don't see why not."

Joei faced Taizen, who was now walking toward them. "Hey, Taizen, do you have any idea where medical supplies are? I believe I've broken my ankle and would appreciate it if you could get me a cast of some kind, maybe some heavy bandages."

"Sure, be right back," Taizen said, quickly running out the door. After a few minutes, he came back with a flexible splint that kept the ankle stable, which Joei wrapped around the injured joint.

"Alrighty then, we're about ready to leave. First, could you guys find a way to get these sub-humans out of the room?" Joei asked the other two.

"Sure. Taizen, you got any ideas where we should put them?"

"I've got a great idea," Taizen said.

***

"Is that all of them?" Boyd asked. Taizen had led him to a trash chute just large enough to fit the sub-humans in, so one by one, they had emptied them out of the ship with it.

"Almost. There's a few more left, so if you want to, you can go back to the deck and let me handle this."

"That works for me."

Boyd returned to the deck.

"Hey, Joei, are we ready to launch yet?" Boyd asked.

"Well, this ended up being harder than I thought it would be. Could you get Taizen for me? He might know how to use this and may even know coordinates for Mars, since I'm not sure I've got the right ones in myself."

"Sure, be right back."

***

"Let's see. I know I remember the coordinates, but I don't have much experience with the actual software," Taizen said as he was messing with the controls on the deck. Joei was looking closely at what Taizen was doing, hoping to pick up something from it.

"Do you have enough to set the destination to Mars?" Joei asked.

"Give me a few minutes to recollect knowledge on the software, and I should be able to."

The next few minutes consisted of Boyd and Joei huddling around Taizen and switching their eyes between the controls and the main screen. Eventually, Taizen seemed more comfortable with the controls, and inputted coordinates, marked by the name "Mars."

"So have you set the destination to Mars?" Joei asked.

"I think so. All we should have to do now is take off."

"But how do we do that?" Joei asked.

"I believe there's a lever here that will initiate the countdown process, which, once finished, will launch the ship into space and toward Mars. This thing basically flies itself, so unless we run into obstacles in space, the ship should mostly do its own thing the whole way there."

"Then let's go ahead and take off!" Boyd yelled.

"Let's see. I think this was the lever," Taizen said, pushing it down. Immediately after, red sirens started going off.

"Destination set. Heading to 'Mars' in T-minus one hundred seconds," the booming, robotic voice said. The giant screen showed a countdown from one hundred, and it was already down to ninety-five.

"So how long will it take us to get to Mars, anyway?" Joei asked.

"Well, with this ship, it should take about two Earth weeks to get there, or a little over thirteen and a half Mars days."

"Well, Boyd, get settled in. Also, feel free to let me tinker with your gear if it needs repairs, since you'll need it in tip top shape for when we get to Mars," Joei said. With that, everyone got settled into a seat and waited for the countdown to end.

"Hold on tight! We may have advanced technology, but this part is still very shaky!" Taizen yelled as the countdown reached zero. The ship zoomed off into space, and for several seconds, the ship shook like a palm tree in a hurricane. Afterward, the ship began to slow down and eventually came to a steady speed.

"Wait, we're already off Earth!?" Boyd asked.

"Yes. Our ships can make it off a planet within seconds. You should be able to move around the ship freely now, as the launch has ended and gravity simulation is automatic," Taizen replied. For the next few hours, Boyd rested, as did Joei.

***

After a few days, everyone had gotten used to life on a sub-human spaceship. They decided to move Zaizo to a storage room since he was too large for the trash chute. Boyd had let Joei tinker at his gloves and boots, and they were now in fully working order again. Taizen, for the most part, kept watch on the ship to make sure it wasn't going off course. On the third day, however, Taizen detected a problem.

"Is that...an asteroid belt?" Taizen asked himself.

Chapter 19: The Space Problem! Asteroid Belts and Space Monsters!

It wasn't long before Taizen saw that it was indeed an asteroid belt.

"Guys! We're about to head into an asteroid belt!" Taizen yelled, turning off auto pilot so he could maneuver the ship through the giant boulders. He strapped himself into the captain's chair. Multiple asteroids blocked their path as they flew toward the belt. They were surrounded, and Taizen was near panic but fought to maintain control. "Hang on, guys! This could throw you for a loop!"

Taizen began to maneuver the ship into a barrel roll. All Boyd and Joei could do was hang on tight to the nearest piece of equipment and hope they didn't get flung around. The next few minutes consisted of more barrel rolls, hard turns, and multiple sideways passes as Taizen dodged and swerved around the asteroids. After what seemed like forever, Taizen finally sat back.

"Is it over?" Boyd asked.

"For now. These asteroids are unpredictable, though. They go so fast that even our ship can't detect them quick e-nough, so we could be in for another loop of that again. There's chairs at the top that are secure, so it'd be best for you both to sit up there while we're traveling through here."

They ran into more, and Taizen had to do it all over again.

***

"I think we're done with this," Taizen said, looking over to the other side of the room. Both Boyd and Joei had passed out. It didn't matter at this point, though, since they were finally out of the asteroid belt. The next hour was quite peaceful, and the two came to soon after. Taizen continued to survey the area, hoping their troubles were over for now. Unfortunately, things were about to get worse. A giant, wriggling worm appeared off the starboard side of the ship.

"What...the heck...is that?" Boyd said groggily. He walked toward Taizen, as did Joei.

"No...I heard they were just rumors, they're actually...?" Taizen wondered.

"What is it, Taizen?" Boyd said.

"You ever heard of *Star Wars*?"

"It's a space slug, isn't it?" Joei said.

"A real-life equivalent, yes."

The three stared at it, getting a good look. The giant worm had teeth, just as Boyd remembered from the movie. They weren't quite as large in real life, however, though this one could move itself around. It wiggled and then faced the ship from afar.

"It saw us!" Boyd yelled, stepping back from the window. The slug seemed to yell out a roar, but no sound travels in space. It seemed like they could hear it, all the same. The slug veered toward the ship, its mouth wide open.

"Unless we can somehow maneuver around it, we're dead," Taizen said, defeated.

"Can't you fend it off with the lasers? You guys used them during the invasion," Joei said.

"With its size, they might have no effect."

"It's worth a try, at least," Boyd said. Taizen looked at the approaching space slug and grabbed an accompanying wheel for the laser guns. The control deck went into attack mode, and Taizen aimed directly for the mouth. Taizen shot multiple times and waited a moment to see what would happen. The slug's mouth was left unscathed.

"We're dead," Taizen said, turning the ship around and trying to fly away from the space slug. The slug was fast, propelling and gaining on them. A rearview screen showed how close it was.

"Think, think! What can we do to escape this slug?" Taizen asked himself aloud. Then he remembered something and started messing around with the controls.

"What have you got in mind?" Joei asked.

"I believe this ship has a few bombs that are more potent than the laser guns. If I can drop one into the slug's mouth, it could do some damage. We'll have to lure it by flying up, though, so hang on!"

Taizen steered the ship upward. Boyd and Joei planned accordingly and grabbed onto the nearest object grounded to the ship that they could find. The space slug, eager to follow, grew closer. When the space slug was close enough, Taizen readjusted and pressed the eject button for the bomb. It dropped from the center of the bottom of the ship and went straight into the slug's mouth. After a few seconds, the slug appeared to cry out in pain and was stunned. Taizen used the opportunity to get away.

"Finally, it's over," Boyd said, dizzy from the maneuver.

***

Nearly fourteen Earth days had passed since the three had taken off. Boyd had gotten more practice with his gloves and boots, feeling confident in fighting whatever would be waiting for him. Joei had tinkered with them to keep them in optimal shape, and with the special cast, his ankle had recovered after two weeks on the ship.

With less than an hour before they expected to arrive on Mars, Taizen called the men to the meeting area on the top deck in the back of the control room. It was accessed via two sets of stairs on both sides and was behind the deck. The chairs here were fixed to the area, and were essentially smaller, less-comfortable versions of the captain's chair. The table was also fixed to the floor.

Taizen started. "Okay, guys, it's time I give you a bit of information on what we're going to do here in less than an hour. Before we can make it onto Mars, there will be a single, rounded ship that monitors who comes in and out of the planet. It's basically like an office made into a small ship. They're very likely going to ask me to identify the ship and require me to use cameras as well. I'm going to need you guys to hide somewhere so we can do this. I'll make something up, since I'm the captain's son, and we should be able to get in."

"What about once we get on Mars?" Boyd asked.

"Well, we're gonna have to disguise you guys as sub-humans, which is going to be very difficult considering you're both short. We could paint you guys with a grayish tone and put you into hoodies, but the height thing is a dead giveaway."

"How about stilts?" Joei asked.

"Then we'd face the issue of trying to make it appear legitimate, since you wouldn't have actual legs. I guess we could get sub-human pairs of pants and make you guys look pretty real..."

"Won't we face the issue of breathing?"

"No, actually. There were giant, transparent domes built around towns and the city of Newtopia."

"Newtopia...?"

"Yes, our main city, where the majority of sub-humans live. Anyway, we're getting off track. I need you two to hide somewhere now; I'm gonna get prepared so that we access the planet."

With that, both Boyd and Joei left the control room, and Taizen tidied everything up so that nothing seemed suspicious. Less than an hour later, the ship approached Mars. Sure e-nough, the round ship was there to greet the ship. Quickly a transmission request came in, and Taizen accepted.

A deep voice came in, "This is Border Guard Kartzen, State your name."

"Taizen Starpson."

"Son of Captain Zaizo, huh? Where's your father?"

"W-well..." Taizen was at a loss for words.

Chapter 20: A Difficult Infiltration! Arrival to Mars!

"Is something wrong?" Kartzen asked. Taizen still didn't know what to say and tried to come up with something on the fly.

"Captain Zaizo had to fight off a tough opponent while invading Earth, and he sustained substantial injuries as a result."

"You're joking, right?"

"No. I'm not. I have video proof to show that he engaged in a battle with a human that managed to injure him."

"Well, this oughtta be something, won't it? Man, he ranked high in the academy, and it seems it's all for naught now. Send it over."

"Right away," Taizen said, searching through security footage from the prison two weeks ago. He selected a sample of video that showed Boyd defeating Zaizo and sent it over. Kartzen watched the footage, and his eyes widened.

"This human...where is he?"

"He was fatigued after his battle with the captain. The remaining soldiers attacked him, and he tried to fend them off. Rest assured, he is no longer an issue."

"So, he was disposed of, I assume?"

"Yes."

"Good. Could you get Zaizo for me?"

"He's resting in his quarters, not to be disturbed."

"He *can* be an angry guy at times. Tell me, though, why are you back here instead of letting him rest up back on Earth? We were to send reinforcements in a few days' time to assist with the invasion. Why not just wait for him to recover?"

"Well, he was gravely wounded in the battle against the human, and our own medical resources on the ship weren't enough to treat him. He agreed that he needed to go back to Mars so he could recover enough to be battle ready."

"That doesn't sound much like Zaizo. He usually is very stubborn when it comes to things like this, so I'd think he wouldn't agree to coming all the way back to Mars just to be treated properly until it was over."

"We made that choice for him. The vast majority on the ship agreed that he would've died from his injuries if he didn't get proper medical attention on Mars. He's in and out of sleep, and has had very little energy to do anything, so he hasn't noticed he's left Earth."

"You made the decision for a captain!? Do you realize how much trouble you could get into for doing that!?"

Taizen was getting impatient.

"Have you forgotten my position? His health was the top priority for us, and although we know it will be a while before the invasion can resume, it's better than the entire thing failing."

Kartzen sighed. "Did you at least leave some troops behind to continue it?"

"Yes, and though the number of troops that are still on Earth is small compared to if the ship had stayed behind, we made sure it would continue to some extent to discourage reconstruction of the invaded cities."

Kartzen had to think about this for a minute.

"Well, I'm not sure what higher-ups will think of the majority decision, but I think I can let you in for now. Just make sure to make it abundantly clear that the intentions were good."

Taizen held back a sigh of relief. "Of course!" Kartzen ended the transmission, and Taizen was cleared. They had managed to get past the first obstacle and could now enter Mars.

"Hey, guys! You can come out now!" Taizen yelled into the speaker. The speaker system sent the message throughout the ship. Boyd and Joei heard it and ran back to the deck.

"The first part is done, now for the harder part...getting you two into convincing disguises. Come on, we'll be landing in a few minutes. We're going to go into the supply room and see if there's leftover clothing, and maybe something we can use for stilts."

***

"This feels...very strange," Boyd said as he walked around in his sub-human disguise. The stilts, albeit short, were still a new experience for both Boyd and Joei, so they were pretty shaky.

"This is bad. If you guys can't get steady with the stilts, they're going to know something's up. We're going to land any minute now, so you hardly have time to get used to them."

"I think I've got an idea," Joei said, "Boyd, try shifting one leg back a bit from the other when you're standing."

Boyd did so, and after a few seconds, the shaking stopped.

"It's working!" Boyd said, now able to walk with courage in his disguise.

"Perfect. Let's get to the hatch. Since we're back earlier than we should be, we should get a quiet welcome, if anything at all."

They went to the hatch and waited for the ship to land. A monitor in one of the corners of the ceiling right beside the hatch showed live video of the surface. It only vaguely resembled the Mars that most people knew; it was covered with structures and buildings, and even vegetation in some areas. In the bottom of the footage, the landing area began to show up, resembling that of both a helicopter landing pad and a parking space, albeit much larger than both.

"I didn't imagine that the city would be this size," Joei said, staring at the monitor and taking in the view.

"Well, fifty years may not be a lot of time for human civilizations, but it was enough for us. This city needs enough space for the majority of all sub-humans, hence its size. We're about to land, so get into character."

Boyd was confused. "What exactly is defined as—"

"Shhhh, we're about to land," Taizen said.

The ship slowed its descent, and the four support legs popped out of the bottom of the ship. Slowly, it touched down on the landing area, and the propulsions keeping the ship afloat turned off.

"The landing process is now complete," Taizen said, walking over to a button. "When I press this button, we'll finally set foot on Mars."

"Well then, press it already!" Boyd said.

"Okay, okay, take it easy."

When he did, the hatch began to lower, and in front of them a sealed walkway as wide as a road led directly to Newtopia, which was in the distance about a mile away. Boyd stood in front of the other two.

"Time to head to Newtopia."

Chapter 21: The City of the Future! Newtopia, Capital of the Sub-humans!

"So, what exactly is our first order of business?" Joei asked as the three walked across the road that led into the city.

"Aren't you guys the ones who are heading this thing? All I can do is help with my knowledge on sub-humans."

"I advise that we find a way to upgrade Boyd's gloves and boots."

"Well, how do they work?"

"Essentially, they use mini-propulsions, which allow them to boost the strength of the person using them. Boyd has been able to bring out the best of their power with his utilization and karate abilities."

"Wow. For human technology, that's quite fascinating. I think I know just the place where we can find some propulsion materials of the right size. We'll need to go to the weapons store."

"All right then, lead us there."

Taizen happily placed himself ahead of Boyd and Joei.

***

"The city's so huge up close!" Boyd yelled as he looked all around him from the sidewalk. Although the city was similar to the one he lived in, it was also very different. He noticed that the sidewalks and the roads were a dark red color, and that the cars on the road were sleek and rounded in design, and used large thrusters over regular wheels.

"Keep it quiet, Boyd. We don't want to attract any attention to ourselves for now. If you think this is all neat, notice how the skies above are clear. Us sub-humans have taken the step to not use any fuels that cause dirty pollution. Methane is our chief fuel source. It's not like we have access to the same fuels that humans do, anyway."

"Speaking of humans, how do you have this much knowledge of them? I thought your first time on Earth was during the invasion," Joei asked.

Taizen got quiet. "Well, we did have a few sub-humans doing undercover work for us beforehand, but we're given some general knowledge on humans in school. We're taught the origin of our society and how humans abandoned us, and are told to hate them. I, of course, see that not all of humankind is evil, and that there's hope for our two kinds to make amends. But still, that's what we're taught from a young age."

"That explains the hatred," Joei said. "So where's this mechanic shop you're talking about?"

"It should be at the last building, at the end of this sidewalk to the left. Let me do the talking so we can find what you're looking for. The guy that owns the shop is one of the top part suppliers and makers in the city."

When they got to the building, they went inside the store, and both Boyd and Joei looked around in amazement. The walls were lined with small bins full of parts. The parts and products that could be seen were impressive, sleek, and modern. There were also a few aisles filling up the space in the store, as well as a cashier's desk right beside the entrance. Then Boyd got a good look at the cashier.

The guy was quite muscular, specifically in the arms, though he had a bit of a belly. Even though he was a sub-human, Boyd could tell that he was middle aged. He wore what looked like a roughed-up trucker's vest and ripped jeans. He had a very thin coat of light-gray hair covering his head. The most obvious trait he had, however, was his jaw. Instead of a regular one, this guy had a metallic appendage that went all the way to the sides of his head. It wasn't bulky, and its shape fit in quite well with the rest of his head. The metallic nature of it was quite easy to see, though. He was slouching in his chair working on a mechanical part with a tool Boyd didn't recognize.

"Welcome to Sparky's Parts and Service, how can I help you?" the cashier said. He hardly took more than a glance at the three, but recognized Taizen. "Oh, the King's own grandson. What are you doing here? I thought you went to Earth with your dad."

"Well, Sparky, some things went wrong, and we had to come back. The Development Team wanted to start work on a new way to make sub-humans stronger in combat. Could you look at these gloves and boots and see if you could find us some parts to help improve them?"

Sparky finally glanced at the three. Boyd had given the gloves and boots to Joei on the ship, so Joei handed them over to Sparky. He took them, adjusted the light toward them, and got a magnifying glass to observe them closely. After a couple minutes, he looked back up at the three.

"They're interesting, but you're telling me the Development Team made this? This seems awfully simple for a prototype of theirs."

The fear of being found out made Taizen take a moment to think about what to say.

"Well, they're not exactly a prototype. Development simply wanted to make a functioning mockup of the weapons using spare parts they had access to and came up with these. We came here to get some new parts so that they could make proper prototypes."

"Ah, that makes sense. It appears the main part that makes the weapon here are these propulsions, correct?"

"Sharp eyes as always, Sparky. Yes, and that's the part Development wants upgrades for. Now that they've made mockups and tested them, they want to take it a step further."

"Hm, okay then. I think I've got just the thing for them," he said, standing up and walking to the end of an aisle where a new product was being displayed.

"Introducing my latest propulsions, the Mark Nines. As per usual with my upgrades, I've made them smaller than the Mark Eights, and more powerful. They're also smaller than the ones currently on the gloves and boots, so they could probably get four on each glove and boot instead of the two on each one now."

"So how powerful are the Mark Nines?" Taizen asked.

"Well, a single attack equipped with four of these could probably destroy a car, and multiple hits would likely take down a small building. Don't quote me on that, though the power output combined with how many you could have equipped onto the gloves and boots would likely be enough to cause that much damage."

"Wow, that sounds perfect for what Development wants to accomplish and will certainly help with the Earth invasion. How much will it be?"

"Well, for each one, it'll be about fifty Subs."

"Not bad, not bad…you mind if I pay you digitally?" Taizen asked, struggling to find any cash on him.

"Now, Taizen, you know I don't like doing digital. It may be what's more convenient for most sub-humans, but cash has always been easier for me to keep track of."

"Well, I can't seem to find any right now, so digital may be our only option."

Sparky gave a heavy sigh. "All right, come on over to the desk, and I'll complete the transaction. You need sixteen, correct?"

"Yes. I'm sure Development can find a way to get four on each, so we'll take sixteen."

Sparky scanned the propulsions, and Taizen tapped his card on the scanner and held it there for a moment, letting the payment go through.

"You let Development know you owe them," Sparky said with a chuckle. "So, who are those two hooded fellows with you?"

Taizen began to lightly sweat, most noticeably on his forehead.

"They're just with me to watch over me and report any suspicious activity. You know Development isn't exactly fond of me."

"I think that's obvious at times," Sparky said, chuckling. "Have a good day, you guys."

With that, the three exited the shop and went a block before relaxing fully.

"Well, that was stressful," Joei said, pulling at his hoodie.

"You should've been me in those moments! I already told you most sub-humans aren't stupid; I'm just glad Development *really* isn't fond of me," Taizen stressed.

"Speaking of which, you and Sparky seemed to know each other well. What's the relationship there?"

"Well, as I said, Sparky's one of the best mechanics in the city, as well as one of the finest part makers. Development has had me be their errand runner to get parts for their projects."

"Interesting, but what is Development, exactly?"

"The Development Team makes weapons for the Sub-human Army. There are obviously other weapons creators, but Development has access to the most parts and has the most skilled creators and scientists working for them. They work directly alongside the army, getting them to be just as the army wants them. As a result, my dad, Captain Zaizo, wanted me to work there, since I wasn't sure what to do with myself. Though I find the weapons they make fascinating, they use me for errands so much. Maybe it's because they see me as a warrior like my dad, and therefore not good for much else when it comes to creating weapons? Or maybe they just don't like me. I don't know."

"Fascinating stuff, Taizen. The propulsions you got look quite interesting, too, and I'm quite excited to tinker with them and see what I can do. I gotta ask, though, what are 'Subs?'"

"Ah, Subs. They're just the currency we use in sub-human society."

"How much are they worth?"

Taizen had to ponder for a moment. "Well, I never did learn what the conversion to human currency was for Subs, so the best way to describe it is that a single Sub can buy you a sizable burger."

"That's...quite a lot, actually. So, where are we going next?"

"Talk of burgers made me hungry, so we should definitely get some food," Boyd said.

Joei glanced back, a bit annoyed.

"Come on, Boyd, we gotta focus on the task at hand. Food can come later."

"Nah, I agree with Boyd. There's a pizza place nearby, so let me treat you guys to some food. Plus, it'll give us some time to think about what we wanna do next."

"Pizza will do," said Boyd, and they headed off.

Chapter 22: A Problem Arises! The Plan to Save the Humans!

Zaizo rattled his chair violently. They'd kept him sedated for the trip, but he'd begun to awaken from his last dose. He had overheard Boyd, Joei, and Taizen when they were on their way to the hatch, and he knew he had to put a stop to it before anything could happen.

I can't believe my son teamed up with those guys! Or are they using him? Either way, I gotta get out of here and contact the Elders before they try and make their way up there, he thought to himself. The bars Boyd had wrapped around him were doing their job well, and all he had been able to do was make himself fall over. He was running out of ideas and wasn't sure what to do to free himself.

Wait, if I charge up energy into my arms, he thought, deciding to try it. He focused energy into his arms for several seconds and tried to pull them out. Although it took several tries, he managed to break the bars holding him and stood up, looking at the door. He went up to it and smashed it down with a few hits.

Hopefully they haven't gone too far, otherwise it may be too late, he thought as he ran down the hallway to the hatch.

***

"Man, space pizza is amazing!" Boyd said as he chowed down on a barbecue chicken pizza, one of his favorites. Joei had gotten a vegetable pizza, and Taizen a regular cheese.

"It's quite interesting how different the pizza tastes, yet how familiar its taste is as well," Joei said.

"I'm glad you guys enjoy it. I wasn't sure how other-worldly food would taste to you, so it's nice to hear. Now, any ideas for what we're gonna do?"

Joei made sure to keep his voice low as he said, "Well, our main goal is to stop whoever's at the top of the hierarchy of sub-humans. I think my first question to you would be this: who is the leader of the sub-human race?"

"Well, the Elder Council are the ones who rule over our society. They're the original eleven who came to Mars and started this society. The thing is, there's a clear leader among them, and that leader would be my grandfather, Elder Starpson, who has now given himself the title of King. As grandson of the Starpson line, I know him, and the Elders well. The other ones seem fine, but my grandfather...well, I always thought he was slightly mad. I know the humans called them all insane, but he really does seem to have a hint of it. His desire to cure diseases has certainly led him to become the most respected among the Elders, though, which is why I say he is considered their king."

"Do you know anything about his powers? He was said to be the strongest among the sub-humans by your father. Would you agree?"

"I would say he is, and that is attributed to his high intelligence as well as his regenerative abilities. Truth be told, aside from those things, the only other thing I know about his offensive capabilities is that he likes using machinery in his fighting style, but he's strong even without it. Then again, I've never really seen him fight, so I can't tell you for sure. He told me about some, and I overheard some things."

"I guess it makes sense. If the sub-humans have no one to fight, their combat abilities may not always be revealed, right?"

"Well...we do have a few enemies. Not as strong as us, of course, but still. You've seen the space slug; I think you can imagine there's definitely life outside us sub-humans and humans. The thing is, the leaders don't ever need to reveal their combat abilities, because no one could get that far with the army we've built up."

"Interesting. Back on topic, I'd like to visit your house, Taizen. I'd like a proper place to upgrade Boyd's gloves and boots so they can pack some more power. How about the Elders? Does the council have their own place of some kind?"

"Yes, they were given a tall palace to live in, though it looks more like a skyscraper. Each Elder has their own floor, with my grandfather's being at the top. If we wanna do this thing, it's best to go straight to the top floor."

"I see. We can plan more later. Let's eat."

***

"Sorry if it's a bit messy; I moved in recently and have yet to put everything where it needs to go. The whole planning of the human invasion took time out of my life, so please don't mind the clutter," Taizen said as they entered his home. His house looked expensive, with technical advancements in all kinds of places, such as self-adjusting light fixtures, a modernized vent system, and, in the kitchen in the back, microwaves that could heat food up in seconds and a talking oven.

"Your house looks...surprisingly normal for a modernized society," Joei said, looking around.

"Well, I guess we use what works and build upon it, am I right?"

Taizen led them to the dining table, where they sat down to discuss plans.

"If you don't mind, Taizen, I think this works perfectly for a worktable. May I use it?"

"Sure, I don't have an issue with that. Where did you get those tools?"

"I grabbed them from the storage room after I got into my disguise. That reminds me; Boyd, could you lend me the gloves and boots? I'm gonna start working on them while we plan."

"Yeah, sure, here you go," Boyd said, getting the gloves and boots out of his hoodie and handing them to Joei.

"So, Taizen, what's security look like in the palace?"

"Well, there're a couple guards outside the building that are there to prevent most people from getting inside. They won't be the problem, though. What will be is once we get inside. There are usually a ton of guards inside the building, mostly on the first floor and the top floor. Even that isn't going to be the biggest problem, though."

"What will be?" Joei asked.

"You see, as I said, each council member has their own floor, starting from the second floor. It's possible that security may notify them of our presence, and if that happens, well, we may have to fight each Elder individually...."

"That's not good. I'm not sure a human's endurance could fight eleven fighters of that caliber, especially if they're comparable to the strongest Elder."

"Actually, only some of them are strong fighters. I'd say about six of them have good fighting capabilities, with the others either having only self-defense or no combat skill whatsoever."

"Why would those Elders stop us, then? Wouldn't they be in for a hard time against us if they don't have combat abilities?"

"Ah, but see, there is a reason for them to stop us: to prevent us from reaching the top floor. If we take out my grandfather, the leader of sub-human society falls. It's unlikely that our civilization would deem the other Elders as worthy to rule over our race. After all, they only played a part in decisions made with this society. My grandfather was the one who ultimately made the decisions."

"So Boyd likely wouldn't have to exert himself as much as I thought."

"Come on, Joei, I brought down the captain of the ship we invaded and dozens of sub-humans that day. Give me some credit where it's due; I can fight for a while if I need to," Boyd said.

"I know, but if we got stuck in a situation like that, we could die. I'm just wanting to make sure we reduce our chances of getting into that kind of situation."

"Sounds like a plan to me. I think that's all for now. Once you've upgraded the gloves and boots, we can get a good idea of our offensive power. You guys let me know when you're hungry for dinner," Taizen said as his phone started ringing. "Lemme get that."

He got up and headed toward the hallway to the left of the kitchen, then entered a bedroom and shut the door behind him.

"Strange, I wonder who he got a call from," Boyd said as he relaxed in the chair. Joei started tinkering with the new propulsions.

***

"Great, this can't be good!" Taizen whispered loudly as he quickly got his phone out of his pocket to answer it. "Hello?"

"Hey, son, you got an explanation for yourself?" said Zaizo on the other end of the line.

Chapter 23: A Decision! The Chase Against the Trio!

"**What** do you mean, Dad?" Taizen asked nervously.

"You know well what I mean. You think I didn't hear you hanging with those humans? Tell me, son, are you a traitor?"

"Answer my question first. How did you get free?"

"Excuse me? Did you just tell me what to do?"

"N-no, I'm just interested in knowing."

"All right, fine; I'm currently walking to Newtopia and have already notified the Elders that the humans are heading toward the city. Now, answer my question."

"Um, well...I'm...."

"Son, you're acting awfully suspicious right now. Answer me, or I'll have to assume you're on their side."

"All right, fine! I decided to help them out a little, but only because I wanted to make them think they would actually have a chance of doing this. I'm about to capture them myself and make sure they're dealt with correctly."

"Wow, son...you're such an awful liar."

"No, Dad, I swear I'm—"

"I'm sending reinforcements to your house right now. You'd better decide to abandon them by then, or I won't hesitate to have you jailed for taking their side."

"No, Dad, you don't need to—" the captain hung up the phone.

Taizen ran into the living room and said, "Guys, we gotta go, like now!"

"Why? What's going on?" Boyd asked as he and Joei stood up.

"My dad escaped the ship somehow! He's calling reinforcements to come to my house, so if we don't leave now, we could be dead!"

"Was that your dad on the phone?"

"Yes, it was! Now we need to get going before they get here! I'm gonna go get some oxygen masks."

"Wait, what—" Boyd tried to ask, but Taizen was already back in the hallway at a closet. Boyd got himself ready to go, and Joei gathered up his tools, along with the gloves and boots, and put them in his hoodie pocket. Taizen quickly came back with three oxygen masks, with small tanks accompanying them.

"All right, take one of these. You'll need them once we leave the city" Taizen said as he passed out the oxygen masks. They went out the front door and ran behind the house. Boyd and Joei followed Taizen as they went farther and farther from the neighborhood. Soon, multiple vehicles parked at the house, and sub-humans started getting out of the vehicles and ran toward the trio. There were barely a few acres between them.

"Great, they're already here! We need to put more distance between us and them, or we'll be caught!"

"Joei, can I use the gloves and boots?"

"I've already started working on the gloves, so those are a no go. I haven't touched the boots yet, so here you go," Joei said as he got the boots out from his hoodie pocket and gave them to Boyd.

"Boyd, don't put those on unless we have to fight, otherwise they'll catch up to us!" Taizen said. Boyd nodded, and they continued running, still far from the dome's border.

Soon, a mini spaceship came from above. A rope flung out as multiple sub-humans appeared and slid down the rope. The three stopped, and Boyd quickly took his shoes off to put his boots on, ready to fight. Boyd used his right leg and stomped it into the ground, propelling himself upward. He managed to reach a sub-human on the rope and went for a spinning kick. Boyd struck him in the jaw, and he fell straight to the ground. He grabbed onto the rope and went for the next one.

"Call for backup! The human is stronger than we anticipated!" the sub-human said as he was kicked in the back of his head and sent downward toward the ground.

"Requesting backup! The human is stronger than originally thought!" said the sub-human piloting the ship. He then set the ship on autopilot and was ready to fight. Boyd, now on the ship, ran toward the pilot, dodged attacks, and kicked him in the back, causing the pilot to fall off the ship. Boyd went toward the door and waved from above.

"I got them!" yelled Boyd as he came down quickly on the rope. Luckily, only one of the sub-humans was still conscious, and Taizen traded only a few blows with him before knocking him out. Boyd landed at the bottom.

"They called for backup, and there's still ground troops chasing after us; we need to go now before more come!

Joei and Taizen agreed, and they started running out of there. The red tint of the rocky ground was all that could be seen beyond the giant, translucent dome that covered the city. All the three could do was continue running. Joei was already getting tired from the run, his ankle throbbing.

"Guys...someone needs to carry me, or I'm gonna be left behind," Joei said, still running, but losing steam quickly.

"Get on," said Taizen as he stopped to let Joei hop on his back. The three started running again. Backup came fast, and soon a small army started coming after them. It wasn't long before they neared the dome.

"Great, what do we do now!?" Boyd asked.

"The dome is a semi-permeable substance, kind of like Jello, that things can come in and out of. It'll take a bit of effort, but we can go right through it, so you both need to put your oxygen masks on and brace yourselves!"

Mere yards from the dome, they put their oxygen masks on, continued running and then slammed into the dome. Although difficult at first, they went through with enough force. They rolled onto the ground, but quickly stood up and continued running.

"How far out will they follow us?" Joei asked.

"In a few minutes here, we should be safe to stop, assuming they don't see us as a threat outside the city."

The army slowed down as they went farther and farther away, until they were out of sight.

***

"What's the status of the humans?" A commanding voice asked into a communicator. The sub-human, frail and old, was still tall in stature. Although balding, he still had some white hair on the back of his head. He wore thick, velvety robes of a dark purple color. Sitting beside him was Zaizo, waiting for the status update as well.

"Unfortunately, My King, they got away. They're beyond the dome, however, so they won't last long," the voice said. The frail sub-human gripped the communicator harder.

"You're sure about this fact?"

"Yes, My King. They disappeared from our sight a few minutes ago."

"Forget it, then. Have some troops keep a lookout in case they return," the frail sub-human said, and ended the call.

"What's the news?" Zaizo asked, thinking about Taizen.

"They got away, meaning we'll have to keep a lookout to see if they return. In any case, thank you for telling me this, son."

"Yeah, you're welcome. I'm just worried about my own son. Surely we can convince him to come back, right?"

The frail sub-human turned to face a portrait of himself and said, "We'd better hope so, because otherwise he'll be little more than a traitor in our society." The portrait had a nameplate above it, reading "James Starpson."

Chapter 24: A Difficult Survival! The Upgrades to Save Humanity!

"So...cold..." was all Joei could say. The three may have escaped the sub-human army for now, but Mars' environment wasn't being kind to them. They had found a large rock with an opening that they sat under. The hoodies were barely helping Boyd and Joei, and Taizen wasn't faring much better.

"We're lucky we're even alive, right now. Though our civilization has warmed things up a lot, it's still usually zero degrees Celsius or a bit below. Without these oxygen masks, we would've been dead within minutes," Taizen said.

"But still, what...do we do now?" Boyd asked, almost feeling too cold to talk.

"We gotta get to the next town fast, otherwise we're going to die out here in the cold. To the left is the city, and if we can find the road..."

"Is that it?" Joei asked, having already stood up, and pointed to what seemed like a road that led to Newtopia, but also led out into the distance.

"Yes, actually. We need to follow the road in order to reach the next town. Hurry guys, otherwise we'll freeze to death!" Taizen said, pulling Boyd up. The three followed the road closely without walking directly on it.

***

"So...cold...so...tired," Joei said, struggling to take steps. Boyd was also having a hard time. The cold was finally getting to them and restricting their movements.

"You guys don't look so good. Wanna hop on my back?" Taizen asked, having stopped walking to check on the two.

"Sure...."

Joei staggered toward him as he fell. Taizen caught him and lifted him onto his back. Boyd also grabbed onto his back and held on as he started walking again.

"Any idea...how much longer?" Boyd asked.

"It's only about a couple hours' walk from the city. We should be there in about an hour," Taizen replied, checking his watch. It was already four PM Mars time.

***

"Finally, I can take this off!" Boyd said, pulling the oxygen mask off and stuffing it into his hoodie pocket. They found what appeared to be the equivalent of an Earth suburban town and were standing on a sidewalk in what looked like a neighborhood. The buildings were much shorter, there were fewer sub-humans around, and the transportation being used appeared to be old. They were like sleeker, smaller versions of a space rover, though with an interior that had seats, steering, and windows.

Joei was astounded. "The vehicles here look..."

"Older?" Taizen bumped in. "That's because that's what we first used when we came to this planet. Similar devices were used by you humans, correct? The designs were based on those, and they worked for a time. Of course, our society evolved technologically quite quickly, and you saw in the city that we now use hovercrafts with mini rocket engines. This is actually the first town that was created when the Elders arrived here."

"That's quite fascinating, though I feel we need to focus on the matter at hand. Are there any good places we can go for me to work on Boyd's gloves and boots?"

"Let's see; if I recall correctly, there's a library here. Maybe they'll have a room we can rent out?"

"Sounds like a plan, but where is it?"

"I don't remember. Let's see if anyone can tell us."

***

"Hello, how can I help you?" The female sub-human asked the trio. She was sitting at a desk and wearing a gray sweater as well as round glasses. She also appeared to be middle aged, though being sub-human, Boyd and Joei couldn't really tell for sure. It was also a bit strange seeing one with such long brown hair, as all the others either had very short hair or none at all.

"Hey, so we're in need of a room to do some stuff in. Would it be possible to rent one?" Taizen asked, leaning onto the desk.

"Oh, Captain Zaizo's son. Sure, for how long?"

"Let's see, maybe until you guys close?"

"Ok, so...about two and a half hours."

"That's it?"

"Well, since you're the son of one of the top captains of the sub-human army, I guess I could give you the keys to lock the place up. Issue is how to get it back to me..."

"How about making a copy? Don't you guys have a 3D printer here?"

"Oh, that's right. Yeah, that should work. Go ahead and get settled in your room, I'll get the key to you in about ten minutes. I'll put you guys in room 1A."

"Sounds good. Thanks for helping us out."

"No problem." With that, the trio found room 1A, and Joei got to work on the gloves and boots.

"I'm not sure I can complete the upgrades in a mere two and a half hours, especially since this is technology that's much more advanced than what we have on Earth. Taizen, do you happen to have any experience with how these work?"

Taizen shrugged lightly. "I've observed Development using older models, but not much outside of that."

He sat down beside Joei, observed the new propulsions, and then attempted to help Joei with putting them onto the gloves and boots.

***

"Ok, solder that, and...was that the last one?" Taizen asked as he gazed at the boot that Joei was soldering one of the new propulsions onto. Boyd made conversation with them whenever he could, but they were hard at work upgrading the gloves and boots.

"After this one, I believe so."

"You guys finally done?" Boyd asked, leaning back into his chair with his legs on the table.

"Just about, yeah," Joei said, "but I'll need to double check that everything is attached correctly. You'll also be testing them in whatever environment is most ideal."

"The gym would be a good idea; using a punching bag to test it out could work well," Taizen said.

"Okay, it seems they're all attached correctly, so let's head to the gym. Lead the way, Taizen."

***

"All right, Boyd, I need you to be prepared for a much stronger force. I have no clue how much power these propulsions pack, so don't overdo it, okay?" Joei said as they walked into the gym, which they managed to get into since Taizen was the King's son.

"Just go and do a casual punch."

"Sounds good," Boyd said as he slipped on the gloves, already having the boots on. He walked over to a black punching bag in the corner of the room. He prepared a punch and went for it. His fist went right through the punching bag and split it in two. The bottom half of the punching bag fell to the ground, and Boyd fell forward into the punching bag, which was filled with soft, white stuffing. The top part of the punching bag flew off, bounced off the wall, and fell on the ground on the other side of the room.

"That was...amazing!" Joei said, running over to help Boyd.

"Yeah...I guess I'm finally ready to be Earth's warrior, huh?"

***

"My King! Some news on the humans has surfaced!" the sub-human servant said to the king. He had been worried over the issue of the trio for a few hours ever since they escaped and wanted an update.

"Let's hear it," Starpson said as he sat at his throne-like chair below his portrait.

"Apparently our undercover librarian at one of the small towns spotted your grandson with two hooded humans, just like the ones that we saw running away from the city."

"That's a *very* interesting development. Have a small army go there and survey the town and capture the trio if they're spotted."

"Right away, My King!"

The servant ran out of the room. Starpson turned his chair to face his portrait.

"I'm not going to let a couple of pesky humans destroy everything I've worked toward."

Chapter 25: Training Again! Newfound Strength!

"Man, the upgrades were a bigger success than I thought!" Joei said as they walked down a sidewalk. They had been kicked out due to breaking the punching bag, but they got what they had come for: a power test for the gloves and boots.

"I feel the punching bag only showed a bit of what the potential of the gloves and boots actually is. A combat situation will show us how good they really are," Taizen said.

"So where do we go next?" Boyd asked, having put his gloves and boots in his hoodie pocket.

"That's our issue right now. If we go back to the city, we're bound to be found. I also think that you're gonna need some training, Boyd. Now that your gloves and boots are stronger, I wonder if a human like you can so easily get used to the newfound power they hold."

"So we need a training place. Question is, where?"

"I've got an idea that should work, though we won't have a lot of time seeing as the Sub-human Army is bound to come after us at some point. I've got Uncle Bonzo who's pretty laid back and chill. I think he'll allow us to stay at his place for a bit so we can train there."

"Sounds like a plan to me. Lead the way, Taizen."

***

A small group of soldier sub-humans entered the gym. They went straight to the welcome desk where the receptionist working there sat. He shook mildly at the presence of the soldiers, who could easily kill him if he did the wrong thing.

"H-hey, sirs, h-how can I help you all today?" The receptionist could barely get the words out.

"Well, we're looking for a couple of humans and have been checking businesses near a certain library that reported them. Would you happen to know about any humans around here, maybe even a couple in your own gym?" One of the soldiers asked.

"I heard they were also with the King's grandson," another one said.

"Wait, really?" the receptionist asked.

"Yeah, you heard something about that?"

"A-as a matter of fact, yes! Three guys, including the King's grandson, came here, two of them in black hoodies. One of the guys in the black hoodies went up to a punching bag and destroyed it in one hit! I kicked them out, of course, but I had no idea they were humans."

The army leader was intrigued. "So where did they go?"

"I-I'm not totally sure, but I believe I saw them go left from the exit when I kicked them out about half an hour ago," the sub-human pointed to his left toward the door.

"Good, good, thanks for the info, little guy. We'll be on our way out now," the army leader said, turning around and heading toward the exit. The rest of the group followed suit. "Boys, we're heading for the humans immediately!"

"Aye, Commander Tenzo!" the group said.

***

"Oh, hello, Taizen," Uncle Bonzo said as he opened the door. He was wearing only some white underwear with a navy blue bathrobe, had a gut, and looked like he had more than a few days' stubble. He slouched as well, and had short hair that was both gray and balding. "What can I do for you?"

"Uncle Bonzo! Good to see you again. We were in town and I thought I'd ask if we could use your backyard to do some testing for a prototype the Development Team created."

Taizen got the gloves and boots from Boyd's hoodie pockets to show to Bonzo.

"Hm, interesting. Does that mean those guys behind you are from the Development Team?"

"They sure are! Development appears to not trust me, so they had these guys follow me to make sure I do my errands properly."

"Uh huh. Why are you wanting to test here instead of testing at Development?"

"Well, this is a more minor prototype, so I didn't wanna bother taking up a spot for a more valuable prototype."

"I see. Well, you guys can come in and head to the backyard if you'd like."

Bonzo let them in. The living room was very simple, a couch chair on the left side with a flat screen TV hanging on the other side. A kitchen was present beyond the living room, and there were translucent doors on the back wall that opened to the backyard. The whole area was quite messy, though, with piles of clothes all over the place and a smoky smell filling the room.

"All right, thanks, Uncle Bonzo," Taizen said as the three went through the doors to the backyard. Aside from the small patio made of a reddish stone, the backyard was empty, and the grass quite dead. It was big enough for what Boyd needed to do, though.

"Are you sure your uncle isn't gonna try to check on us out here in the back?" Joei asked.

"You make a fair point. I'll distract him and make sure the curtains lie over the doors so he can't see you. I'll come up with some kind of excuse so he doesn't bother looking."

Taizen stepped back into the house. Uncle Bonzo had gone back to sitting on the couch, watching TV.

"Already inside? I thought you needed to test the prototype."

"My two supervisors decided to test it themselves. They advise not to go near the doors or the backyard in general while they're testing, since it could get dangerous."

"Ah, okay. My backyard's already dead enough, so it's not like this is gonna do much else to it."

Taizen pulled one of the curtains back a bit and gave a thumbs up. Boyd saw it and got to work.

"You'll need to learn to get used to the power these gloves give off now that they're stronger than before," Joei said, sitting down on the patio floor. Boyd nodded and tried going for small punches at first. The gloves were so strong that they pulled Boyd forward several feet, face planting into the grass.

"This is gonna take a while," Boyd said, getting back up. *At least with the first version of the gloves, it was easier to let my body move with the punches, but how do I manage it with these...?* Boyd thought. He decided to try a few different things. First, he tried swinging his fist down so he would stop after making a punch, though this resulted in him slamming into the ground. After several attempts, he saw this wasn't gonna work. Next, he went for a swinging technique, to see what would happen. On his first attempt, he was sent spinning in the air and fell onto the ground right on his face. Even after a few attempts, it still caused him to spin around multiple times.

Nothing is working. Is this too much for someone like me? Boyd thought, not quite sure what to try next. He decided to lie on the ground and gaze up at the sky. It was already dark, with the two moons starting to come up. Within a few minutes, he fell asleep.

"Boyd," Joei said, rolling his eyes.

***

"Captain, we've got a problem," Tenzo said through a communicator. A sub-human captain in the cockpit of a ship picked it up.

"What's the problem?"

"Well, we've been following a lead, but it hasn't gotten us anywhere. We've been going through the town and haven't seen any sign of the fugitives."

The captain tightened his grip around the communicator. "I was afraid of this. I'll need to make an announcement so that every sub-human in Motern Town is looking out for them. That way, we can find them."

"Sounds good. Thanks, captain."

"You're welcome," the captain said as he hung up. "Time for a universal emergency message."

Chapter 26: Is this It!? Discovered by the Sub-human Army!

Boyd was rudely awakened to Joei's face telling him to wake up!

"Uhhh, Joei?"

"Sorry, Boyd, you fell asleep. I know you may be tired, but you need to get used to those gloves and boots. Sleep can come after you can get those down."

Boyd dizzily got up and shook his head as Joei went back to sitting on the patio floor. He thought for a few minutes about what to do next and got an idea. *It may be a bit ridiculous, but I've got to at least try,* he thought. When he went to punch, he brought his arm upward, lifting his body up. He was prepared for it, though, and made a shaky landing. After a few tries, he was completely stable upon landing.

"I'm astounded. You got that down even more quickly than you did with the first iteration of the gloves. The fighting spirit in you shows."

"Thanks, but I'm not done yet. I still gotta find a solution for the boots."

With fists, it's easy to swing upward, but feet are a different story, Boyd thought, moving his legs around in different positions. He thought up something that might work, but only trying would confirm it. He went for a kick, then tried doing a flip. The force swung upward, then looped right back down. He failed to land on his feet the first time, but after a few tries, he managed to do it.

"Looks like you've already mastered the power of your new gloves and boots, however unconventional your methods may be."

"I'd like to try doing it a few more times, but yeah, I think I've got these down," Boyd said, lifting his fist into the air in triumph. He was sent flying into the air and back down onto his back. "Urgh...."

***

Taizen was looking through some notes on his device for info when he got an urgent notification from his phone.

"What's this?"

He pulled the notification up. It was an audio message.

143

"Attention all sub-humans in Motern Town, this is a town-wide emergency. Two humans have been spotted in the town disguised as sub-humans. They wear black hoodies and keep their heads covered. All sub-humans who are currently in Motern Town must evacuate immediately. I repeat, all sub-humans in Motern Town must evacuate immediately," said the deep voice from the audio message.

"Hey, wait…" Bonzo said as Taizen ran toward the translucent doors and opened them.

"Guys, we gotta get out of here, now. An announcement was just made on you two, and now every sub-human in the town is gonna be looking out for us. Let's jump over the fence."

The two went toward him and followed suit. They jumped on the left side of the fence and went toward the sidewalk at the front of the houses and started running.

A few seconds later, sub-humans started pouring out of the houses, having little more than food and water on them. Many saw Joei and Boyd and screamed, running in the opposite direction. Taizen glanced back and saw them, but also saw a small group coming toward them. The tall, muscular sub-humans far behind him were armored and armed.

"Uh, guys? We need to speed up," Taizen said, making increasing his pace. Joei and Boyd glanced behind and saw them as well, making their paces faster, too. The leading sub-human ran up quickly to them and did a tall flip, landing right in front of them, facing them.

"What's up, boys? I'm Commander Tenzo, and I'm gonna be y'all's personal trainer today. Step one, I beat you each to a pulp."

Tenzo rushed straight toward Boyd with an uppercut. Taizen stepped in and blocked his attack.

"You'll have to get through me first if you want to take these humans," Taizen said.

"So, you really have become the humans' ally, huh? Guess I'll have to beat you up as well."

He went in for a jab at Taizen. The two traded blows, but Taizen was struggling to keep up. Boyd quickly took his gloves and boots out of his hoodie pocket and put them on. He waited for Tenzo to come in for a blow, then struck him in the gut, sending him flying several yards away and landing on his back.

"Thanks, Taizen, but I think I've got this now."

Boyd stood in front of Taizen. Tenzo stood up and started walking toward him.

"So, you're the strongest one among them, I see. I'll make sure to go all out against you," Tenzo said, dashing toward Boyd. Boyd cranked his arm back and slammed his fist into Tenzo's. Tenzo was slammed onto his back.

"I used to struggle against sub-humans of your caliber, but I'm beyond that now. I'm stronger, so why don't you go ahead and give up?" Boyd told him. Boyd walked over, as Tenzo had barely gotten on his feet. Tenzo went in with his right fist, but Boyd pushed forward with his foot and slammed him back into the ground.

145

"It's over, Tenzo. Why don't you tell your soldiers to surrender now so we can end this?"

"I refuse. As if I'd give into the likes of you! Plus, I don't need to, anyway. Why don't you take a look in front of you?"

Boyd looked up and saw multiple small ships just outside the translucent dome of the town. Below the ships were what looked to be around a hundred armored sub-humans in a square formation.

"On each ship, except for one, is a commander of the Sub-human Army. On the center ship without one is a captain. I figured you'd be pretty strong, so I brought some backup. If you try to run away, you're finished."

Tenzo started laughing maniacally. Boyd picked him up, put his fist into his face, and slammed him back into the ground.

"If you're looking to capture us, we're not going down without a fight!" Boyd yelled, putting his fist out toward the army.

"So be it, tough guy. You're going down," said the captain of the center ship through the speakers.

Chapter 27: A Difficult Battle! The Trio Vs. the Sub-human Army!

"**Joei,** hop on my back!" Taizen said. Joei grabbed onto Taizen's shoulders and hoisted himself up. Taizen got close to Boyd, back to back. There were sub-humans coming from both directions.

"Those ships will be problematic, so I'm heading towards them first," Boyd said, then started running toward the army. He went right through the translucent dome and looked toward the center ship.

I gotta take out the captain first, or else I risk us getting captured, Boyd thought as he ran toward the army. He noticed that as he got closer to the ship, it seemed to lower itself toward him, until eventually it was on level ground with him. Then he noticed the ground feeling lighter and looked down.

He had somehow managed to lift himself into the air with his boots and was now as high as the ship. As soon as he noticed, he started falling rapidly. He screamed the whole way down before he landed on a sub-human soldier, instantly knocking the soldier out. He had landed right in the center of the army.

"It's one of the humans! Get him!" one of the soldiers said before the entire army started dogpiling him. The captain saw what was happening just below him from the cockpit and slowly facepalmed before putting a small communicator to his mouth.

"What the heck are you doing, soldiers!? Our orders were to capture the human, so do it with professionalism!" the captain commanded the army.

"Yes, Captain Arpmin!"

The army got off Boyd. One soldier quickly locked Boyd's arms with his own, and another locked his legs with his arms as well. Boyd shook his arms, activating the gloves and knocking the soldier down. He then pushed off the ground with his arms and held them up. The propulsions went off again and slammed the soldier in the face, knocking him onto the ground.

Boyd crouched down and shot himself up into the air with his legs, holding his right arm up. At that moment, he felt like a superhero. His fist tore right through the bottom of the ship, and he slammed into the ceiling, falling onto the floor.

"Well, well, look who decided to fight me," said Arpmin, walking over to him. Boyd had fallen into the seating area of the ship, with seats that lined the walls. Boyd stood up and took on a fighting stance.

"I'll have you know that I've heard about your strength. The strength to take out Zaizo, I heard. I'll make sure to go all out against you and take you out in the most professional and elegant manner possible."

Arpmin raised his right arm out. Attached to his arm was what seemed like a futuristic version of a sniper rifle.

"A gun is interesting, but that won't be enough to take me out."

"We'll see."

Arpmin narrowly dodged one of Boyd's attacks and let off a shot from his gun. Boyd narrowly dodged in return as the captain fired off multiple shots. He jumped above them and came at the captain by kicking off with both his legs. Boyd managed to give him an uppercut to the chin and flung him through the cockpit windshield; breaking the glass and sending him falling to the bottom a hundred feet down.

"Catch me, my soldiers!" The captain yelled. The soldiers ran and managed to catch him.

"All right, soldiers, great job." He grabbed his communicator. "Commanders in the ships, get out here!"

Each of the remaining ships spat out rope ladders, from which multiple commanders started sliding down. The four ran over to the captain and stood beside him.

"Go into formation 'Cannon!'" said Arpmin. They followed suit, and two lifted the captain up by his arms. The other two waited until he was lifted horizontally from his arms and put their hands around his shoes, one commander for each shoe. The captain bent his knees and began charging up energy.

"All right, on the count of three. One, two, three!"

Arpmin pushed off as the two in the back also pushed him forward, and the two remaining commanders pushed his hands to give him an extra boost. The captain was sent flying toward the ship he'd fallen out of, smashing through the cockpit windshield and slamming his fist into Boyd's face, bringing the captain down onto the floor and sending Boyd to the back of the ship. Boyd quickly got back up.

"No more. I'm ending this," Boyd said, running back toward Arpmin for a strike. The captain came back with a counter-strike and picked him up, throwing him out of the broken windshield. Boyd fell and the commanders caught him and slammed him into the ground. The captain jumped down to join in.

"Pummel him, boys."

Boyd could barely stand up before they started throwing punches at him. He went back and forth around the small circle of commanders, being punched around repeatedly. Boyd blocked his face as they continued. Eventually, when Boyd was facing one of them, he went in for a punch, knocking the commander down. The captain came and punched Boyd back to the remaining ones, who slammed him into the ground and held him down. The captain also helped restrain him.

"It's over for you, o' futile one."

***

Taizen was struggling to defeat all the commander's soldiers, with Joei's added weight to his back being an issue for him. Now he was on his last one.

"Give up, already. You're obviously too tired to fight me properly," the soldier said to Taizen.

"I don't care what you think, go down already!" Taizen said as he came in for another hit. The two traded a few blows before Taizen's legs began to shake. He went for the gut, and Taizen fell onto his back, knocking the wind out of Joei. The soldier stepped forward.

"You're done." He went in for a hit as Taizen kicked both of his legs out at the soldier's gut. He stumbled backward and fell onto his back. Taizen got up, as did Joei.

"Is he...?"

"Yup, he's out cold."

Taizen looked over to where Boyd was fighting, only to see him being restrained by multiple sub-humans. Joei looked, too, then attempted to run toward where Boyd was. Taizen held him back by his arms as he flailed about.

"What are you doing, Taizen!? Boyd's in trouble!"

"If we go into that group of commanders with a captain, we'll be captured as well."

After a few seconds, Joei stopped flailing and Taizen released him.

"Well then, what's your plan? We can't just leave Boyd to fend for himself."

"I have an idea, but you'll have to follow my every move if we want to make it work."

Chapter 28: Boyd Captured! The Plan to Save a Friend!

"Taizen, you're crazy!" Joei was being carried by his friend, who was about to jump onto the ship. They had waited for Boyd to be captured and carried onto one of the ships so that no one was looking back.

"Come on, Joei, we talked about this. I have great muscle strength, so my boosts should be enough to get us up on the ship.

"Yeah, emphasis on should—agghhh!" It was all Joei got out before Taizen went for a high jump. As he soared through the air, he started slowing down at the bottom of the ship and barely made it to the top. Taizen landed and let Joei climb off his back.

"Well, we made it, didn't we?"

"I wasn't trying to prove a point. I was just trying to be safe."

They looked around at their immediate surroundings. The top of the ship was very similar to an airplanes', so there wasn't a lot of room to stand on, as it started sloping on each side after several feet. They sat down and got settled.

"How on earth did they not immediately know we had landed on the top of the ship?" Joei asked.

"These ships are used exclusively on Mars. As strange as it may seem, the security on them is pretty light since it's not really needed. You have to remember that our society is still very young in comparison to any on Earth, so our population is lower and therefore can't produce as many materials. Any security is saved for the important things. There aren't usually too many issues, as we are the only race on the planet."

"Well, what's our plan to get Boyd back?"

"It's a work in progress, but the basic idea is that we'll need to disguise ourselves as security guards to make it into the cell room. He'll probably be held in a temporary cell area until they're ready to execute him, so we'll need to act fast. Luckily, if they're taking him where I think they are, we should be able to get to him. For now, we'll need to wait."

With that, Taizen laid on his back, and Joei followed soon after, and they were carried on the ship back to Newtopia.

**

"Let me go already!" Boyd yelled as he attempted to free himself from the shackles that held him. He had large metal balls that encased his hands and feet that were attached to metal ropes, which were secured to a metal frame. Needless to say, Boyd had had no success with freeing himself so far. He had just left the ship and was being transported to a short building, which appeared to be a jail of some kind. Joei and Taizen carefully peeked from the top of the ship, ready to make their move.

"Once they enter the building, I'll take out both guards. You'll ride on my back to stay safe, so go ahead and hop on," Taizen said, ready to pounce.

"O-okay, just don't get me killed."

Taizen jumped straight down from the ship as soon as Joei was on his back. Joei couldn't help but scream the whole way down as Taizen slammed himself on top of one of the guards, digging him into the ground. The other guard tried to fight Taizen but ultimately got pummeled by him.

"These outfits should work for getting inside," Taizen said, holding up the coat the guard had been wearing. Joei was already getting his guard's coat on.

"Indeed. I'm glad I kept the stilts with me now, because there's no way I'd be cutting it in there as a shorty."

Joei got his stilts out of the hoodie he had taken off. He put on his cap and lowered it so it covered all but his mouth.

They both got the rest of their new clothes on, prepped themselves, and headed toward the building.

"Don't say a word once we go inside."

Joei nodded, and they opened the doors. The building was quite large for a jail, with a ceiling that went all the way to the third floor, and two metallic, spiraling staircases to the left and the right, each leading to the second and third floors. There was a receptionist a few feet away, who was sitting there minding his own business.

"Oh, you two. What do you guys want?" The receptionist asked without looking at them.

"We wanted to know where the captain was, given we're guards of his ship and all," Taizen said, trying not to look directly at him.

"Hm, but aren't guards supposed to guard the ship and stuff? Not watch over a captain."

"Well, you know how he is, wanting to have order in everything. He asked us to check up on him frequently."

"Oh, did he now? I suppose I can't argue with that. He's on the basement floor, he should be putting the prisoner in cell 7-A."

"Okay, thanks."

They began to walk away. The receptionist finally glanced at the two and quickly noticed something was off.

"Hey, wait a minute—you two come back here."

They slowly went back to the desk and continued not to look directly at him.

"I knew it, you're not the guards, you're Taizen and you're—" Taizen slammed his fist into his face, knocking him out. The two let out a sigh of relief.

"It seems like these disguises aren't working too well after all," Joei said.

"Well, it's better than nothing, right? Now quickly, we gotta get down there before security calls actual guards to come get us."

Taizen pulled Joei toward the door that led downstairs. Yet another spiral staircase lay behind the door, and at the bottom was a long hallway. The place didn't appear to be well maintained and was covered in smooth, red stone. To the left were cells that were barely the size of a car, and the whole place looked much older than the rest of the city.

"Now, where's Boyd's cell...."

"It seems like the cells are in ascending order from one, and they go all the way down to 'E' before moving up to the next number. From what I can tell, we shouldn't be too far off from him seeing as we're on five..." Joei said, looking at the cell labels. It wasn't long before they made it to the sixes and saw 7-A up ahead.

"Be very quiet, Joei. There could easily be a guard coming at any given moment if we're not careful."

They went up to cell 7-A and saw Boyd sitting in the middle of the back wall, looking knocked out, with multiple bruises on his face and a swollen cheek.

"Boyd, we're here. Do you have any clue where your gloves and boots are or where some keys may be?" Joei asked. Boyd slowly looked up at the two.

"I'm glad you guys are here, but you need to hurry. I saw a guard room around halfway through coming through this hallway. I don't know where they put my gloves or boots, but it's worth looking there."

"I know where that is. I'll be right back," Taizen said as he started running toward the room. Sure enough, right at the first cell, 5-A, was a room to its left. The room was about the size of a regular office and had a rectangular window that faced the cells. The guard inside was older and had a short, gray beard. He appeared to be asleep, and the desk was cluttered with a computer and stacks of papers. Taizen tip-toed toward the desk and slowly opened the drawer. Sure enough, inside were many objects which looked to be from prisoners, including Boyd's gloves and boots. As he started taking them, he saw the guard open his eyes.

"Hrm? Wh-who's there?" the guard said groggily. Taizen punched him in the face and he fell backward, taking his chair with him. Taizen took the gloves and boots and started running back to Boyd's cell.

158

"Here, Boyd, break through the bars so we can get out of here."

Taizen held the gloves out.

"I can't reach you! You'll have to do it yourself."

Taizen gazed at the gloves for a moment, then put one on and punched right through the bars. The bars broke and bent, and Taizen was sent flying forward onto the ground of the cell, but the job was done. Taizen handed the gloves and boots to Boyd, and Boyd punched through his shackles, freeing him.

"Good, let's get outta here before someone finds—" Arpmin held Joei in a chokehold.

"I thought I heard some noise down here. One move, and your friend here is dead," Arpmin said.

Chapter 29: Escaping the Jail! To the Palace We Go!

In that moment, Boyd felt himself veer off into another world. He saw Arpmin dodging one of his attacks and then crushing Joei's neck immediately after.

Wait, does this mean Joei's guaranteed to die? Boyd thought as he came to the realization that he was having a vision. The vision ended, and Boyd knew there was only one thing he could do.

*If the captain dodged to the right, then....*Boyd crouched down, ready to pounce at any moment.

"You think I kid? Try it, and see what happens," Arpmin said. Boyd pounced right toward the captain, and he dodged his initial attack.

Now!

Boyd went in for a right hook just as the captain was about to crush Joei's neck. He went for the nose and crushed it. Boyd drove him into the ground, sending a couple teeth flying.

"Boyd, that was incredible. How'd you do that?" Joei said, sprawled on the ground.

"My vision told me where the captain would dodge. Hey, I'm sure there'll be guards here soon. Come on."

Guards started coming from both sides of the hallway, blocking them off.

"Taizen, put Joei on your back, and let's take the shorter hallway beyond this cell."

Taizen acted accordingly, and they started running. A couple dozen guards blocked the way, but Boyd simply used one of his legs to uppercut the guard in front, then followed it up with a walking Propeller Propulsion, taking out most of the guards. He finished off the last few with some swift punches and kicks.

"You've gotten quite a bit stronger, Boyd. Now you're taking out guards effortlessly," Taizen said as they ran toward the spiral staircase on that side of the hallway.

"Well, these upgraded gloves and boots have helped a lot. We gotta get out of here fast. What's the plan now?"

"We're going to have to go directly to the palace from here. Now that we're right in the middle of the city, that's our safest bet."

They reached the stairs and headed up. As they were getting to the top, Boyd realized that more guards were coming from the top of the stairs.

"Hang on, guys," Boyd said as he started running faster. He came in with several uppercuts in a row, throwing the guards to the bottom of the stairs, where the guards from the other side had already reached. They finally got to the base floor again, but more guards were waiting for them at the entrance. Boyd gave each one a swift punch or kick, and they escaped the building.

"Okay, where's the palace?"

"Let me pull up the location on my device," Taizen said, quickly pulling out a device that resembled a smartphone and started messing around with it.

"Head left."

***

"My King! My King!" A servant ran into Starpson's throne room. He turned around.

"This had better be good."

"It is! The human has escaped! The other human and your grandson appear to be with him!"

"I see...and why hasn't he been handled yet!?"

"We have been working on that, but the one human with special equipment has been able to make it through every guard we send out!"

"And what of Arpmin, who was supposed to oversee his capture and make sure he didn't escape?"

"He...was reported to have been taken out in one punch by the human with special equipment...."

Starpson grabbed him by the shirt and quickly lifted him up onto his level.

"What!? I thought he struggled in his battle with Zaizo, and Arpmin didn't even give him trouble?"

"We don't know, My King! Perhaps the human has received upgrades to his gear...."

The king slowly put his servant down.

"Perhaps he has. But by who?"

"We're unsure. Captain Zaizo also has informed us that one of the humans has familial relations with traitor Parett. He's his son."

"He neglected to tell me that fact when I saw him earlier. So, he's related to him, huh? What's their current trajectory?"

"Toward this very palace! What is your command, My King?"

The king put his hands together and smiled.

"Have every available guard and soldier surround the palace. We cannot let them through under any circumstances."

"Yes, My King. I will let the guard and army services know right away!"

As the servant left, King Starpson turned to glance at an old photo of him and the other ten Elders. Another one was also in the picture, but his head was blackened out with marker.

"Parrett, I won't let your lineage take me down. Your traitorous son shall die here."

***

"We're getting close to the palace! Just a little more to go!" Taizen said. Still, there were a bunch of guards that managed to stay on their trail even on one of the busiest streets in the city on a night like this. Taizen and Boyd parkoured over the hovercrafts and maneuvered their way around the crowds of people on the sidewalks. They were just a block away from the palace, and they could now see the gate that stood around a tall, fancy building, which almost looked like it was made from rubies. There were fewer citizens around this area, so it was easier to get through.

"Wait..." Boyd said, looking in the distance. He saw that tons of guards and soldiers, all in a large crowd, surrounded the gates of the palace. They seemed to number in the hundreds, and didn't appear ready to back down.

"They've already gotten that many guards around the palace?"

"Well, it looks like we have a problem."

Chapter 30: Breaking into the Palace! Engineer Master, Sammy!

"**Great,** how are we gonna get through that line of defense?" Boyd asked as they continued running toward the palace.

"There might be a way. You remember what we did that one time when we were being chased by sub-humans and how we escaped, right?" Joei said, still on Taizen's back.

"Yeah, but you think I can do it with both of you on my back?"

"We'll need to wait until the right moment for us to get on your back, but the gloves and boots should be powerful enough for the job."

Boyd and Taizen nodded, and they soon came upon the massive number of guards and soldiers.

"There they are! Get them!" One soldier yelled, and the whole mass started charging toward the three.

"On the count of three," Boyd said, crouching down.

"One, two, three!"

On three, Taizen quickly got onto Boyd's back, and he pushed off with his boots. At first, they barely got off the ground, but the next instant, the boots activated and sent the three flying into the air. The guards were in awe at the feat, but unfortunately the trio was on track to hit the wall rather than make it over. Boyd kicked with his feet again and started flying toward the ground on the other side of the palace.

"Taizen, hold on tightly to Joei, and make sure the two of you land safely in the palace grounds."

Taizen nodded, and Boyd dropped them toward the ground. Taizen flipped multiple times through the air and came to a safe landing with Joei on his back. Boyd braced for impact and activated the boots right as he came down, making him only bounce up a bit in the air before landing on his back.

"You okay, Boyd?" Taizen asked, walking over to him to lend him a hand.

"Yeah, just not used to doing landings like that."

They got a quick look at the area. The ruby palace was surrounded by a sprawling lawn, with flat red rocks embedded into the ground forming a path to the palace entrance. There were exotic trees in multiple places, especially around the path. It was other-worldly, a giant garden out of a fairy tale.

"All right, let's go," Boyd said, and they headed toward the palace. Quickly they realized that the gates had been o-pened, and the mass of guards and soldiers were behind them. They soon approached the palace doors, an entrance covered with an awning supported by pillars. Guards started coming from inside the palace as well, and they had to fight their way through them, throwing the occasional punch or kick. By the time they reached the doors, Joei was dazed, having taken a few hits while clinging to Taizen's back. They opened the giant doors and looked around.

"We gotta try to make it straight to the top, though I know the Elders will put up a fight," Taizen said. The first floor of the palace was quite large, almost the size of a warehouse. It looked like a cross between a reception hall and a fancy living room, with fireplaces on both ends, several couches, and what looked like a large monitoring station in the center. They heard a ding and saw guards come out of sliding doors.

"That way."

They ran right at the guards. Sure enough, it was an elevator, and they punched their way through. Once inside, Taizen glanced at the floor numbers and pressed the highest one, Floor Twelve. As the elevator door closed, the mass of guards and soldiers were already entering the palace. A guard managed to barely get his arm through the gap as the doors slid closed; Boyd punched the arm, and they shut with a snick. For a few seconds, they heard intense banging coming from the other side, until the elevator began to go up.

"Okay, so remember, each Elder will try to stop us on every floor. Get ready, Boyd," Taizen said. Right after he said that, they heard a ding, and the small display showed they were on the second floor.

As the doors opened, they were shocked to see that no one was waiting for them. What they saw instead looked like a mini warehouse, filled with giant shelving units. They formed aisles, and large hunks of metal and machinery lay haphazardly around, including on some of the shelves. There were also long, modern-looking workbenches full of tools and smaller metal materials and machines.

"Um, where's the Elder to stop us?" Boyd asked as they took a few steps forward. Then they saw it: to the far right of the room was a massive silver machine.

The machine had giant tracks for movement that were divided into two legs and two arms with double-pronged claws. At the center of the machine was an oval-shaped cockpit, with a clear dome you could see through. Inside was an older, female sub-human, wearing thick goggles of some kind and with a head of curly black hair. The machine started slowly moving toward them, and Boyd took a fighting stance. After several seconds, the machine stopped, and the dome opened.

"Well, hello! If it isn't the human I've heard so much about. The one that managed to take out the king's own son? I'm impressed," the sub-human female said, lifting her goggles up to her forehead.

"Who are you?" Boyd asked, maintaining his fighting stance.

"Pardon my lack of manners—I haven't introduced myself. My name is Samantha, but everyone calls me Sammy. I'll keep this short: I'm the engineer master for sub-human society. I've played a part in many of the technical advancements in this society, and I've made several devices for our own King Starpson. He's better at controlling these things than I am, but being the creator, I'm pretty good myself. This is the E-7000, the latest self-defense model of mine that I keep stored for whenever anyone tries to infiltrate the palace, like you guys."

"Interesting. What's the name supposed to mean?" Joei asked.

"E stands for Execution, and the number stands for the amount of strength it's got. This one's got a strength of over seven thousand kilograms."

"That's cool and all, but let's not waste any more time, shall we? I got a job to do, and I guess I'm taking you down first," Boyd said, running toward Sammy. He brought his right arm back to punch, but the machine simply swat him away with one of its arms. Boyd was sent flying to the other end of the warehouse, where he managed to make a safe landing on his feet.

"Sounds good to me. If I can wear you down even a bit, my goal has been achieved."

She put her goggles back on and closed the hatch. The machine opened its pronged claws and let off lasers from them. Boyd dodged through the multiple laser shots as he managed to knock back one of the arms, sending the machine off balance. The arm simply caught its balance and righted itself.

"This machine may look bulky, but it's quick."

"You talk a lot for someone who's fighting," Boyd said, going in for another attack.

"Yeah, you're right. Let's finish this."

She swooped the right claw and grabbed Boyd by his torso. Boyd tried to release himself, but the claw had too tight a grip on him.

"Let's see, shall I crush you, or shoot you?" Sammy asked, looking between both claws. "You know what? I think it'd be easier to guarantee death by laser, so let's do that," she decided, charging it up.

"Boyd!" Taizen and Joei yelled. Joei fell off Taizen's back and ran to help his friend.

Chapter 31: A Stressful Awakening? Second Elder Howard!

Boyd continued to try to free himself in what he thought would be his final seconds. Taizen moved toward the machine, knowing he likely wouldn't make it in time. Boyd wasn't sure what he could do, and with the stress piling up on him, all he could do was scream. When his stress was at its highest and the laser was about to fire, Boyd emitted several pinkish waves that radiated outward. They sent the machine flying to the right side of the room, and it released Boyd. It slammed into the wall, causing some cracking in the surface wall. Boyd managed to land safely, hardly aware of what he had done. Taizen and Joei looked confused as they ran over to him.

"Boyd, what...was that?" Taizen asked.

"Honestly, I'm still not sure. It happened back when I was fending off those hundred sub-humans on the ship and a desperate situation came up. It seems to only activate occasionally, at my most desperate times."

"Well, if you're fine, you should finish off that machine. Don't wanna exert yourself too much, no?"

"Yeah, you're right. I'm not holding back this time."

Boyd crouched down where he stood. As the machine started rushing toward him, he sprang into the air. He started bouncing all over the place like a pinball, getting quicker and quicker each time he bounced onto something.

"Heh, you think a little speed's gonna help you here? All I gotta do is track you and—" before Sammy could finish, Boyd blitzed through the transparent cockpit dome, breaking it into pieces. He started pumping fist after fist into the machine, going at it repeatedly. The machine could barely right itself. Then, he aimed for the bottom of the cockpit. He slammed his fist into it, and the force caused Sammy to fly out, hitting her head on the ceiling and coming down with a crash. She struggled to move a few seconds later, and by the time she tried standing up, Boyd had run over to her and pinned her hands behind her back. He then picked her up by her arms.

"Tell us: How do we get to the next floor?" Boyd asked, staring at her.

"I'm not telling you. That would be abandoning sub-humankind, after all."

"Well then, let's make a guess. Joei! How about it?"

"Well, it's possible that they're using a simple exploit to keep the elevator on the same floor, likely something that keeps the button that calls for an elevator on each floor activated. Destroying the call button might work," Joei explained. Taizen seemed happy with that response and went over to smash the call button into pieces. Sure enough, the elevator dinged, and the three knew what to do.

"Simple as that, huh? Thanks for the battle, but we gotta get going now," Boyd said, letting her go.

"I won't let you get away!"

Boyd rushed to get into the elevator with the others, and the doors closed before she could get to them. The elevator then continued up until it was stopped at level three.

"Okay, guys, get ready," Boyd said as the elevator doors began to open. Before them lay a pearly white laboratory, with chemicals and glass bottles lined up on multiple white tables. Toward the back of the room, they saw what looked to be a scientist of some sort, with a white coat on, as well as short, gray hair, and a pair of glasses. He was also quite short. He was messing around with a few glass bottles, but after a few seconds, he turned around to look at the three.

"Oh, how delightful. It's you three," the scientist said, a bit surprised. "My name's Howard, and I happen to be the assistant to our science and health director, King Starpson himself."

"Oh, so you're strong then?" Boyd asked, taking a few steps forward.

"Well, it wouldn't be wise to reveal my abilities, now would it? Just fight me and see."

Howard picked up two glass bottles. Boyd concentrated on him, and was able to briefly see a future where he used the bottles to make poison gas that would knock them out. Boyd then sprung at him right before he did so. He quickly but carefully stole the bottles from him, and set them on one of the counters. Before he could reach for them again, he pinned Howard's arms to his back.

"Pretty weak, I must say, even if you are smart. Tell us about yourself, and maybe about some weaknesses of your king?" Boyd said.

"If it'll stall you, I'll gladly say what I'm allowed to say. Though I'm not the main director of the science and health of sub-human society, I have made a few significant contributions. I was able to figure out how to completely isolate viruses before they could do damage to the body. With my scientific knowledge, I also helped create propulsions that were small, but also strong enough to be used on devices such as our transportation vehicles. I even—"

"All right, you know what? You really aren't being very helpful to us. How about you give us some juicy information on the King himself?"

"No can do; that would be betraying my own kind!" Howard said as a pit opened underneath him. He kicked Boyd away as he went through it.

"I guess that's it, then. Let's move on," Boyd said. When Taizen destroyed the call button, a green gas started to emit from the walls. A recording of Howard's voice blared throughout the entire room.

"You fools thought I didn't have a backup plan? Think again! You'll all be poisoned and die in this room."

Before the recording was over they booked it into the elevator and closed the door right before the poisonous gas could reach them. It quickly went up, and was stopped on the next floor, now level four.

"All right, let's see who's next."

Chapter 32: Level Four! Marty the Elite Constructionist!

As the doors opened, the team saw a very interesting sight at the other end of the room across from the elevator doorway. It looked a lot like a cafeteria, with commodities like a refrigerator and other kitchen appliances on one side, and a couch with a TV on the other side. This was only part of the floor, however. They could see another room toward the back, like a workshop, with a long worktable and tools as well as wood and metal materials. An old sub-human was working busily at the table. He had a yellow hard hat on, and he wore safety goggles as well as blue overalls with a dirty white long-sleeved shirt under it. He didn't have a hammer in his right hand; a hammer *was* his right hand. He looked up and saw them standing in the breakroom. He stopped his work and walked over to the door between the rooms, opening it.

"So, you've made it here, eh? Looks like not even Sammy could do in the sub-human-stopping human. I must say, I'm impressed, but I'm keeping my introduction short so we can fight. I'm Marty, head of construction for all of sub-human society. I've helped build the structures that make our civilization what it is today. Though I don't specialize in technology, I did have some expertise in it when it came to what we used in our buildings. I'm proud of what we've accomplished as a society, and I won't let you guys ruin what we've built," Marty said. He pulled up his sleeves to reveal metallic coverings of some kind, and with a push of a small button, his left arm turned into a small shield, and his right turned into what looked like a mini jackhammer.

"I lost my right hand in an accident that occurred on construction. With some help from Sammy and my own recommendations, I got some combat gear of sorts. I use my gear on my right arm to help with building, though it also doubles as a weapon. I use the gear on my left for special situations like this. Just try to defeat me, human. It's not gonna be as easy as you think."

"That's for me to decide," Boyd said, coming in for a left hook. Marty blocked with his shield, and the punch didn't even leave a dent. Boyd dropped down to give an uppercut kick, knocking Marty into the air. When Boyd came in for a jab, Marty used his jackhammer hand to shove it out of the way. Boyd tried his other fist, but Marty blocked it as well. The two continued to clash, Boyd trying to get hits in but being unable to, as was Marty. After a minute, they jumped to opposite sides of the cafeteria, Marty beside the workroom door, Boyd beside his friends.

"Can't you see? You'll have to try harder than that a-gainst me."

"Oh, that was my best though..." Boyd said, looking sad. The next moment, Marty saw him disappear. Then, he suddenly saw Boyd reappear.

"Propeller Propulsion!"

Marty was able to put his shield up, but this time the move left a dent.

"Heh, looks like you were holding back after all."

He went in for a counterattack. Boyd dodged, and they went back to fighting. Block after block, dodge after dodge, they traded punches back and forth.

I can't keep doing this, or I'll lose too much steam. What to do? Boyd thought.

Then he got an idea. He concentrated on Marty and had a vision that he would block to the right. Boyd went for his left and caught Marty off guard. He made a blow to his head and knocked him to the ground. Boyd took advantage of this and followed up his initial punch with a kick to the back, knocking Marty into the ceiling. He started to fall again as Boyd slammed his fist down into Marty's gut. He broke the floor beneath him as he was smashed through it. Marty, now embedded into the ground, looked as if he was knocked out. He reached toward Marty to pick him up and Marty tried to jackhammer his hand. Boyd quickly lifted his hand away.

"I...will not...let you ruin our society!" Marty said raspily, opening his eyes and lifting himself out of the ground. Boyd went for a kick, but Marty blocked. Boyd was getting tired of the shield, so he went in with a fierce jab to the side of the shield, breaking it off. He then punched Marty into the wall and followed up with a flurry of punches to his entire body. With each punch, the wall crumbled more and more, until that part of the wall gave in and Marty broke through it. He fell onto the ground, and only a small thud could be heard when he fell to the bottom.

"Is he...?" Boyd trailed off, looking at Taizen.

"I doubt it. Sub-humans are very hardy, so he's probably still alive. That should be the last we see of him for now, though. We should be good to go to the next floor."

Taizen broke the call button, and they got one last look at the break room, now a mess, as the elevator doors closed. On the ride to level five, Boyd got an idea.

"Hey, wait, couldn't we break the call button on each floor we stop at and skip through levels that way?" Boyd asked.

"Maybe, but I doubt any of the Elders would make it that easy."

When they reached the fifth floor and the door opened, Boyd wasted no time and went for the call button to destroy it, but a sub-human in a white coat grabbed his arm.

"I wouldn't do that if I were you..." the sub-human said, leering at Boyd.

Chapter 33: #2 Doctor Beth! And Ted Too!

Boyd got a quick look at the sub-human. She had a serious gaze on her face, and her light brown hair was put up in a bun. She also looked as old as the other Elders they had come across. She seemed very formal, with rectangular glasses and a gray, collared shirt underneath the lab coat. She wore formal pants of a lighter gray color. Even her shoes were simple, pointed, black shoes that looked as if they were made of faux leather. In her other hand was a syringe, one that was about to be stuck into Boyd's arm.

"Oh no you don't!" Boyd said, seeing the syringe just in time and kicking her across the room. He saw now that the entire room seemed like a cross between a doctor's office and a laboratory, with desks with all sorts of beakers and mixtures on them in the center. She had landed on her desk, knocking it over.

"Well, I'll be, you really are a big—" was all she could get out before Boyd had sprinted over to her and tossed the syringe from her hand, smashing it into pieces. He then took her hands and put them behind her back and held them there.

"Let's make this simple: Who are you and what do you know about the king?"

"If you want to waste your time with me, that's fine. The more time wasted, the more likely we succeed. My name is Beth, and I specialize in the medical field. I'll be blunt, unlike the others, and say I don't take interest in combat, even for self-defense. My knowledge of and skills with the sub-human body are second only to our own king. My skill and expertise has led to the cure of many ailments, such as neurological disorders like—"

"You know that's not what we're looking for. How about you tell us about your king?"

"Why, that would be traitorous! Such an action would be treason! I would never do such a thing!"

"All right, then. Let's go guys," Boyd said, putting her down as they walked toward the elevator, smashing the call button before entering it. Beth ran after them, but Boyd pushed her away as the doors closed.

"Man, some of these Elders seem like they have knowledge that would be valuable to us. It's a shame we have to beat them up. Honestly, I wonder if there's a way to convince them to make peace with us humans," Joei said, pondering the thought.

"Not currently. If we want to have any chance of making peace, we'll need to take out my grandfather first. Maybe then they would listen."

They were stopped on the next floor, now the sixth.

The room was full of what seemed to be supercomputers that formed four small aisles. In the middle of each wall was a large monitor, displaying some kind of code. The one right next to the elevator had a sub-human typing on it at a long desk with a digital keyboard. He had short, thin hair that was a light gray color, glasses, and wore a dark-blue, collared shirt with gray pants and black shoes.

"Already here? I wasn't expecting you so soon," the sub-human said, turning toward them. "I'll keep things simple: My name is Ted, and I'm essentially the greatest computer programmer for our society. Now that that's out of the way, this is Sub-Android 1000, a self-defense bot Sammy designed for me. I did all the programming for the A.I. myself, though."

Ted turned behind him and they saw a small door open vertically to reveal what looked like a robotic version of a sub-human without clothes. The entire body was a metallic silver, with places where the joints were revealing some of the wiring, though they were covered up with translucent pipes.

"Target acquired: prepare yourself, human," the sub-android said to Boyd as it stared at him. The voice was almost indistinguishable from a regular sub-human's.

Boyd went for Ted, but the android got in the way and blocked him with its forearm. The android followed up with a quick counter punch that sent Boyd soaring across the room into the wall on the other side. He got up as the android came for him and this time, he went for a punch of his own. The android barely budged, however, and gave him an uppercut to the head. Boyd took the opportunity to flip his feet upward and bounce downward toward the android, giving a side blow to the head that knocked it down. It came back up and went for a kick. The constant punches and kicks the two traded with each other went on for a minute until Boyd managed to gain the upper hand.

No more holding back, Boyd thought as he concentrated on the android. He saw it was going to try to grab him by the neck, and he managed to avoid it and land a blow on the android. This time, a kick, and Boyd avoided it and got his own in. This continued several more times. Boyd was having issues, however. It was getting harder and harder to focus as the android attempted to go faster, until eventually—

"Got you," the android said as it grabbed Boyd by the neck. He gasped for air as the grip got tighter and tighter.

"No need to crush his neck, Sub-Android. I'll open your compartment so that you can throw him from this floor. A puny human like you probably can't survive a fall from this height, could you?" Ted said, motioning his hand toward the small space the sub-android had come out of. The space unfolded to reveal the city of Newtopia outside. The android took a baseball pitcher's stance and raised Boyd's body up as he continued to struggle to break free. He then curved his throw back before launching him forward. Boyd went flying as the android sent him at a speed higher than he had ever gone before. He was out of the building in no time and started falling down quickly.

"Boyd!" Taizen screamed as he rushed toward the opening.

Chapter 34: The Last Stance Against the Sub-Android! Rachel, Social Media Expert!

Boyd knew it wasn't over yet for him.

I can do this, Boyd thought as he was falling. As he got close to the ground, he readjusted his body midair and kicked the air before he could hit it. He was wobbly in his execution at first, but he got the hang of it quickly. Slowly, but surely, he was kicking the air and was making progress.

Joei, Taizen, please be okay by the time I get up there.

***

Taizen could barely attempt to stand up before the sub-android punched him back down. He was already bleeding some from his face but refused to back down.

"Boyd..." Taizen said weakly, trying to get up again. The android punched him down again. Ted laughed at the sight.

"Why do you keep getting up? You're clearly no match."

Joei wiggled as he was being held by the collar by Ted.

"Let me go!"

"You're so weak, I don't even need to bother keeping you restrained beyond this. Knock Taizen out, will you, Sub-Android? My apologies, Taizen, but I'm going to let the King decide what to do with you. I'm sure he'll have you executed!"

Ted laughed after he said it, and the android readied a punch. Just then, a metallic fist punched Ted to the back of the room, smashing him into the wall. Joei fell to the ground and was dazed. The metallic arm stretched out to Joei.

"Boyd!"

"Sorry for the close call. You okay?"

"Yes, but Taizen!" Joei said, pointing over to him as he was trying to get up. The android had stopped what it was doing to look over at the two. It pounced at Boyd, and he countered with a block.

"I think I got an idea."

He went right for the android. It blocked him, but Boyd used the opportunity to tackle the android to the floor. He grabbed it around its chest with his left glove, and around his head with his right. He shoved into the ground to keep the propulsions activated.

187

"If I can't defeat you with attacks, I'll destroy you instead!"

He started pulling the head apart from the body. It took everything he had to keep the android on the ground. The pipes around the neck began to stretch, and the metal framework began to separate. He exerted a quick pull, and the android head went flying to the other side of the room. The android's body went limp, and he could finally relax. He then glanced over at Ted, lying on the back wall, and ran to restrain him. He lifted him up by the hand.

"I won't say a word beyond what I've already said!"

"We'll be heading out, then," Boyd said, letting him go.

"Already ahead of you," Taizen said, smashing the call button for that floor. The three walked inside, and the doors closed before Ted could reach them. "Almost halfway through already. You're doing great, Boyd."

"Thanks, but I couldn't have done it without you guys."

With that, they arrived on the seventh floor.

When the elevator doors opened, they saw what appeared to be a wealthy person's apartment living room, except more modern. There was a big, rounded couch that sat in the center of the room facing the left side. On the wall was a giant, thin TV underneath a hologram fireplace. To the right was a kitchen with an island in its center and a fridge in the back corner. The entire back wall was a window facing the city of Newtopia. Sitting on the couch was a female sub-human with long, brown hair. She was wearing a red V-neck shirt with jeans and black slippers. She was browsing on her phone, then glanced over at them.

"Aw, shucks, you're already here? Oh well," the female sub-human said as she stood up from her couch. "My name's Rachel, and I'm in charge of all of the social media sites we sub-humans use. In fact, I created them myself to engage and entertain users as much as possible. In fact, I—"

"That's great and all, but we're more interested in info about your king. Are you gonna tell us anything? Or put up a fight?" Boyd asked.

"Nah, I'm not gonna hurt you or anything," she said, putting her hands up, "In fact, I got some gossip on the king I'll gladly share with you."

"Wait, are you serious?"

Chapter 35: An Ally in Disguise? Blake, Entertainment Extraordinaire!

"You heard me correctly. I can give you some info on the king, but there's a catch: You can't harm me," Rachel said.

"I'll only do that if you try to fight us."

Boyd sat down on the couch. Both Joei and Taizen were hesitant, walking near him without sitting down.

"Give us a moment, won't you?" Joei asked, looking toward Rachel. He then looked at Boyd, whispering, "What are you thinking? How can you trust her so easily?"

"There's little risk in hearing her out. I can just knock her out if she becomes problematic," Boyd whispered back.

"You're not wrong, but still, you need to be careful."

"I will be."

He turned to Rachel. The other two took a few steps back, deciding just to listen.

"Since you've agreed to cooperate, I'll explain: Our king, as you may know, is leader even over us Elders. How did he become so? I'll tell you how—he's the smartest of all of us. He's a mastermind in all areas of science and math. Of course, he does have his specialties, but the point is, he was able to stand out among us eleven. There's a reason he's been able to back up his dream of curing all diseases, even if he hasn't accomplished it yet. Still—he's a total megalomaniac, and some of us are not happy about how he rules—quite literally—with an iron fist."

"You said literally—does he fight with an iron fist? What are his combat skills like?" Boyd asked.

"Good question. Truth be told, our king's combat skills are truly exceptional, though his actual strength leaves a lot to be desired. Where his strength truly lies is in his machinery. We Elders who specialize in creating equipment like that, such as Sammy, have created some for him, though he's smart e-nough that he's created a few of his own. They usually range from weapons to actual mech suits of all different sizes. With one of those mech suits, his power is greater than any sub-human could hope to be."

"This sounds interesting. Can you elaborate?"

"Unfortunately, I didn't have a hand in the creation of it, nor have I ever seen it. All I know is, he's only ever used it once in testing. I heard his strongest punches from that thing could take a chunk out of mountains."

Boyd's jaw slowly dropped at hearing that. "So, how do we defeat him?"

"Get him angry. If you get him mad enough, he may lose his cool and not focus on strategy as much. That's your key. If he happens to pull out that mech suit, you're likely going to be defeated. That's all I can give you."

Boyd nodded and stood up from the couch.

"Well, that wasn't bad info by any means. Thanks for helping us out."

"You're welcome. Don't tell anyone I gave you that info, or else I could be in a fair bit of trouble."

"Fair enough. See ya if we end up defeating your King."

"Yeah, see ya."

The three headed toward the elevator. Rachel deactivated the call button with headphones and allowed the elevator to continue going up. As soon as they were in, the doors closed, and they started going up. Rachel lay back on the couch and made a call.

"Yes?" The voice asked over the phone. Rachel started laughing slowly, until her cackles became hysterical.

"Oh, boy, was that good. Your plan worked. They actually fell for it!" Rachel said, still chuckling.

"Yes, yes, but why all the laughter?"

"Well, King Starpson, I talked of your most significant feat, and the human with gloves was hardly fazed. He seemed to fall for the anger tactic, which is good. It just makes me laugh that they think they can defeat you!"

"Well, you're not wrong. Even if this human has some strength, it pales in comparison to what I can do. Little do they know, anger is one of my greatest weapons. Get a livestream ready, and let the entirety of sub-human society see what happens when someone tries to defy us."

"Sounds good, My King," Rachel said, hanging up the phone. She still was chuckling a bit after all that.

***

King Starpson turned his throne chair toward the side of his room opposite the wall where his large portrait was located. He pushed a button on his chair, and a gap opened on the wall, revealing a smaller, white room full of weaponry.

"Parett's son, or my own grandson—it won't matter once I'm armed. Not even this 'Boyd' can defeat me," Starpson said to himself, smiling.

***

The three had reached the eighth floor, and when the door opened, they saw what looked like a theater. Rows of small, well-cushioned chairs lined the room, and at the end appeared to be a stage, with soft, velvety red curtains closing off whatever was on the other side. The chairs were packed to the brim with sub-humans, young and old. The room was quite loud with chatter. It only took a few seconds for them all to start staring over at the three. They murmured quietly with each other, some concerned, others gossiping.

"This is so odd. What kind of Elder would live in this?" Boyd asked as they walked through the aisle the chairs made. He wasn't sure what to think of this.

Suddenly, two stage lights turned on and the light illuminated the bottom center of the still-closed curtains. An announcer's voice blared from speakers: "Introducing, the one and only entertainment extraordinaire, Blake!" The red curtains opened, revealing a sub-human wearing a black tuxedo with a red bowtie and a white, collared shirt. His short hair was black and slicked back, and he wore a top hat with a white stripe at the base. The audience roared in applause for him.

"Thank you, thank you," Blake said as he bowed to his left and then his right. He adjusted his top hat. "It looks like you three finally arrived. You know what that means?"

"Oh no..." Taizen said.

"It means it's time for everyone's favorite sub-human game show, Death Round!"

Chapter 36: Death Round! A Show Like No Other!

"**What** do you mean 'Death Round?'" Boyd asked, walking up to the front of the stage.

"All right, let me explain. Contestants will participate in three fights, and if they win all three, they get themselves the handsome reward of a thousand subs! If they lose even one, well...they're dead. As for you, the only reward you're getting if you beat all three is leaving with your life. Folks, I may be a great host, but I'm no fighter."

He pretended to fight by putting up his fists and trying to land a blow, but let himself jerk backward a bit as if he was knocked down. The audience laughed at the skit, and he took a small bow. Boyd wasn't amused.

"If you want a fight, I'll give it to you directly!"

Boyd went for a punch, but Blake jumped into the air and was quickly hoisted by some invisible lines, whisking him from the stage. A few seconds later, two screens on each side of the stage lit up, and Blake's face appeared on them.

"Sorry, folks, it seems like our contestant for today is a bit rowdy. Let's get him started on his first opponent!"

Four Lucite-like walls came down, and one smacked Boyd into the center. They closed in on each other, creating a translucent room on the stage. It was barely enough room to fight in. The first opponent dropped through the top of the room, which was quickly closed off with a translucent ceiling.

"Boyd!" both Taizen and Joei yelled as they saw him being trapped. Boyd glanced over at them with a grin. Though they wanted to help, they knew at this point it wasn't possible. All they could do was watch.

It's like a caged fight, Boyd thought as he looked around. Then he got a look at his opponent. He looked like a sub-human on steroids, as each of his limbs were supersized and buff, with only his head looking normal-sized. He was bald and had on only a white tank top and jean shorts.

"First up is our classic fighter, the mean, buff legend, the Crusher!"

The crowd went wild, and the Crusher slammed his fists together.

"The Crusher? That's a bit of a generic name, don't you think?" Boyd asked. The Crusher chuckled slightly.

"You'll pay for that remark," the Crusher said, riled up and ready to go.

"All right, the battle begins in three, two, one, go!"

Boyd found the Crusher to be very weak, as each punch he threw at Boyd was easily dodged. He played along, dodging a few more attacks before going for his counterattack. He went for a grab of one of the Crusher's fists, then jumped into the air, going behind him. He then used the downward force along with his gloves to bring the brute into the air and then land back on the ground with a crunch. The Crusher was sprawled on the floor, dazed.

"Incredible! With just one attack, the human has taken down the Crusher! That's one win for the human!" Blake said, surprised at the feat. The crowd was booing Boyd.

"What can I say? I didn't get here because I'm weak," Boyd boasted. The crowd booed harder, and started throwing food at the translucent arena.

"All right, folks, calm down, let's go to the next round!"

A pit opened underneath the Crusher, which he fell into. The next opponent dropped down, and with it the ceiling quickly closed again. "Introducing another frequent in Death Round—he may be skinny, he may be small, but he's no one to take lightly! It's the Chopper!"

The crowd applauded harder for the Chopper. This one was the exact opposite of the Crusher, being a skinny, smaller sub-human. He was dressed in some sort of white karate gi with no sleeves, and had no shoes on, either. He had short, black hair, and a black belt around his head. He took a fighting stance.

197

"Do not take me as some brute, human. I shall be a better opponent for you then he was!" the Chopper said, gesturing with a taunt.

"All right, folks, get ready, get set! Three, two, one, go!" Blake said, and the two went at it. The Chopper was faster than the Crusher had been, and was more calculative with his moves, too. He was able to dodge some of Boyd's attacks, and the two traded blows.

This guy still isn't strong enough for me, Boyd thought, knowing he was holding back quite a bit. When the opportunity arose, he went for a grab and got the Chopper by the throat. The Chopper countered with a headbutt, knocking Boyd down. He tried to go for a grab as well, but Boyd kicked him across the room, knocking him into the wall and falling onto the floor. Before he could stand up, Boyd went for an uppercut, then kicked him around the room, Boyd leaping at him every time he was sent flying. He ended it with a fist into the ground. The Chopper had been knocked out cold.

"Amazing! Folks, we may have a true fighter on our hands. The human has taken down both fighters with ease! The human wins this round!" Blake said. The crowd got angrier this time, and started insulting Boyd, throwing more food. Some even tried to grab at Joei and Taizen, though they kept their distance.

"If I'm trying to save Earth, wouldn't it be pathetic to lose to weaklings like these?"

The crowd became furious, and security guards around the seating area had to start calming people down.

"Folks, folks, let's calm down. We still have one final opponent left!"

A pit opened under the Chopper and swallowed him, just as it had the Crusher. The final opponent dropped through, and he seemed deranged. One of the sub-human's eyes was almost entirely closed, as if swollen, while the other was wide open. His grin was missing some teeth, and he had short, black hair. Though normal in height for a sub-human, his arms were quite bulky, and in his right hand was a mace of some kind.

"Our final opponent is a doozy! Previously a Sub-human Army commander, he was sent to prison after being too harsh on some of the soldiers and killing them! Deemed insane, he now fights in this arena to reduce his sentence! Give it up for ex-commander Skull!"

The crowd went as wild as they had ever been for Skull, and he let out a crazed laugh.

"A human? In this arena? You'll surely have your head smashed in by me, weakling," Skull said, heckling.

"Did he say 'ex-commander?' Buddy, I eat those for breakfast."

Skull showed visible anger at that statement and could barely contain his killing intent.

"It's time, folks! Three, two, one, go!" Blake said as the final round started. Skull rushed toward Boyd, coming down with his mace. Boyd narrowly dodged, and Skull did the same, though Boyd had an easier time. This continued for a few more times until the two took opposite sides of the arena.

"Wow, a human fast enough to dodge even me? Color me impressed. No matter, see if you can dodge this!"

Skull began to swing his mace around him in a circle. Although it started slow, he began to pick up speed, and he quickly spun around like a tornado, bouncing around the arena at breakneck speed. Boyd had a harder time dodging, and eventually fist and mace met. The equal force made both fly back, though Skull still had plenty of momentum. He came spinning back at him, and Boyd was still on the floor.

"You're finished, kid!"

Only one thing left to do, Boyd thought as he concentrated for a moment. A vision kicked in, and he saw that Skull simply lowered his mace so that it would squash him. The vision ended, and right as Skull was about to do so, Boyd kicked him in the head with both of his boots. He then grabbed onto the mace and slammed him into the ground. Before he could get back up, Boyd slammed the mace into his back. The mace flew across the other side of the room, and Skull was knocked out. He had punctures in his back, and blood was pouring from them as well as from his mouth.

"Insanity! The human has knocked out the final opponent with his own weapon! We have a winner for Death Round!"

Finally, the crowd got out of their chairs and started running toward the arena. Taizen held onto Joei as they jumped onto the top of the box.

"Boyd! We gotta get out of here!" Taizen said, banging on the ceiling of the arena. As the crowd of sub-humans pounded, kicked, and slammed into the walls, the arena soon fell apart. Boyd grabbed both Joei and Taizen and leaped across the room. The sub-humans quickly saw what had happened, and started running toward the elevator. The call button, now visible, was smashed by Taizen as they made it inside.

"An unfortunate tragedy...you all won't get past our King, though," Blake's voice wafted over the crowd.

The elevator doors closed. Luckily, no sub-humans had reached the elevator, so the three rode in peace.

"Eight floors cleared...I'm glad we've made it this far," Boyd said.

"If it weren't for your determination, I don't think we would've," Taizen said as the elevator came to a stop on the ninth floor.

Chapter 37: Stewart, Gaming Innovator! A Pierce Like No Other!

The elevator door opened, and the three saw that the room was dark. The only thing that lit it up was a giant screen on the back wall. The other two were lined with multiple shelves, and they all held different kinds of video game consoles and games, ranging from discs to cartridges. In the back of the room, they saw a sub-human sitting on the floor playing some kind of old RPG video game. In front of him was a shorter shelf that held a much older console on it. He was more heavyweight compared to others they had seen and had short, balding gray hair. He wore a T-shirt with shorts and no shoes. He looked behind him and saw the three standing there.

"Oh, it's you. The human and his inventor friend, plus the traitor. I've heard a fair bit about you three," the sub-human said as he stood up. The team stepped out of the elevator.

"You with the gloves, you took down a captain and have caused quite the ruckus since you arrived here, am I correct?"

"Yeah, I'm trying to defend my world. Is there something wrong with that?" Boyd asked, taking a fighting stance.

"Heh, the conflict between humans and sub-humans is indeed a simple, yet simultaneously complicated, issue. Not that it's my place to get too involved in it anymore. My name is Stewart, and I dabble more in the entertainment side of technology. I've used my intelligence to innovate gaming as we know it. I'm a bit of a gamer myself, if you couldn't tell by my collection."

"Yeah, that's great, but I don't care right now. What can you tell us about your king?"

"You probably know by now, but that's not info I can give away. If it means you gotta beat me up, I don't care. Just don't expect me to get knocked out without trying to fight back!"

He pounced toward Boyd, who didn't move until Stewart got close to him, then he smashed the sub-human into the ground.

"A true gamer, I see...you didn't break anything in this room."

Stewart passed out.

"That was easy; it seems like he didn't know how to fight," Boyd said as he smashed the call button. "At least he was a nice break from the last floor."

"As I said, a good portion of them don't have much of any fighting experience whatsoever. A lot of them use machinery or other people to become stronger," Taizen said as they stepped into the elevator. The elevator doors closed, and they started going up. It came to a stop on the tenth floor.

The doors opened, and they saw what looked like a detective's office. The room was quite dark, as well as crowded. Shelves lined the walls on all sides, filling up most of the wall space. They were all stuffed with papers, folders, and books. Toward the back of the room was a desk, also covered in papers and folders. The only other thing on the desk was a small lamp; it was all that lit the room. Sitting there was a sub-human in some kind of black trench coat, wearing a matching black fedora as well. He seemed to be looking through one of the folders. He then looked up at the trio.

"Not now, please, I'm working on something," the sub-human said, looking back down at the folder. Boyd slammed his fist into the desk.

"I think you've got something a lot more important to worry about, buddy," Boyd said, looking right at him. He continued looking through the folder. Boyd put his hand on his shoulder. "Did you not hear me? We're here to get to your King. We want some info on him."

"I have nothing of the sort to give to you. If you keep pestering me, I'll have to move you out with force."

He still hadn't looked up from his work. Boyd dove at him, and the sub-human grabbed his head and slammed it into the desk, breaking the flimsy piece of furniture in half. "Don't take Detective Pierce lightly, he'll make quick work of you."

Boyd got up and jumped back. "You're quicker than I expected, but don't expect to get a lucky shot like that again."

"Lucky shot? I'm a detective; I need a bit of combat skill to be able to fend for myself. Get outta here."

He lunged at Boyd. He dodged with relative ease, and he let himself dodge a few more times. The attacks sent papers, folders, and books flying throughout the room. Then Boyd made a jab at his back, knocking the wind out of him and slamming him into the ground. Boyd then got right on top of him.

"Now, talk."

"Look, I'm just a detective, kid. All I do is solve mysteries and help with ongoing crime investigations. Just because I'm the best detective of sub-human society doesn't mean I know everything. All I know for sure is, you humans owe us for what you've done."

"We're just gonna leave, then. Don't try to stop us," Boyd said, walking away from him.

"Are you feeling tired yet?" Taizen asked.

"Not really. I can't be too tired, or else I'd be unable to take on the king."

He smashed the call button. As the pieces fell to the ground, the three walked into the elevator.

"At least the brief elevator rides are a bit of a break."

"That leaves one more Elder besides my grandfather then..." Taizen said as the elevator went up.

"Who is it?" Boyd asked.

"Oh, you know...the king's wife."

"Wait, what?"

Chapter 38: Wife of the Sub-human King!? King Starpson, in the Flesh!

"That's...very interesting. Does that make her queen of the sub-human race then?" Boyd asked.

"I've never heard her called that. I'm pretty sure she's got the same influence the rest of the Elders do," Taizen said as the elevator came to a stop.

The doors opened to reveal a seemingly normal apartment room, aside from the modern changes that came with sub-human society, such as smaller, more efficient lighting and a super-slim, translucent flat TV hanging on the right wall. Toward the back in the right-hand corner was a small kitchen, and the other corner seemed to lead into a hall-way. The first half of the room they walked into was a living room, complete with a couple of couches, a table in the center, and a virtual fireplace that gave off real heat. In the kitchen was a female sub-human cooking something on the stove. She wore some kind of silver sweater with black sweatpants, and had her brownish-gray hair in a ponytail.

"She certainly doesn't look the role," Boyd whispered. She looked over at the three and groaned.

"Already here, Taizen? Please don't let your friend hurt me; I'm working on something right now," she said as she continued cooking.

"Grandmother. It's been a while."

Boyd looked back and forth between them. "Well, I'm interested in a couple of things: Some info on the king, who I've heard is your husband, and whether or not you're going to fight us."

"No, I'm not. I may be Claire, the wife of King Starpson, but I'm basically treated like an equal to the rest of the Elders. You'd think he'd treat me as more significant, but nope! It feels like he doesn't care, honestly."

"Look, I'm sorry about that, but is there any info you can give us on the king?"

"You already know the answer to that. Besides, it's not like I know much more beyond what the Elders do, I'm basically treated just like they are. I worked alongside Beth, though. Back in the day, we were the two doctors of our society. Now, although we may be some of the finest, we've kind of retired from that job. Being an actual society now, we have plenty of doctors who now do our job. Ah, but those older days were good...."

"I don't have time to talk like this. If you won't hurt us, though, will you let us go to the next floor?"

"It's not like fighting back is gonna do much, so go on. I'll let my husband deal with you. Even if he's not the best person, at least he can take you down."

"Yeah, yeah, we're just gonna go on up, then."

Boyd smashed the call button.

"Taizen, you dirty traitor," Claire said under her breath as the three walked into the elevator. Taizen frowned a bit at that as the elevator doors closed. The elevator quickly went up, and Boyd's heart began racing. He had to make himself take deep breaths to keep it in check.

"You worried, Boyd?" Joei asked.

"You think? From what I've heard, this guy is incredibly strong and can heal himself! I know I have strength as well, but this matchup will probably be my hardest yet."

Finally, the elevator stopped and the doors opened. In front of them was a short hallway with tall red doors that were closed. The hallway itself was dark gray, as was the floor. A red carpet lined the middle of the hallway. As they walked through it, they knew they were ready for whatever power lay behind those doors.

"You ready?" Taizen asked.

"As ready as I'll ever be."

Boyd stepped toward the doors and pushed them open.

The palace room was quite sizeable, comparable to a school cafeteria in size, but with a taller ceiling. To the right was a giant, circular table, which was built into the wall. Cushioned chairs that numbered a dozen accompanied the table. Toward the back of the right side were tall, brown shelves, with an assortment of folders and books nicely organized on multiple different compartments. To the left was a work area, with a few desks on the front and back walls. In the center of the right side was a giant, red square carpet, and on the wall was a virtual fire-place. Above the fire-place hung a gold-framed portrait of a sub-human. On the bottom of the frame was the name "James Starpson." The left side had worktables, five of them in total. They all held folders and papers nicely kept in place. On the center of the left wall was a square opening leading to a small room that gave off a whitish-blue light. It was full of gadgets and mechs of different sizes, all sunken into the wall and available presumably when they were needed.

Coming out of the room, in a tall, rolling throne, was the King himself. He had put on a black jumpsuit like the ones worn by the sub-humans from the invasion, except this one had cuffs outlined in a shiny red. He wore a red king's robe with the usual white trim, and a shiny red crown with black jewels on four sides of it to complement the robe. His hair was silver, though short almost to the point of a buzzcut, and he was balding as well. He had a maniacal look on his face, and Boyd saw he was wearing silver metal gauntlets that went all the way to his elbows. The king laughed deeply.

"If it isn't the human warrior, Boyd. To say I've heard a lot about you would be an understatement. You put a halt to the invasion on Earth, defeating my best captain through sheer willpower. Now, you've come to our home planet, and have somehow made it this far, managing to escape my masses of guards and soldiers, plus getting through all ten previous floors and all the other leaders of sub-humankind. Tell me, Boyd, what makes you think you can defeat me?" Starpson asked, looking at him.

"Nothing is guaranteed, but with how far I've come, why should I quit now? I've fought my uphill battles and eventually won. What makes this different?" Boyd asked.

The king laughed slowly. "The difference? Oh, the difference? You'll soon enough see the difference. I'm going to take you down without even needing to use my full power. My smarts, combined with my mastery in machinery and the sciences, have allowed me to rise above the rest, becoming the leader of sub-human race. My natural leadership is what allowed us to thrive on this planet, where life for us was thought to be impossible. I have created the ideal, modern society which will only continue to grow. And you!" he said as he pointed to Taizen, "you thought you could just throw away your ideals for these weaklings without punishment? I'll have you publicly executed once I've taken down Boyd. I'll show sub-humans what it means to betray their own kind."

"Your kind has killed humans for mere rejection! My father was the only sane one of you all!" Joei yelled as the king glanced his way.

"You are mistaken, youth. Mere rejection wasn't all. Yes, they rejected my ability to cure every disease despite my plan of how to accomplish such a task, but humankind also greatly impaired our ability to live. They forced us to go down this path of revenge! Your father could not see that, and for that, he is and will always be a traitor. But alas, an argument of this kind is pointless. Not only are you all to die soon, but such explanations will never be understood by the likes of humans."

Starpson stood up from his throne and pressed a button on the left arm of the chair. Suddenly, mechanical arms sprang out of the walls and began to take everything out of the room, and the roof and walls began to open, sinking into the ground and opening Starpson's room up to the outside. It was as if the room was now an arena. The night sky covered the area in darkness, save for the two moons that glowed from above.

"Now, let's get this over with, shall we?"

Chapter 39: The Start of a Grand Battle! Boyd Vs. King Starpson!

Boyd didn't have time to marvel at the arena the king had created. He was already coming at Boyd, and he swiftly dodged the attack. Starpson's speed with the gauntlets put him off. He dodged a few more attacks before Starpson got a kick in. Boyd quickly recovered and came in for a counterattack. Starpson blocked it, punching Boyd in the face and knocking him to the ground. He continued to land blow after blow on Boyd, and he couldn't block due to Starpson's speed.

I gotta concentrate, Boyd thought as he jumped back and calmed his mind. He saw Starpson would land a blow with his left hand. Boyd acted accordingly and dodged his attacks.

"Oh? Is this the 'future sight' I have heard about from Captain Zaizo? Certainly impressive, but it's only a delay to my victory!" the king said as he came in for another punch. Boyd knew he would have to use his opportunities as attacks rather than dodges, so attacks he landed. Such concentration was difficult in succession, but he managed to do it again and started landing multiple blows on the king. The king managed to block most of the attacks though, and little damage was done to him. He continued to try to get in blows on Boyd, with Boyd barely managing to keep his concentration enough to use his visions. Finally, the two jumped back.

"I was worried. I thought the Elders had lost for nothing, but you aren't quite as weak as I had thought. My old body alone won't be able to keep fighting with just this gear, but we're far from done here yet."

A small, circular pit opened behind Starpson, and he jumped through it. Boyd tried to run toward him, but the pit closed right after he dropped through.

"Did he run?" Boyd asked.

"I don't know. I've never seen him in action before," Taizen said. Moments after, a larger, square pit opened, and up rose Starpson, now in a suit that covered his entire body. The only part visible was his face through a shield melded to the rest of the suit. It looked quite mechanical, yet was thin enough to fit onto his body like clothing. Nonetheless, the silver suit looked more threatening than the gauntlets he had worn minutes prior. Right after, a large drone came flying in and flew high above the arena, but close enough to see them well.

"Hey everyone! It's Rachel here, and that invader you all heard about? He's fighting our very own King Starpson! King, what's up?" she said from the drone.

214

"Hello, citizens of Newtopia. Watch as I pummel our invader to death, and show everyone what happens when you mess with sub-human society!" He then took off the attitude and looked toward Boyd. "Congratulations, you've made me need a stronger means of killing you. How does that make you feel?"

"Who cares? I'm here to take you down!"

Boyd launched but was blocked. Starpson came back with a punch much quicker than before and followed up with a quick series of attacks, so fast that Boyd was unable to block. He face-planted into the ground, and he couldn't get up before he had the wind knocked out of him. Starpson began toying with him, picking him up and throwing him across the arena.

"Funny how weak you are when faced against a greater power such as me," Starpson said, running at Boyd. Since he was thrown across the arena, Boyd had enough time to get up and run toward him as well. With the stakes high, Boyd threw a fist at his face. Moments before landing, his metal glove had a pinkish essence to it, and when it connected, the energy burst out where he landed. It destroyed his face shield and went right through into his face. The king jumped back a bit and checked his nose. "You...fool! You imbecile! You...made me bleed! Hahahahaha."

The king's eyes turned vicious, and his head jerked in an unusual manner. The blood on his nose vanished, as if he was never hit. He walked toward Boyd.

"What's...going on?" Boyd asked. The king got lifted onto his toes and disappeared. Boyd looked around, but saw no sign of him. A jab to the face, and he was knocked back. Kicked in the back, he fell onto the ground. An uppercut to the chest, and he was sent flying into the air. It was all happening so quickly that Boyd only saw a blur.

"Anger strengthens me, child. Your seemingly little victory was nothing more than a boost to my power."

He punched Boyd back down into the ground.

"Then that means—"

"Yup! I lied to you! Did you really think I was helping you? I would never help someone trying to take down our society!" Rachel said from the drone as she laughed maniacally. Boyd didn't have time to be angry over the betrayal. Starpson was coming right for him.

C'mon, concentrate, there must be something I can do, Boyd thought as he went to focus. He shifted into a dreamy realm, and saw Starpson going for his face. He looked for anywhere he could go for. *The neck trick won't work, not on such resilient armor. Wait,* Boyd realized as the vision ended. It was happening for real now, and Boyd knew what to do. Before Starpson reached for his face, Boyd aimed for his crotch. He landed with a kick, and it stopped Starpson in his tracks. Starpson landed, and staggered for a few moments.

216

Go time, Boyd said as he went for the broken face shield. The punch landed, and he went for it a few more times. With each hit, Starpson's face got more and more bloody. Eventually, Starpson was in a daze, but managed to block the next attack. He jumped back.

"Fine," Starpson said with a crack in his voice, "I'll just...do this." A pit opened behind him. Boyd saw what was about to happen and tried to go for him again. Starpson jumped through the pit before Boyd could get to it.

"Not again! Come out and fight!"

Boyd banged on the floor where the pit was. Suddenly, the whole arena began to shake. Boyd looked behind him and saw it. A giant pit opened up, and out came a sizable mech. This one had two mechanical arms and legs, with a cockpit center where the king had settled, his face completely healed. It was similar to Sammy's mech, though this one was larger and had actual moving legs as opposed to tracks. In its right hand was a handle, but with the push of a button on the side, a glowing light came out of it in the shape of a blade.

"Do you still care to fight me?" Starpson asked, his voice booming through the mech's speakers.

Chapter 40: The Fate of the Fighting! Boyd Vs. King Starpson Ends!

Boyd stood there, dazed, as the mech built up speed toward him. Boyd snapped out of it, narrowly dodging the mech.

"This may not be as fast as I was before, but I can hit you a lot harder, and you can't hurt me!" Starpson said, going for another attack. Boyd continued to narrowly dodge his attacks, trying to keep up as much as he could.

"I don't care what it takes, I'll take you down if it kills me!" Boyd said, lunging. He went for a double punch, and the mech didn't budge, not even a tiny dent.

"I told you; I'll be winning this. This mech has great offensive power, with a defense to back it up. You'll be saying goodbye here."

He swung the saber around. Boyd had to jump back and start running from the mech to dodge. He decided to jump into the air to think of a plan.

Great offensive power combined with a rock-hard defense, Boyd thought. *How do I get past it?*

"You think you're safe in the air? This mech is able to convert the power we sub-humans can store in our bodies and release it as electrical energy."

The mech jumped into the air. It caught Boyd off guard, and he quickly dropped onto the ground.

That's right! If I can just break the glass covering the cockpit, I can get to Starpson! But only if I can catch him off guard.

Boyd had a plan, at least. Whether it would work, he would have to find out. He continued dodging a few more times, then focused on a vision.

No opening. He dodged and tried again. *Still no opening. How can I break through to him if I can't even get an opening?*

Then, it happened. He saw a vision where there was a small opening. *It's risky, but I can't pass this up.* Boyd went for it, putting all his power into his punch. Pinkish energy emanated from his fist before it landed, and he slammed his fist into the glass of the cockpit. Unlike before, however, the glass only cracked and didn't fully break through.

"You sure are smarter than you look. Does it matter, though? This glass is tougher than what was on my suit. You'll need to catch me again if you want to defeat me, and that won't happen," the King said, jumping away from him. He still went for attacks on Boyd, and Boyd had to continue dodging them. He was beginning to drive the king into a corner with his offensive ambition. His visions, however, were beginning to become blurred. He knew he was tiring it out, but he had to do this. Finally, another opening came. He went for a kick this time, the only way it would be executed quickly enough. He smashed through the glass and grabbed Starpson by the neck.

"You were saying?" Boyd asked as he began choking Starpson. The old man gasped for air, putting his hands on his neck. Just as Boyd was about to crush his neck, the mech's arm swatted Boyd away, throwing him across the arena and onto the ground.

"Bwahahahaha!" Starpson laughed. "You really thought you could kill me that way? I can control this mech just by thinking about the action. Truly the technology of the future! And you decided to try and stop it."

"I wasn't going to stand there and watch you murder everyone I know and love! Not to mention all of humankind!"

"It doesn't matter when humankind is plagued by the disease of rejecting anything too advanced. Too smart. Even rejection of that which could eliminate sickness from the world. I showed them I could do it! And they called me crazy and tossed me aside. Me! They shall all die for their mistake, as will you. But first, I think I shall lower your spirits."

Starpson looked toward Taizen and Joei. Boyd knew exactly what was about to happen and started toward his friends. The mech managed to reach them first, and grabbed onto Joei.

"You, you disgusting rat. You TRAITOR! Though I hate Taizen now for his betrayal, you are the one I despise the most. A direct relative of the one who betrayed us so long ago, Hoover Parett."

Even though he was being choked out, Joei managed to say, "You...were the one who abandoned my father! He was...the one who wanted to...give humans a second chance, but you didn't even care!"

"Who cares? He chose wrong, therefore betraying us. You shall die now as punishment of his bloodline."

He began tightening the grip around Joei.

"Wait!" Boyd yelled, "Please! Don't hurt him! Kill me instead."

"Don't say that...Boyd. Saving humanity is what's...most important," Joei squeaked out.

"Oh? Someone else wants to die for Parett's son? And the biggest threat at that? Very well, if they both agree to leave and never return to this society."

"Joei, Taizen, please accept! This is the only way left for us."

Joei was upset. "How...can you say such a—"

"We accept the conditions," Taizen interrupted. Starpson threw Joei toward Taizen, and he caught him. Joei tried saying more, but was muffled by Taizen's hand. Boyd started walking toward the mech, and the mech met him and scooped him up.

"This is what happens when anyone goes against our ideals!" Starpson said. "Now, you shall die, but simply letting you fall off the building wouldn't be enough. Let's make this fun, shall we?"

Starpson gripped Boyd by his right arm and held him at the edge of the arena. Taizen shook his head as he started running toward the mech. Starpson swung down with his saber, slicing Boyd's right arm off. Blood started pouring from the wound as Boyd began to fall off the building.

"Boyd!" Taizen said, but he could barely comprehend what had happened before the mech came toward Joei and grabbed him.

"Sorry, but I don't keep agreements with the enemy."

Taizen wasn't sure what to do.

Chapter 41: A Disaster! The Conflicted Rebel!

"**So,** Taizen, how does it feel to betray your own kind, seeing as your allies have lost miserably?" Starpson said as he began to tighten his grip around Joei. Taizen looked up and knew what he had to do first. *Sorry, Boyd.*

"Give Joei back!" Taizen yelled, moving toward the mech's hand that was holding Joei. He was swatted away with the other hand. He slid off the edge and started falling off.

"Joei!"

"Now, to deal with you."

He crushed Joei with his mechanized hand. Blood started running through all the cruel metal fingers. After he finished, he dropped Joei off the edge.

"Let this day be remembered in infamy! No matter how strong someone may be, they cannot deal with my overwhelming power! All will bow before our ideals, lest they be dealt with if they don't!"

Starpson looked up and made a hand gesture, which Rachel recognized as a sign to end the stream.

***

Falling, Taizen tried gaining more momentum in order to get to Boyd, but time was running out. The fifth floor, then the fourth floor, Taizen still wasn't close enough. He pushed off with his feet toward the building and was almost to Boyd. Third floor, then second floor, Taizen gave it one more push and he managed to reach him. He pushed off against the building while holding Boyd, and the two were slowed by one of the trees in the palace garden. They fell into the grass, Taizen breathing heavily. He got up and checked on Boyd. His breathing was slowing, but he was somehow still conscious.

"Taizen, thanks...how's...Joei?"

"I don't know yet, but let me get you situated, and we can deal with that in a moment."

Taizen took off the security guard shirt he had on. He ripped it up and began wrapping the pieces around Boyd's wound. He wasn't sure how much longer Boyd could survive like this, but it couldn't be long.

He then looked up at the skyscraper and saw something falling. He realized it was Joei and ran toward where he was going to land. He wasted no time and began charging up power in his legs, then jumping. He managed to catch Joei and fell back onto the ground. He was horrified by what he saw. Joei's entire body was dented all over the place, and he was soaked in blood. He barely resembled the Joei he had seen mere minutes before. He checked for a pulse and couldn't feel anything. He checked back over at Boyd and noticed he was unconscious.

What am I supposed to do!?

Taizen put the two down side by side. Boyd was sure to be dead soon without some sort of medical attention, and Joei seemed like he was gone.

It's...over....

Suddenly, he snapped.

No! Taizen, it's not over yet for you. You can still save them, even if it means you have to do something you don't want to. You've gone soft, and now it's time to show the sub-humans your true self, Taizen thought. He knew of one way to save both. He glanced at the palace and saw guards beginning to pour out of the doors. He took Boyd's black hoodie off him and put it on. It didn't fit, but the concealment was all he needed. He quickly put Joei on top of Boyd, then put them both on his back, concealed by the black hoodie. He put the hood up and started running.

"Hey! Get him!" one of the guards said, pointing over to Taizen. The guards started after him.

Even with the midnight darkness, they still see me? Taizen thought, giving a sigh as he continued running toward the gates. The guards were gaining on him, and some guards from the other side of the gate had spotted him and attempted to take action. Taizen's brain racked over a way to get over the wall, something plausible. As he reached the gate, he realized: *The trees!* He started running toward one and jumped up to the top of one of the higher branches. He felt the weight of Joei and Boyd as he struggled to make the jump. He looked up to the top of the wall and knew it was a long shot. Then Taizen had a realization.

The boots! Taizen reached to his back to grab the boots off Boyd. The guards had seen him go into the tree and were quickly approaching. The boots were too small, but it didn't matter. The time to act was now.

He made the jump just as the guards were reaching the branch he was on. The propulsions activated, and Taizen wasn't prepared. He shot up into the air and easily made the jump over the wall. Now he had to deal with getting down. Taizen looked around, trying to find a place to land. He realized he couldn't reach any nearby buildings and had to fall onto a parked hover car. He braced himself; as he landed, the entire top of the hover car was smashed through by the impact, and the cushioned seats combined with the advanced airbags saved Taizen. He quickly took the boots off and put them in his hoodie pockets. He looked behind him. The guards had seen his trajectory, but were tens of yards away from where he was. He thought about getting away in the car he had landed in, but it was destroyed and wouldn't be usable.

Do it, Taizen. It's not like you have any obligation to them anymore.

He shook his head, not wanting to do this, but he knew there wasn't another choice. He started running on the sidewalk, punching down any civilian that got in his way. He didn't see any more parked hover cars, but he did see one going in the same direction he was. When it got close, he jumped for the passenger window and punched his hand through it. The glass broke and he saw the young sub-human driving it. He looked much like he did, and was of a similar age, too. Taizen hesitated.

"What are you doing!?" the sub-human asked, eyes wide. The hover car started swerving. Taizen sat up and held his face near the sub-human's face.

"Stop the car, NOW!"

Taizen's fist shook. The sub-human followed his orders and stopped the car, then put his hands up beside his head.

"Now, where is your self-defense gun?"

"I-I-In the middle compartment. Here," the sub-human answered, opening the console between the front seats. He pulled out the gun, which had two small barrels attached to it, standard for a self-defense gun. Taizen swiped it from his hands and put it in his pocket.

"Good. Now, get out of the car."

"But—"

"I said get out of the car!" Taizen yelled. The sub-human nodded quickly and got out of the car. Taizen took Boyd and Joei out of his hoodie and set them in the back. He climbed into the driver's seat and shut the door. He drove off, not sure how far behind the guards were. He only had one destination in his mind.

***

Taizen pulled up to the building and parked. He was lucky to have eluded the guards, but he knew it wouldn't be long before the King attempted a city-wide search for him. But that didn't matter. What mattered right now was the building in front of him. He put Boyd and Joei back in his hoodie and walked to the door. Though the place was closed, it didn't matter to him. He took his gun and shot through the glass door, breaking it into pieces.

"Sparky! I've got some business with you!"

Chapter 42: The Ultimate Upgrades! Can Joei Be Saved?

If Taizen knew one thing about Sparky, it was that he made his home within his own shop, which was made clear from the room in the back with the label "Bedroom." From the back, Sparky left his room and came toward the front. Taizen was quick to point his gun at him.

"Hey now, what're you doing, Taizen?" Sparky said, putting his hands up.

"Let's make this simple. You know I'm a traitor now; it's been plastered all over the news here from what I can tell. You're gonna help me out with something, and if you don't, I can't guarantee your future."

"Okay, okay, what do you need?"

"I know your skills as an engineer, so I think you can help me."

Taizen took Boyd and Joei out of the back of his hoodie and held them up.

"You brought *those* two? If this is regarding helping them, I refuse. That's blatant treason on sub-human society."

Taizen pointed his gun at him again. "Do it, Sparky. Help me save them, or die for your pathetic loyalty. Did you ever think for a moment that maybe the rulership we are under was corrupt? Even for one second that maybe, just maybe, we were—"

Sparky groaned. "All right, fine. I'm not open to hearing your corruption shtick. I'll lead you down to my workshop." He waved his hand at himself, then went over to his computer on his cashier desk to enter a special code. After doing so, an opening on the right wall opened, revealing a door. Sparky went to the door and opened it, and Taizen followed, putting Boyd and Joei back into his hoodie.

They went down a metallic spiral staircase, which led to a room the size of a basement. There were multiple workbenches with a bunch of materials and tools on them, as well as a few medical chairs. To the left side of the workshop was Sparky's main work area, having the largest workbench of the lot. It was covered with blueprints, tools, and materials.

"What's with the medical chairs?" Taizen asked.

"Well, I used to work for a company that created prosthetics, and also would do procedures to attach said prosthetics. These happened to be leftover, and I took them for myself."

Sparky motioned him over to one of the chairs as Taizen took his two friends out of his hoodie.

"Boyd here's lost one of his arms, and I'm pretty sure Joei is dead. I need you to use whatever knowledge you have to help me out here. You may not be on my side, but nonetheless, you're helping."

Taizen put Joei on the left chair, and Boyd the other. Sparky took a good look at the two for a minute.

"Your friend here on the left is finished. His body is destroyed, and I don't see how we can save him from this state. On the other hand, your friend on the right looks rough, but he can be saved. I can give him a prosthetic, and he should be good to go."

Taizen pondered what he said for a moment and got an idea.

"Hey, wait, since you're an engineer, I think I've got another idea. How about you make Boyd here some upgrades to his current gear? He's already having to get his arm replaced, why don't you make it a propulsion arm while you're at it? You seem to know a bit about that kind of technology, so I think you could make him some very powerful gear."

"You want me to create a weapon for not just a human, but one who wants to take down our own ruler? Are you out of your mind?"

Taizen got his gun out and pointed it toward Sparky. "Why don't you make that decision for yourself?"

Sparky was a bit shocked and didn't retaliate. "You truly are a madman, but I can't do anything about that. Just know I'm not doing any of this willingly, and given the chance, I'd betray you without hesitation. I do have the ability to make some stronger gear for your friend here and, in fact, I've been working on the Mark Tens already. I still have a fair amount of work to do, but I plan on making them a few times more powerful than the Mark Nines."

Sparky then perked up and went looking in a storage room beside his main workbench.

"What are you doing now?"

"Your dead friend may have a chance after all. I remember the company I worked at had created a prototype for the ultimate prosthetic, one that could save just about any sub-human, provided their brain was still intact."

Sparky continued to go through the storage room until he found it. The prototype he spoke of looked like the sub-android Ted had used, but cruder and simpler in design. It only somewhat resembled a sub-human and was more robotic, having skinnier arms and more simplistic hands, and having the same pattern for the legs and feet. Its body was cylindrical in shape, and the head was the least robotic part, looking much like a sub-human's head, though the forehead was taller.

"Here we go. If we can get his brain out of his body and hook it up to this thing, he may be able to live again. This prototype was scrapped due to concerns over the severe mental issues of being inside of a robotic body, and I don't know much beyond that."

"That's…amazing, if it actually works. Issue is, how would we go about doing such a thing?"

"Well, let's just say I don't work on all of my gear by hand," Sparky said, pointing at the center of the ceiling. A bunch of robotic hands attached to a base could be seen, having different tools to cut, seal, and hold items, among other things.

"It's an older model of the auto-surgeon. Of course, I don't use it for that anymore, and with all the creative minds out there that have made software for it, you can get it to perform engineering work as well. Of course, since it *is* intend-ed for medical use, there's probably a piece of software that allows it to perform a brain transplant, which is exactly what we'll need. That, combined with the prototype, could give your friend new life."

"Well, then, I'll have you tasked to do that. Meanwhile, I'll check on Boyd."

Sparky nodded and walked over to the computer on his workbench to start researching software. Taizen went over to Boyd's chair.

"Boyd?"

Taizen shook him lightly. Boyd remained unconscious.

This day has been rough on him, so I'm not too surprised, Taizen thought, checking for a pulse. Though weak, he still felt one.

"Found something," Sparky said, bringing the computer over to Taizen. "Someone managed to steal the latest software used for this kind of stuff and made it publicly available. I'm gonna plug the computer into the auto-surgeon and let it do its thing. Your friend is already dead without this method, so there's not really any risk."

"Alrighty then, how about you work on Boyd's new prosthetic afterward? Might as well, since this thing is gonna be doing all the work, right?"

"That's correct. I'll get to work on that after we get this set up, though the propulsions will have to come later, since those will take time to work on."

"All right. Just remember one thing." Taizen turned Sparky around to face him. "Don't try to sell us out through your job. The consequences will be dire if you do. If I have to disguise myself and be by your side to assure that, I will."

Sparky nodded quickly and readied the computer.

"Go ahead and bring your friend over here." Taizen went over to Joei's chair and folded it down so that it was flat. He then rolled it over to the center of the auto-surgeon.

"All right, get your other friend out of that chair and place the prototype on it. Same position and stuff as the first one." Taizen followed directions, placed Boyd on the floor, and rolled the medical chair to the center as well. He bent it down flat. Everything was ready.

"Only one thing left to do. I'll go ahead and execute the software, then I can begin work on that prosthetic." Taizen was both excited and nervous.

Please, Joei, get through this. I don't want to say goodbye to a friend so soon.

***

Hours had passed. Morning had just arrived, and Sparky had been awake through it all, working on the prosthetic and then attaching it to Boyd's arm. Taizen had fallen asleep at the entrance, but had woken up soon after the auto-surgeon had completed its work. He got up from the floor and saw only the robotic prototype, with its forehead tinted red from the blood.

"Where's Joei's body?" Taizen asked.

"That's an interesting way to say 'good morning' to someone. As you may have seen, the surgery is completed, so I've disposed of the body. It seems to have worked, as the brain appears to be attached. The only thing to do now is turn on the prototype and see if he becomes conscious."

"That's great! Let's test it, then."

Sparky bent the chair upward so that it was in normal position again, then put his hand on the back of the prototype and flipped a small switch.

***

Joei opened his eyes, and noticed he wasn't on top of the palace anymore. He wasn't even on Mars anymore. It was his dad's old workshop. Tables lined the center of the room and were packed with all sorts of metal pieces, including a project that was actively being worked on. The walls were lined with shelves, full of all sorts of things, from notebooks to folders for previous projects. He even noticed the cot in the corner of the room his dad would sometimes sleep on.

Then he saw him. It was his dad! He was near the entrance of the room, combing through one of the shelves. He had the same curly hair as Joei, though brown instead of red. He was wearing the white lab coat that he always wore, alongside gray pants and black shoes. His face was similar to Joei's, except that he had a short beard. He looked over at Joei.

"Hey, son, long time no see."

Chapter 43: Joei's Dad!? The Start of a Revolutionary Flashback!

Joei was shocked at first, then curious.

"Wait, is this a dream, or...?"

"That I can't answer. Why don't you sit down on one of the barstools so we can talk?"

Joei obliged, though he was still wondering what was going on.

"Is it really you, Dad?"

"Well, it sure looks like me. I wanna know son, what happened?"

"Let's see, I was on top of a palace on Mars—"

"Say what now? How did you get to be on Mars?" his dad asked, leaning in with a curious look. Joei then explained to him everything he had learned about the sub-humans up to that point, as well as his experience with Boyd and Taizen.

"That is...a lot to take in, though it appears I made the right decision not to continue on with that friend group. Anyway, what were you saying before?"

"Okay, so the last thing I remember is being in the hand of the mech of their king. After that, nothing. I woke up here and am talking to you now."

Joei's dad leaned on one of the tables, lost in thought.

"Dad, am I dead?"

"That's also a question I can't answer."

Joei started looking around at the workshop and examining multiple items.

"This is great, though! Now that I'm here, we can do new projects together! We can finally be together again and make whatever creations we can think up!"

"I'm sorry Joei, but I don't think we should do that," his dad said, grabbing one of the projects from Joei.

"Why not? If I'm dead, then it doesn't matter. It's been so long, Dad..."

Joei's eyes began to water. His dad put the project down and sat at one of the barstools.

"I understand that, but I have a feeling that this isn't it for you. You seem to have found some great friends, ones who are finally taking full advantage of your inventions. I may have died trying to accomplish my goal of bettering society with my creations, but that doesn't mean this has to be it for you. Isn't your dream the same?"

"I mean, yeah, but...I don't wanna lose you again."

"It's okay, son. Your journey isn't over yet, and as your father, I want you to keep doing what you've been doing. Come over here," his dad said as he walked over to the entrance and opened the door. Joei followed, confusion forming on his face as the door opened to nothing but a white void.

"There's nothing out there..."

"Not yet. You have to make something out of it."

"What do you mean by that?"

"That's all I can say, Joei. Now, you need to make your decision."

Joei pondered it for a minute, tears forming in his eyes, then looked toward his dad.

"Y-you're right. I need to keep going. They still need my help!" Joei said, hugging his dad as the tears began to run down his face.

"I'm proud of you, Joei. Always."

"Goodbye, Dad."

Joei stepped into the white void.

***

The two stood back and waited. Several seconds passed. There wasn't any sign of movement.

Please, Joei... Taizen thought. Several more seconds went by. No movement.

"Great. Looks like the technology has either aged too much or never worked in the first place. I'd say I'm sorry, but I don't care aside from whether it works or not. Not to mention that I was forced to—"

Suddenly, the prototype's eyes lit up a warm yellow. After several seconds, the machine began to make small movements. The head began to lift slightly.

"Joei!" Taizen said, running to the chair. The robot glanced at Taizen.

"Huhhh...?" The robot slurred. The machine had a generic, slightly robotic voice. He looked around at his surroundings slowly, then back at Taizen. "T...Taizen...?"

"Yes, Joei! It's me!"

"W...what's going...on?"

"Well...we lost the fight, but we're okay! We're still waiting for Boyd to wake up, but he's alive. I'm just glad you're finally awake!"

Joei looked down at his body and realized that something was wrong. "Hey, Taizen...what's up with my body?"

"Please, don't ask about that yet...can't you just be glad you're alive?"

"Get me a mirror, Taizen. Or show me where one is."

"But Joei—"

"Taizen, please! Something feels very wrong, and I need to see for myself if you did what I think you did."

Taizen sulked as he went to get a handheld mirror and handed it to Joei. He held the mirror up and saw an unrecognizable face staring back at him. A robotic one.

"I'm...I'm..." Joei said before screaming, shaking his body violently.

***

"How's the search going?" Starpson asked. He had his throne turned away from his servant, who he had called in for this matter.

"Not well. We haven't seen any sign of Taizen or the humans since midnight. We still are continuing our search, but we've already covered a fourth of the city."

"Ah...that's unfortunate, isn't it?" Starpson said, turning his throne around to face his servant. "You know what'll happen if your search squad fails to find them, correct?"

"Well...."

"I'll have you executed! I must ensure they all are dead before I can finally rest. Seeing as they all fell from the top of the palace, I don't know the state of the humans, so let's change that."

"Y-yes, My King."

"Let's add a few dozen more men to your squad, so we can make the search quicker. Go tell my army you have my permission to do so."

"Right away, My King."

"Now, you may leave."

"Yes, My King," the servant said as he left the room.

"Taizen, I'll make sure you're dead if it's the last thing I do, and anyone else who defies me."

***

"All right, calm down, Joei," Taizen said, crouching down to the ground where Joei had fallen. Joei had tried to run around, but due to not being used to his new body, he had fallen onto his back as soon as he tried to stand up.

"Why? Why am I still alive? I mean, I didn't want to die yet, but being kept alive like this? This doesn't feel right, doesn't feel right at all."

"I didn't want to lose you, Joei. I'm sure Boyd wouldn't have either. It's a miracle the revolutionary technology of our society could bring you back. Your real body had been deformed, and you were dead. This was the only way to keep you with us."

"Even so, and despite how fascinating this is, it's making me feel sick. Where's Boyd?"

"He's over here. From the looks of it, you'll need some help walking.'

He hoisted Joei up. Joei tried to walk without Taizen but kept losing his balance. He gave up and let Taizen help him. They glanced at Boyd, who was still unconscious.

"Your friend will wake up soon. That cut was clean, though I'm not surprised, considering who made it. I also didn't have any issues installing a prosthetic arm on him," Sparky said, working on the propulsions.

"How long has he been out?" Joei asked.

Taizen checked his phone. "At least six hours, as it's now 6 a.m. here."

"Well, I just hope Boyd wakes up soon."

Suddenly, Boyd moved his head. The two immediately caught on and stared at him for a moment. He opened his eyes slowly.

"Boyd!" They yelled.

Boyd stared at them for a bit. "Taizen...?"

"Yes! You're finally awake! You've been out for a while, so I was hoping you'd wake up soon."

"What's with the robot?"

"Let's talk about that in a moment. First, you remember what happened last, right?"

"Yeah, I lost my arm," Boyd said as he looked toward where his arm had been sliced off, only to see the prosthetic.

"Wait, what...?"

"Yup, you got a prosthetic! I've forced Sparky to help us out, so he gave you one, and also handled Joei as well. This robot...is Joei."

"What!?"

"Hey, Boyd..." Joei said. "I know this may seem weird, but yeah, Taizen kept me alive through this machine. I still don't feel too good, but I guess I'll have to get used to it."

"What...what happened to your body?"

Taizen jumped in. "I'll explain. Essentially, Joei's body was crushed, and he was dead. Sparky had an old prototype of a robotic body that could keep someone alive solely through their brain. We had an Auto-Surgeon do the job and transferred Joei's brain to this machine, and now he's back."

"W-wow. So it's a miracle he's even here with us then...."

"Exactly. Anyway, Sparky's working on some upgraded propulsions that'll be installed on your new arm, and you'll also get a new glove and new boots. You're gonna become stronger than you ever were before."

"All right, but won't I need to learn how to use this new prosthetic?"

Boyd tried moving the fingers on it, and found it to be effortless, as if he had never lost the hand. He was shocked.

"Nope. As you just saw, our technology has allowed for prosthetics that require zero therapy of any kind to use. The nerve filaments mimic neurons exactly. It'll allow you to get right back into action," Taizen said.

"That's great, but what do we do now? We failed to defeat the king, and surely they'll up their defenses after what's happened," Boyd asked.

"I'm not sure. Presumably, we'll need to do the same thing again, going through all the floors. At least you'll be stronger, though, so we can get through them faster."

Boyd sat up and moved to the side of the chair, making room for the other two so they could sit down as well.

"I just wish we knew why the king holds this much hate toward the human race. I know that they keep saying stuff about rejection, but there's gotta be more to it, right? Something we don't understand...."

"Well, there is a story I've failed to tell you two, mostly due to time restraints. Since we have more time now, how about I tell you both about the origins of the sub-human race?"

245

"Didn't Zaizo kind of give us a rundown of that story though...?"

"Yeah, but it *was* basic. Would you be able to give us a more detailed story?" Joei asked.

"Yes. I've gotten information from all sorts of places, including school, my grandfather the king, and even the other Elders. I have plenty to tell you two."

"Well then, how about you begin?" Joei asked, and Boyd nodded.

"All right then, let's see...where do I start? Oh, of course!"

***

"Mayday! Mayday! We've failed to slow our ship down enough! We're set to crash in one minute!" a human said. It was Claire. There were eleven people on the ship, all being the Elders when they were initially human, and she was right beside two other people, with Sammy to the far right, and James in the center. He had decided to be the main pilot for the ship, seeing as he had gotten the most time with the manual. The parachute had been activated too late, and the entire squad was panicking, except for James.

"We're not dead yet. Tell everyone to put their helmets on and head for the exit. We'll rip the parachute off this thing and use it for ourselves," James said, pointing toward the others, who were seated in the back. Claire nodded.

"Guys! Put your helmets on! We're gonna go to the exit and head for the parachute! Go!" Claire yelled, putting her helmet on. The rest of the eleven put their helmets on quickly, and started running toward the exit.

"On the count of three, we open the hatch! One, two, three!" James said as he opened the hatch. The chill of the rushing air outdoors threw them off for a moment, but they persisted. James grabbed onto the side of the wing and reached for Claire, who was behind him. The eleven formed a chain, and they quickly crawled on the wing until they could stand up, and ran for the parachute. When they reached it, James motioned to Marty.

"Come here, Marty. You're the only one strong enough to detach the parachute from the ship. Use your hammer!"

Marty nodded and got it out of his suit pocket. He went to the parachute and started swinging away.

"My timer says fifteen seconds!" Claire said.

"All right, hurry everyone!"

Claire nodded, and Marty continued to hammer away at the parachute. Two of the four ropes had been detached, but it would be close.

When he was down to the final one, James said, "Everyone hold on to each other!" He made sure to grab hold of the parachute ropes, and everyone else held onto each other in a linked line. Marty took a final swing at the last rope as it broke. Marty had made sure to hold onto James, and the ship went flying down, but the parachute slowed their descent.

"We did it!" Claire said after they'd landed, and everyone cheered. Their cooperation had gotten them out of another bad situation.

"Now we just need to hope the ship hasn't gotten damaged too badly, or else we'll lose precious resources needed for our survival," James said, already moving on to the next issue at hand.

Chapter 44: Landing on Mars! The Beginning of a Civilization!

"The ship appears wrecked from here," Marty observed. The group decided a shelter would need to be built, and thought the ship would be their best resource for that.

"We need to start stripping the ship of its materials. With proper craftsmanship, we can create something that won't require special gear to survive in. Marty, I'll leave you to the job of building that. We'll need it as soon as possible if we want to last out here," James said, "The rest of us will gather surviving resources on the ship."

"Sounds good to me. I think I can make a blueprint for something like that, and with the technology the ship has, I'm sure we can make it work."

They started walking toward the ship.

"You take the front side, and we'll enter the ship from the other side," James said as they approached the ship. Marty got out his hammer and started smashing through the metal.

I just need a few large pieces to build this thing, Marty thought as the other ten walked toward the hatch, which would require a bit of a climb. James started first, as usual, and held out his other hand as Claire grabbed on, and the line formed. They slowly climbed up the ship and reached the hatch. They had to force the door open, seeing as the power wasn't working, and saw the state of the interior.

A few seats had come loose, and their parts were all over the place. The windshield was severely cracked, and the interior was quite dark. Still, there was enough light to make do with collecting resources.

"All right, let's get some groups going, shall we? Firstly, Claire and Beth, I'll have you two gather medical resources. Sammy and Ted, you two can gather scraps and electrical parts from the ship. Howard and Rachel, find some scientific resources. Blake and Stewart, you two salvage food and water. Pierce, you can help me check up on the other groups, and maybe find some additional resources with me," James said. Each group nodded and went off to complete their assignments.

"Leaving me with you, eh? Do we *really* need to check up on them? I think they're smart enough to fend for themselves," Pierce said.

"As someone who's taken up the leader role, I want to make sure progress goes well for each group. Plus, any resources they don't find, we can find instead. Like...ooh, look here!"

James had spotted a photo. He quickly picked it up and brushed the debris off.

"I didn't realize I'd lost this when we were landing."

The photo was of the eleven of them around a park bench in various poses, from standing, to sitting on the bench, to lying on the ground. They were all smiling in that photo, taken only about a year ago. It was all before their rejection. Before *he* betrayed them.

"Of course, the photo. You shouldn't lose that. That's a great memory."

"Indeed, though now that I think about it, I'll need to mark Parett's face out later. We were so focused on getting all the resources ready and stealing the ship that I didn't think to do it. Anyway, let's look for some materials, shall we?"

James put away the photo. Pierce spotted a journal and picked it up.

"Isn't this the journal you were talking about? The one you were going to use to keep track of our progress here?"

"Yes, it is! I didn't record much while we were on the ship, but I'll certainly be writing in it a lot now that we're here. Later, that is. Let's focus on the task at hand."

***

After a while, the eleven had finally gathered resources for Mars. Though the resources had to be packaged to survive the conditions, they still ended up with plenty. Marty had managed to salvage a large pile of metal and other materials for the shelter. He also built a giant box out of some scrap metal to temporarily store supplies.

"You guys can just put your resources in here for now," Marty said, lightly tapping the box. The rest of them nodded and started putting their resources into the box. Marty walked a bit of a ways away from the ten and started clearing out an area of debris and small, red rocks. Once it was smooth, he took a piece of metal he fashioned into a share point and started drawing.

"What're you doing here, Marty?" James asked behind him.

"I'm drawing up some plans for the shelter. We may not use it for long, but it needs to be habitable without a spacesuit. Otherwise, we can't eat, survive, or thrive."

"Oh, all right. I was wondering why you had walked away. Carry on, we'll help once we're finished storing our resources."

Marty nodded and continued his drawing.

***

"So, how long is this gonna take to build?" Sammy asked. The eleven of them stood around the blueprint Marty had created, which was a simple, one room place with the essentials: a toilet, light fixtures, and an airlock door so air wouldn't get through if they entered or exited the shelter.

"If we all work together non-stop, about a day," Marty said.

Rachel was shocked. "A day!? How are we supposed to go to the bathroom without a toilet? Not to mention, after all that work, I'm *starving*."

"Relax, we have those waste bags inside our spacesuits, remember? In case of emergencies, we'll need to use those to relieve ourselves. Plus, if we all get to work soon, we'll have it done in no time," James said.

"But what about air? You can't just build a shelter and expect it to have air, even if it's shut off from the rest of the atmosphere," Sammy said.

Marty nodded. "I had thought about that. We'll need to get oxygen supplies from the spaceship. After that...."

"You haven't forgotten about electrolysis, have you?" Howard asked.

"Electrolysis...?"

"Yes, electrolysis, the process of creating air through water. We can create a current that allows water to be split into hydrogen and oxygen, allowing us to have a source of air. It's not finite, either, as our own waste can be used to create air through the same process."

"Sounds odd, but I'm not picky on how I get my air. That'll cover the oxygen issue for now. I don't believe there's any other issues to cover with the shelter, at least that I can think of. Anyone got any issues that you think need to be resolved here?"

Everyone shook their heads.

"All right then, let's get building!"

Everyone cheered as they stood up and started heading toward the box full of materials. Marty followed behind. Materials were moved near the blueprints, and tools were provided to Marty, who cut down the giant metal sheets he had salvaged and started forming the outer pieces of the base.

***

"All right, people, we can do this! Just a little farther!" Marty said as he was helping lift a part of the hatch from the spaceship. They were nearing completion, save for the oxygen supply; all they needed to do now was attach this piece of the hatch to the rest of the shelter. They were mere yards from it, though the twenty-hour marathon of building the place had worn them down. Ted and Rachel had to quit due to exhaustion and were sitting inside the shelter.

Once they reached it, they started placing the hatch part down. "Slowly, slowly!"

The hatch piece slowly dropped as it was finally put into place. Marty quickly secured it, making the shelter complete. James sat down inside and recorded something in his journal.

"You really like that journal, don't you?" Rachel asked, looking toward James.

"Well, I'm quite excited for whatever adventures Mars puts us through; our journey, our development of a civilization. I want to build a society where no genius has to feel left out, and one without disease as well. It's quite important to document these things for archival purposes later down the line," James said.

"It's just like you to plan ahead, farther than any of us."

"We can't sit back and relax yet, though. We gotta get that oxygen supply now," Marty said.

Chapter 45: Rapid Development! The Otherworldly Creature!

"**Come** on! Just a little more!" Marty said as they pulled the last oxygen supply out of the spaceship. The apparatus was a giant metal container that was attached to the ventilation system, which supplied oxygen to the whole ship. There were others, but they had been emptied on their way to Mars. Marty had to seal it off before attempting to carry it back. It took all eleven of them to lift it high enough to carry it. It wasn't easy, but they obviously needed oxygen to survive.

"We're lucky it was low enough for us to reach without having to climb for it. I don't know how we would've gotten to it that way," James said, panting.

"Well let's be glad it wasn't, all right? Let's get this to the shelter!"

Marty's confidence pushed the others to try their hardest as well. Though the trek was slow, after half an hour, they managed to reach it. Once it was in its designated place, they slowly set it down, and everyone fell onto the ground, some sighing and others panting.

"Our suits can't have much more air. Let's get this thing installed so we can finally eat and rest," James said, standing up. Marty nodded and followed. The rest went inside, while James, Marty, and Sammy stayed to install it.

"It's basically already where it needs to be; we just need to hook it up, and verify that air can't escape," Marty said, looking at the sealed hole. "Our first step is to solder the tube from the oxygen supply to the shelter to make sure air can't leak from there. Can I ask you two to check around it to make sure there aren't any spots for it to leak from?"

"Sure."

They both started their inspection. Marty went to get a soldering tool he had used earlier and started working on the tube.

***

"I dedicate this toast to all of us, who put in the utmost work into constructing this shelter in as quick a manner as we did, and especially Marty, who came up with the blueprints for it. Cheers!" James said, toasting with every other person. They had finally finished it, and air flowed through it safely. Though their dinner consisted only of a small steak for each of them, they had decided to splurge on a glass of wine. They had managed to find a fold-up table and chairs, though some had to sit on the floor. It didn't matter, though, as they were all glad to have finally established a base.

"I appreciate the credit, but all our work is just as important as mine," Marty said. Everyone dug into their food.

"So, Howard, how will you go about creating a sustainable source of air?" James asked. "You mentioned before that you would need to create a current that would separate oxygen from water. Is such a thing possible within the few days of oxygen we have left in the storage?"

"Easily. It's simple enough to be a home experiment. Of course, I won't be lazy with it, but the point is, I can get something done by tomorrow."

"That's great. Of course, a sustainable source of oxygen is only the bare minimum for survival. We'll also need food and water."

"I'll need some of our water supply to start the O2 process, but after that we can start with some planting and filtering. I can help get those arranged, though I'll also have to take a bit out of the food supply to do so," Beth said.

"And you know me. If there's something that needs to be built, I'm your guy," Marty said.

"Great! Then that means I only need to figure out how to start our civilization for now. Buildings for all of us would be great, of course, but we'll need to explore around Mars and find resources we can use to make materials. We can even make our own dreams of future advances in the technology and scientific realms come to fruition. That's a bit too far off for now, though, what we need to do first is...." James trailed off, not wanting to say anymore.

"Produce offspring?" Claire asked, looking happily at James. He looked back reluctantly, knowing she was right.

***

In ten years, the eleven knocked it out of the park. Not only had they established a small town, but they'd even gotten their population to increase to a few dozen. With their methods, Beth and Claire made sure genetic diversity wouldn't be an issue, and four couples would be enough to ensure the population increase. Motern was the perfect starting point for them. They wanted to eventually establish a city, but it would be at least several years before they could start moving toward that. Their offspring were still children, after all.

They had all been thrilled when Marty had found a reddish ore toward the surface of Mars that would be the perfect material to build with. They built a mine to obtain a readily available flow of the ore, which they dubbed Martinite. That wasn't the only resource they had found, of course. There were those similar to ones on Earth to use for other purposes, such as metals, and the properties necessary to make glass and plastics. It took their combined knowledge to create their growing society, and they were proud of it.

Their society wasn't the only thing that had advanced, however. They had noticed significant changes to their bodies.

First, their skin had turned to a grayish tone, making it appear dead. Their bodies produced less hemoglobin due to the atmospheric changes, so the human pinkish hue decreased.

259

The colder environment and distance from the sun also contributed. They had also become thinner and had started losing muscle mass. Beth had narrowed it down to being an issue of gravity, and they decided mandatory exercise would need to be in place if they wanted to keep their strength. They had become taller as a result, and their fingers and toes became longer. They had also noticed their noses began to sink in, and their nostrils became longer. Their offspring had the same traits, though the differences in their noses were more pronounced. They were happy about the changes, though. It made them feel stronger.

The hardest part was figuring out how to create a town. Howard had worked with Claire and Beth to make a substance like Jello that was able to hold air in while allowing physical items to pass through. They planned to use it to construct a dome. The resources of Mars, as Howard had put it, were simply fascinating. It took a year to create a plan and construct the dome barrier, but it was well worth it. It allowed them to go outside and build their town without the need for spacesuits, and it was incredible to live freely again. Their children certainly appreciated it.

"So," James said, sitting at the dining table of James' house with Claire and Marty, "when can we expect another expansion of the town?"

"Soon, I'm sure. Our children need a proper school, even if we're smart enough to teach them ourselves. Other than that, it'll be a few years before we can open businesses. The kids need to grow up and learn how to work hard, and we need to set up a currency, too," Marty said.

"That's a good point."

James wrote something down in his notebook.

"You still write in that thing, huh?"

"It's a useful tool, writing our history down so we can eventually teach it to our children and to remember it ourselves."

The door to the house opened, and Sammy ran inside.

"James! You need to come quickly. Arpmin spotted something beyond the barrier, said it looked like a little capsule and that it fell from the sky," Sammy said, panting. James nodded and stood up to head outside. He followed Sammy and saw nine-year-old Arpmin standing there already, staring at the thing that had crashed.

"Boy, where's the capsule?" James asked. Arpmin pointed, and sure enough, there was a capsule of some kind made of metal, though it was too far away to see much more than that.

"We'll need to suit up. Have Marty come, too, since he's the only one who's got any fighting strength."

Sammy nodded and headed toward her house. James ran to his house to get his suit, and the two met back with their suits on and oxygen tanks ready.

"I'm ready," Sammy said, giving a thumbs up.

James smirked. "Good, let's go."

They moved to the barrier. Although it gave some resistance, eventually they went right through.

"You guys can't go without me, can you?" Marty said, standing behind them. The two turned around quickly, startled.

"Of course not. After all, we need somebody who can actually fight," James said, moving behind Marty, as did Sammy. The three walked toward the capsule, and as they got closer, they noticed it looked a lot like an escape pod. When they arrived, Marty noticed something.

"There's a door, and it's open...."

Something pounced out of the pod. It went for Marty, covering his face as he was slammed into the ground. James and Sammy ran toward him, but the creature swung them away. Marty wrestled with it for several seconds before pinning it to the ground.

The black, octopus-like alien resembled a human in its shape, walking on two tentacle-like legs. It wore was a black jacket that covered its body and its arms, which were also like tentacles. The large octopus head extended out of the neck of the jacket. The creature pulled out a gun of some kind and pointed it at Marty. He reacted quickly by throwing the creature behind him, sending him in the direction of the town.

"That's not good. We gotta get it before it tries to do something in the town!" James said as he got up. The other two nodded and got moving. The creature noticed the town as it stood up and started running toward it. They tried to catch up with the creature, but it was too fast. It went right through the dome with ease, noticed Arpmin, and dashed at the frightened child.

"Not the kids!" James yelled as they approached the dome. The creature pointed its gun at Arpmin. The three had gotten through the dome, but now they had a new problem.

"Don't do it!"

The creature spoke an unrecognized language, sounding angry and making motions toward the kid. Arpmin stood there, shaking.

"Don't kill him! Just tell us what you want. We can't understand you," James said. The octopus creature rolled its eyes and cocked its gun.

"NO!"

Just then, right before it took a shot, another kid shoved Arpmin out of the way. That boy was shot through the head and fell to the ground, dead.

"Quinn!" James yelled as tears started pouring from his eyes. "My son!"

Sammy had to hold him back as Marty's anger welled, and he jumped at the creature, punching it in the face and stealing the gun. He then pinned the creature down again.

"You think you're some smart guy, huh? You're paying for this now!" Marty yelled. The creature said something as Marty shot it in the head, killing it. Blue blood poured from its head. Marty got up and put the gun in his pocket. Sammy let go, and James ran to Quinn's body. Blood poured from both sides of his head where the bullet had gone through. James picked up his body and cried into it.

"These creatures...will pay for this...even if it means we need to become battle-ready, we'll do it. They won't get away with this!" James yelled, continuing to cry. It was clear: they needed to build defenses, and create offensive strategies as well.

Chapter 46: The Conflicts They Faced! Flashback End!

A month had passed. They had to bury the only deceased member of their society, but James wouldn't stop there. He would give those octopus creatures their due. After the incident, they had gotten a transmission. They recognized the language as the same as the one the octopus creature had used, and despite not being able to understand it, they could tell the creatures sounded furious. It was all the sign James needed to start building their society's offensive and defensive abilities. Sammy and Marty could help build weapons, with Ted doing programming. Beth, Claire, and Howard would all help create chemical weapons, such as gases and explosives. All of them, of course, were also to learn self-defense, and get stronger than ever before. This was also to apply to the children, who would undergo training so that they could at least defend themselves. He didn't want to lose another one.

It was likely that any day now, those creatures would come, and if they weren't prepared, they would get wiped out. The kids weren't to get involved in combat unless it was for self-defense, meaning the eleven would have to become strong enough in their own ways, in such a short amount of time, in order to take them down. Without knowing what these octopus creatures packed, it was the only thing they could do.

"I finished some of your fighting gear," Sammy said, walking over to James. He was sitting on the couch, writing in his journal.

"So you have. Let's see what you came up with."

He saw the gear she was holding, gauntlets that went up to the elbows, yet were not bulky.

"Say, the technology here reminds me of...Parett's propulsion gear idea that was tossed around."

"Don't get the two mixed up. These don't work like that. These bad boys take the air from the energy of a punch and push it out of a few small pipes. They'll give it an extra 'oomph' while still allowing you to use them without much training.'

Sammy handed them to James.

"I'm also working on getting you some armor as well. We really need to work fast to get preparations complete so we can be ready anytime they come after us."

"You've done a great job, Sammy. Let me know when you've completed the armor. I'd also like to check up on everyone else to see how progress with their weapons is coming along."

"Gladly, though I will say they're coming along great! Marty wanted something that could serve as both a construction tool and a weapon, so we've been working on that to success. That's just one example, though. I'll be glad to show you it all tomorrow morning."

266

"That sounds good. You can go home now."

"All right, see you tomorrow."

James nodded and made a quick wave as she exited out the front door. It was nearly midnight, and he wanted to get some sleep. He finished writing in his journal and then went to bed.

***

"James! James! Wake up!" Claire yelled as he woke up. She was shaking him before he pushed her away.

"What is it, Claire? You don't need to shake me like that." James glanced at his clock, startled.

"Outside! Sammy noticed it as she was working this morning. The octopus creatures may be here!"

James thought to himself for a moment. "Where's everyone else, then?"

"Everyone's getting ready for the worst, and the kids are being put in the bunker area. We need you to come and get ready with us."

"Thanks for waking me up. Tell everyone I'm coming." Claire nodded and ran out of the room. James got into new clothes.

The gall to come to our planet! You won't overtake us that easily.

267

James went outside and saw the other ten talking with each other near the edge of the dome, so he walked toward them. He noticed something new had landed beyond the dome, though this time it looked like a ship.

"All right, what have you guys come up with?" James asked.

"I'd like to lead us into battle. I know we've all trained ourselves, but I still don't want you guys to get hurt," Marty said.

"I don't see an issue with it. Any other details?"

"We're doing this to defend our town. Let's keep it *and* ourselves from being destroyed."

Everyone nodded before they noticed creatures coming out of the small ship. Sure enough, they were the same as the octopus creature that had touched down a month prior.

"All right, everyone! Marty will lead us into battle! For Mars!" James yelled as everyone rallied and screamed a war cry in response. Fully geared, they ran out of the dome, one by one. Dozens of octopus creatures poured out of the ship, armed with several kinds of guns. Marty tackled the first one, drilling right through it and lopping its head off with his small, but sharp, shield. James punched a few into the ground, and the rest attempted to stay out of combat, fighting only when necessary. Marty and James were doing quite well taking care of the initial crowd, but soon, things changed.

Another dozen exited the ship, and these were different, not only in size but also in strength. James and Marty began to struggle, and a few of the others joined in. Sammy started throwing a few of them around with the small mech she was using, and Ted had created a humanoid robot that punched down a couple. It took much longer to get through this batch, but eventually they overcame them. Finally, an octopus creature larger than the rest came out. He wore battle gear that included machine guns on his back as well as brass knuckles with spikes on the ends. His octopus hands shook as he spouted more of the unrecognizable language of the species, pointing at James.

"I don't care what you have to say, you're going down," James said as he threw a gauntleted fist. The creature slammed James into the ground and attempted to thrash him with brass knuckles. Marty came in to shove it with his shield as he pushed his drill into the creature. It winced before activating its machine guns, causing Marty to move out of the way. Sammy ran in with her mech and the creature turned its machine guns off and lifted the mech off the ground. Though it took a second, the creature lifted it all the way off the ground and threw it at the sub-humans. They got out of the way as it crashed into the red dust. Sammy got out, dazed as she fell down.

"I'm fine, guys...just fight without me," Sammy said, giving a thumbs up.

"We need to team up on him to win. Surround him!" Marty yelled as the rest of them ran at the creature. Though they weren't equal in strength, they knew they would be e-nough to take down this creature. They started piling onto him, punching and hurting it in whatever way they could. After several seconds, the creature pushed all of them several feet away from it as it yelled a low, bubbly cry.

"What are we gonna do? This creature clearly over-powers all of us combined," Rachel said, groaning.

Howard pulled out a syringe. "I've got an idea. If we can create an opening and stick this into the creature, it'll daze it enough for us to take it down. I figured it was too inconvenient a solution unless there was no other way."

"Well, it's our only option now, so let's do it," James said. He grabbed onto Howard and hoisted him onto his back. He advanced on the creature as it came in for another strike. How-ard was thrown onto its back and he slammed the syringe into the creature, pushing the liquid down inside of it.

The creature winced as it threw Howard away, but the damage had already been done. After only a few seconds, the creature's movements began to slow, its eyes heavy. Marty yelled as he came in with his drill, this time going for a fatal blow. He drilled through the back of the creature's head, which sent blue blood and guts everywhere. The creature fell to the dirt and quickly died. The eleven yelled a cry of victory as they fist bumped and gave each other high fives. Even Sammy joined in, having recovered from the initial shake the fall had given her.

James breathed heavily as he said, "Well, we did it. Our offenses worked!" Everyone cheered to that, being glad the fight was finally over.

***

The eleven had decided to celebrate with an outdoor party, with a campfire complete with some rocks to sit on. There had been space in the dome which would be used for other buildings later on, but for now, it would be their party space. James had decided to use the octopus spaceship for resources as well as any potential technology they could utilize. Marty had already started work on taking the ship apart, finding materials to use for later projects. The bodies of the octopus creatures would be burned and used as fuel and fertilizer. Their entire population was at this party, all happy for their first offensive victory. They decided to come in for a toast before eating.

"I would just like to say that I am proud of everyone here today for what they've done. Marty, you were a real force in that battle, being the main attacking menace throughout. Sammy, you built all of us either armor or weapons, and for that I can't thank you enough. Howard, you gave us the serum that allowed us to defeat their strongest soldier. The rest of you were valiant warriors who came in when things seemed bleak. Kids, your obedience in not coming out of the shelter even when you were worried about us is admirable. The point is, we all did something here today, and I'd like to toast that," James said. Everyone yelled "Yeah!" and toasted with him.

***

Taizen paused, bringing everyone's thoughts back to the present. "Though that was their first conflict, it wasn't their last. The octopus creatures came back fifteen years later with greater offenses, but by this time, the eleven of them had developed a bigger civilization. Motern was already fully complete by then, and Newtopia had become the new hub for their society. They easily overcame the octopus creatures this time, and in fact, the eleven of them didn't need to get involved, as by then, the first wave of the Sub-human Army had been developed. Some humans tried to come to Mars a few years after that, but the few who did were utterly destroyed before they could arrive in a city per James' command. James' heart had started hardening ever since the loss of Quinn, leading to a worse relationship with the other ten. They had established themselves as 'Elders' at this point, with James convincing them that since they were the ones who started the society, they should be the absolute rulers of it as well. He didn't even want to be called James anymore, preferring 'King' or 'King Starpson.' He started to blame the humans for what had happened to Quinn and took it upon himself to build up offenses to one day invade Earth and take it as his own. He began to hate them so much that only a few years after the octopus creatures had invaded their society, he dubbed his own kind as 'sub-humans,' as due to their physical differences, they had strayed from humanity and became a sub-species of human. One that lived on Mars, and one that was much stronger. It's all led up to where we are today," Taizen said, finishing the story.

"Wow, that was...a lot. It certainly explains everything we've witnessed so far," Joei said.

"Agreed. Phew. Anyway, how's the propulsions for my new gloves and boots coming along?" Boyd asked, looking over at Sparky.

"Seriously? That was a lot of good info that could help us out," Joei said.

"They're just about finished. How about you come over here and let me attach them to your new arm?" Sparky said, signaling for Boyd.

Chapter 47: Insane Upgrades! The Plan to Beat the King!

Boyd stood up and walked toward Sparky, keeping himself cautious of the sub-human. Sparky presented the glove for the left arm, which looked like Boyd's prosthetic, except being a gauntlet. He also had some propulsions in his other hand.

"All right, hold still while I attach these," Sparky said, putting down the gauntlet and picking up a soldering tool.

"So, just how strong are these new propulsions?" Boyd asked.

"These Mark Tens are significantly better than the previous iteration. From my calculations while building them, they theoretically have the power to destroy large buildings in a few hits."

Boyd's eyes widened at that, and a grin covered his face. After a minute, Sparky said it was attached.

"You'll also notice that these have a bit of additional functionality: They're able to swivel around from a base joint that I added to the design to make them more convenient. Previously, they were stuck in place, but now they move around wherever you want them to."

Boyd held up his prosthetic arm and looked at it. The propulsions fit in quite well, and sure enough, they moved around, too.

No more trying to resist the force these give off. Now I can just bring it back in no problem.

"I'll go ahead and attach them to the other arm, so give me a minute for that."

He sat down at his workbench and began the soldering process. Both Taizen and Joei marveled at Boyd's prosthetic.

"They look great!" Taizen said.

"These might be your finest upgrades yet," Joei said, looking at Boyd.

"Might be? I'm getting more power, plus convenience. Of course they're the best I've had so far. The question is, where can I test these out?"

"I got a punching bag upstairs in my room. If you need to use it, go ahead," Sparky said, finishing the soldering process. He handed the gauntlet to Boyd.

"Thanks," Boyd said, turning to Taizen and then whispering, "Why is he being so nice? He's our enemy, no?"

"Well, you remember how I said I forced him to help me, right? Basically, I had to threaten him with a gun. It wasn't pretty, but it got the job done."

"Wow. I didn't take you as someone who would do something like that."

"Yeah, well, desperate times call for desperate measures, what can I say?"

Boyd started up the stairs, and the two followed. Taizen helped Joei up the stairs, as he was struggling. They found the back room and went inside. Sure enough, in the bedroom, there was a black punching bag in the corner. Boyd went up to it, concentrated, and threw a left hook. His arm went right through the bag, and he brought his arm back in. A perfect hole through the bag, with no fall.

"W-wow. My fist felt like butter going through this punching bag...and it was also easy to bring it back in. I may not need much training with these; they seem easy to control."

"That was quite impressive, Boyd. We've come a long way from my poor excuse for a lab, haven't we?" Joei said.

"Don't beat yourself down. Without you, I would've thought I was crazy and probably ended up dead from the invasion. You're the main reason I've gotten this far."

"Well, thanks, Boyd," Joei said as they went back down. They gathered around Boyd's medical chair.

"I'll start work on modifying your boots, but I'll need to set up shop upstairs soon, so they probably won't be done until tonight. We'll see if the King's troops try to search for you guys here. If they do, I'll do my best to get myself out of the situation, without betraying you, of course. Not like I have much choice..." Sparky said, trailing off as he started work on the boots.

"After hearing that story, I've got an idea we could try. Not just to take down the king, but maybe make peace with the sub-humans as well," Boyd said.

"That's unusual. You usually let me or Taizen come up with ideas. What've you got?"

"All right, so, if what we heard is true, Starpson is a bigger threat than we imagined. Like, seriously, the power to take pieces out of mountains is no small feat. I imagine even my new upgrades won't be enough to overpower him if he brings that power out, so we gotta play this smart. We'll get to the top of the palace the same way as before, though after that, I don't have any details. If we have to go up against a mech like he had before, or even bigger, it'll take all three of us to take him down. Taizen would serve as a distraction of sorts, someone to take the King's attention from Joei. I'd give a sign, let's say a thumbs up, and Taizen would have to jump onto the mech and allow Joei to get inside it without him noticing. Joei, you're the key here. I don't know what kind of technology is packed within those mechs, but maybe you could break inside and start doing some damage, whether it be by hacking or by knowing what the right parts to destroy are so the whole mech stops working. I, of course, will also serve as a distraction, but also as someone to do some damage to the mech."

"That sounds like a solid idea," Joei said.

"I'm not done yet. There's another part to this plan: Making peace with the sub-humans. I'm much less sure about this part, because the conflict and grudge the entire race holds against us isn't necessarily something that can be erased easily. Rachel had a drone that flew in to record our first match; I'm sure it'll be back again when we go after him. We can use this to our advantage, though. Starpson has clearly evil tendencies that he hides from most of sub-human society, but if we can bring them out in him, it'll allow everyone to see his true side. I would give a speech of sorts acknowledging this evil, and then trying to be understanding, talking about what ultimately caused Starpson to turn: Quinn's death. I would discuss how humanity isn't always open to change, and how we could be ambassadors for them, convincing the humans that they're not all bad, just misunderstood, and how the sub-humans have i-deas that could help human society greatly in development."

"That's...a very interesting idea, Boyd, but I see a couple problems: first, there's no guarantee the drone will be there a-gain. Without that, there's no way to get the message out there, and that half of the plan banks on that factor. Second, this doesn't seem like a compelling-enough argument. I'm not sure that sub-humans would want to bet everything on us being ambassadors, even if we expose Starpson for his corruption and try to be understanding toward them," Taizen said.

"That's why I said 'possibly.' There's no guarantee it'll work, but with where we are, is there anything else we can do?"

"Good point. I'm in, even if there's uncertainty here."

"I'm just pleasantly surprised you were able to come up with such a plan, Boyd. It's worth a try," Joei said. Sparky got ready to go up to work when banging noises started coming from the entrance to the shop.

"Don't tell me...." Sparky said as he started up the stairs.

"Let us in, Sparky. We got something to ask you," a voice called out.

Chapter 48: Sparky's Confrontation! The Escape!

Sparky opened the door and saw a group of sub-humans in black military jumpsuits. His suspicions were correct: they were from the Sub-human Army.

"Hello, can I help you?" Sparky said, keeping his composure.

"Yes, actually, you can," the leader of the group said. He was similar to the others in looks, except his hair was a bit taller and shot up like a mohawk. "I'm Commander Mervin, from the Sub-Human Army. We're looking for the king's grandson Taizen and a couple of humans. Surely you've heard about them?"

"Yes, of course. The king made quite the example out of them, didn't he?"

"He sure did. Issue is, we couldn't confirm the status of any of them. They've disappeared since the fight occurred, and we're looking to see if they're taking refuge in any part of the city. Would you happen to know anything about where they are?" Mervin asked, leaning in toward Sparky. He stood there, sweating slightly at the thought.

"We gotta get out of here," Taizen said, grabbing the boots. "We'll finish the job of attaching the remaining propulsions to the new boots later."

"Wait, why? Sparky won't rat us out if you've threatened him, will he?" Boyd asked.

"I don't know. What I do know though is that these guys are smart. They know what to look for in lying suspects and may pick up on any signs. We have a plan; the only thing left to do is to finish these boots up, get you comfortable with them, and execute the plan. There's gotta be some kind of way out of here, but where could it be...."

Boyd and Joei took the hint and started checking around the room. They messed with the walls, touching them for any signs of a hidden door. Joei was exploring the small area underneath the stairs when he felt the wall go flimsy. He tore through it to reveal a door. The other two heard the noise and gazed at Joei's discovery.

"Interesting. I didn't expect it to be as straightforward as a door," Taizen said, walking toward it. Boyd put on his other glove so that both his arms were ready for combat. Joei opened the door to reveal a dirt tunnel, held up only by some metal bars every few feet. They could see another door at the end of the tunnel a dozen yards away. They ran toward it, and Taizen cracked the door open. It revealed a tiny dirt room, with a ladder at the back and a hatch on top. They entered and Taizen climbed up, unlocked the hatch, and opened it up. He saw an alleyway, which was between Sparky's shop and a neighboring building.

"Bingo. Let's be careful so we don't get spotted."

***

"You're sweating quite a bit there, Sparky," Mervin said. Sparky wiped his forehead with his hand.

"Sorry, I haven't seen any sign of the three since Taizen came with a couple of guys yesterday. I had no clue at the time he had betrayed the king. Had I known, I would've stopped him."

"Hmm." Mervin stared at Sparky for a few seconds before saying, "You're lying. Your voice is wavering a bit, and your body is showing signs of it, too. Answer me, why have you done this? Did you do it on purpose, or were you threatened?"

"I...I...I can't do this anymore! They're on the bottom floor, assuming they haven't escaped. Now please handle them. If they figure out I ratted on them, they'll kill me."

"Don't focus on that. We'll handle them, then take you directly to the king. We'll see what he says about this, even if you were forced into it. Come on, boys! Search the bottom floor!"

***

Taizen, Joei, and Boyd watched as the group entered the store alongside Sparky. They took the opportunity and headed in the opposite direction.

"Can we go behind one of the buildings? I wanna get a feel for these new propulsions. Plus, Joei could use the time to finish my boots," Boyd said.

"Sure."

They went in between the two buildings to their right. They headed to the back and got settled.

"We can't stay here long. Someone will find us at some point, so let's move it."

"Wait, I don't have a soldering iron," Joei said.

"I got the portable one from Sparky's workbench. Here you go," Taizen said, digging it out of his pocket and handing it to Joei. Though Joei's new hands were awkward, he made do with what he had, and started soldering. After he was done, he handed the gloves to Boyd, and he started practicing with them. A few minutes later, Boyd had already stopped punching.

"These new propulsions are nice! I can bring my arm back in after punching, so I hardly needed any practice. The fact they move around now too really does make everything easier."

"Good to hear. I'm almost done with the boots," Joei said, not looking up. After a few more minutes, Joei stood up to hand the boots to Boyd.

"Thanks. I'll make sure I can use these as well before we execute our plan."

He put them on and started to kick. Sure enough, it came very easily to him, with the propulsions moving his leg back when he wanted it to. Five minutes later, he was ready.

"You've come a long way, Boyd. Let's finish this together," Joei said, standing up.

Boyd nodded, and grinned. "Let's go give King Starpson what he deserves."

They cheered as Taizen pulled up the location of the palace on his phone.

Chapter 49: Return to the Palace! The Second Confrontation!

They had decided collectively to let Taizen lead the way, seeing as he was the one with the way to the palace. They ran behind the buildings, though it wasn't long before they had to go out into the open. It didn't matter now. All that mattered was getting to the palace and executing their plan.

"Luckily, Sparky's shop isn't that far from the palace, so we should get there soon," Taizen said. Soon after, they entered a busier area where they could *definitely* be seen, so they were bound to be discovered by the king soon. Sub-humans started looking over at them and pointing. Some yelled, while others made calls.

***

"King! King!" the sub-human servant cried out as he ran into the king's room. King Starpson had woken up recently and looked over at the servant from his throne.

"Charging in without permission? This had better be urgent."

"It is! Very urgent! Taizen and the two humans have been spotted! They're moving toward the palace just like yesterday," the servant got out before Starpson's phone started going off. He answered, seeing as it was one of the commanders searching for the fugitives.

"An update?"

"Yes, My King. I believe we've found a lead. We managed to talk Sparky into giving us information, and it seems they were last spotted at his shop. He's told us he was forced into helping them, so their current status is unknown. I'm having a team bring Sparky to you so you can talk to him about his fate," the commander said over the phone.

"I would like you all to return to the palace. The three have apparently been spotted already, so a search is no longer needed."

The king hung up the phone. He started twitching as he looked over at his servant. He shook as he grabbed the servant and threw him across the room, past the entrance door. "Their strength could have improved! I will not have this! Get in contact with my engineers and tell them to get my super mech ready. I'll be preparing until then."

"Y-yes, My King!" the servant said, quickly standing up and running to the elevator.

"Only a few blocks left to go!" Taizen said. They were now having to dodge the many sub-human citizens that got in their way. It was clear they wanted to protect their king.

"What I'm wondering is if we're even gonna have to go inside the palace. If he's got another mech up his sleeve, it could be bigger than the last one, and there's no way it's fitting inside," Boyd said, jumping over some hovercrafts.

"We can't get caught up on details like that now. We just have to get to the palace and hope for the best." They continued running for a few more blocks until they got to the block that headed directly to the palace. When they got closer, they noticed that there weren't any guards by the gates.

"That's strange…" Joei said as they stopped at the gate.

"That's odd, but we can't focus on it. You two hop on my back. Hopefully I'll have more control now that my propulsions can move," Boyd said, crouching down. The two grabbed onto his back as Boyd counted down from three. When he got to zero, he jumped, going higher than ever before. He was able to propel himself toward the ground, this time jumping back up when he got near the ground. He started kicking one leg at a time until, eventually, it was as if he could jump on the air. He got low enough to the ground and landed on both of his feet.

"Wow, these new upgrades are more impressive than I thought," Taizen said as he got off Boyd. Joei followed suit.

"Well, I had done it accidentally when we were facing those ships back in Motern town, so I wondered if I could do it *and* have control over it. It seems like I can."

They started running toward the palace doors. Strangely, there were still no guards to be seen. They got inside, and there wasn't a single sub-human on the floor. They stood there for a few seconds, looking around.

"What's going on...?"

"I don't know. I haven't seen anything like this before. Usually, the king prefers to be heavily guarded and not engage in combat unless absolutely necessary. Unless...." Taizen trailed off, then coming to a realization. "Unless he considers you to be a genuine threat. Maybe he doesn't want any distractions, just a match against you, so he can do the job with his own hands."

"Interesting. All we can do is head up to the top floor and see," Boyd said, heading to the elevator. The other two followed as they went inside the elevator, pressing the twelfth-floor button. Since they had broken the call buttons yesterday, the elevator went straight up, skipping past the first floor, second floor, third floor. It continued going up each subsequent floor until they reached the top.

"No...defense...of any kind," Taizen said, mouth open in shock. They stepped out of the elevator and headed toward the familiar palace hallway. Boyd threw the large doors open.

"Hello!? Anyone home!?" Boyd yelled. The entire room was dark. It was the same room as before, with the throne chair turned backward. It slowly turned, revealing King Starpson. He wore battle clothing similar to the night before, but seemed to be wearing a backpack of some kind.

"No need to be so loud, is there?" Starpson said, giving an evil grin. "I must say, I'm quite shocked you three have managed to stay alive after what happened last night. Especially you, Parett."

"I won't allow you to talk badly about my lineage. Boyd here will make sure of that."

Boyd nodded toward Joei, then faced the king again.

"Of course, the main attraction. Boyd," the king said, eyeing Boyd.

"Nah, don't call me that anymore. I've had an upgrade. I think I've earned the name Psyborg."

Joei and Taizen looked at Boyd in confusion, as did the king.

"Oh. Your visions plus the replaced arm. You think you're clever, aren't you? I'll let our final fight squash those sentiments," Starpson said, pushing a button on his throne chair. Like before, the entire roof, as well as the walls, opened to the outside. A drone was already flying above, getting ready to record the fight.

"Meet me in the front of the palace. Smile for the camera while you're at it."

He grinned as he activated a button on his backpack, revealing it to be a jetpack. He quickly flew down to the front of the palace. They weren't quick enough to catch him.

Then they saw it: Four ships were flying down, carrying a mech suit. It was much bigger than the one the king had used before. It appeared to be over half the size of the palace and was bulky, too. It had two legs and two arms, as well as a cockpit where the head would've been. It was similar to the earlier mech, except its arms and legs were longer in proportion to the body. Its body was pill-shaped. As the mech reached the ground, the four ships released the chains and let it drop. The entire area shook for several seconds. They could see the king flying toward the mech, with the top of the cockpit opening for him. He flew into it, taking off the jetpack and sitting down. The cockpit top came back down, and the mech started to move.

"Ready to fight me?" Starpson asked, his voice coming out of a speaker from the mech. The mech made a taunting motion with its right arm.

Chapter 50: Final Battle Start! Psyborg Vs. The King!

"I'm not gonna back down now, am I?" Boyd asked as he let himself fall off the side of the building. He quickly jumped off the wall toward the giant mech, going at a speed quicker than he ever had before. The mech went in for a punch as the two collided fist-to-fist. Despite the size difference, it took a few seconds before the mech could push Boyd away. He was sent rocketing to the ground, but he was prepared and bounced right back up for another collision. This time, Boyd went for the head, but the mech's arm swept him away.

"Your little power increase is meaningless. Now that I'm in my most powerful form, there's nothing you can do against me," Starpson said, sending the mech in for another punch. Boyd dodged by jumping, and made sure to go high enough so that Joei and Taizen saw him. As Boyd went for another hit, he made a quick thumbs up that the two of them could see.

They took the sign, and Joei hopped onto Taizen's back, waiting a moment for an opening. Boyd and the king went fist-to-fist again, with Boyd being blown away again by the force.

Taizen saw the opening and jumped at the mech. Boyd jumped back up and tried going for one of the mech's legs; the mech simply kicked him away. The distraction allowed Taizen to hop onto the shoulder of the mech. It only took a moment before he was spotted.

"Trying to help, I see. Stay out of this fight!" the king said, slamming Taizen with the mech's hand and sending him flying into the trees. He managed to land on one, and despite being off the mech, the first part of the plan had been completed. Joei had hopefully not been spotted, and would be able to enter the mech's internals. Boyd had bounced back up and went for an arm, hoping to keep him distracted.

The king's eyes darted to where Joei was. "Did you really think I wouldn't notice something trying to hijack my mech? I have sensors all over this machine to prevent such issues. How about I send you out of this world a second time?"

The mech's left hand went toward its right shoulder, where Joei was. Though Joei tried to run, it was too fast for him. As the fist neared him, Boyd hopped to where Joei was and pushed the hand. It was taking everything the gloves had to keep it away. Boyd got a quick idea and tried pushing off the mech's shoulder with his legs. The boots activated, and the arm was swiftly pushed away. The force shook the entire mech, and a few seconds later formed a crack in the cockpit glass. Starpson stared at it for a moment as he started shaking and laughing maniacally. Joei took his chance and moved lower down the mech.

"Ohhhohoho, now you've gone and done it! How DARE you damage my precious mech! You think you're so powerful now, don't you? Well, let this be known: No one messes with me! Not you, not Taizen, not even sub-humans! I'll show you what true pain is!" Starpson yelled, his eyes looking crazed. He sent a fist toward Boyd, but he simply dodged.

As he focused on Boyd, though, the mech became faster. Boyd tried powering his punches up with his boots, but the mech easily shrugged them off and countered with stronger punches. Joei had started the process of creating an opening on the mech when a hand started coming at him again. "I told you; you can't hide from me!"

Joei decided to let go and drop to the ground.

"Boyd!" he yelled as he fell. Boyd was close enough and was able to send him flying upward before Boyd was punched away. Joei managed to grab onto the bottom portion of the mech in between the legs and noticed something. *Is this...an entrance to the inside?*

Though it seemed too good to be true, it appeared to be a hatch, with a handle and circular shape around it. Joei's robot body could *barely* fit if he managed to get inside, but there was some sort of lock on it.

Meanwhile, Boyd waited for the next fist to come before he started running on it, getting closer and closer to the cockpit. As he approached it, the mech sent him flying upward. Boyd pushed upward with his boots as he quickly flew at the cockpit.

He narrowly avoided the fists coming at him as he attempted to smash through the cockpit glass. Though he bounced off as soon as he slammed his fists into it, the glass cracked severely from the impact.

Joei had found that simply destroying the lock with a few tools he had brought allowed the entrance to open, and he was inside the mech. The only issue was that he didn't recognize a lot of the technology inside. He was surprised to see how much space there was, with wires hanging everywhere, and circuitry lining the walls. He couldn't just start cutting random wires. He would risk killing himself and maybe even Boyd if he were to do that. He had to go about this carefully and find a way to shut the system down without causing it to explode. *Carefully....*

Starpson started fuming at the sight of his dome all cracked up. Then he saw the alert that something foreign had entered the mech. He started shaking violently, and his whole head turned the color of a rotten tomato. He said no words, but quickly slammed Boyd into the palace, knocking him through one of the floors. He rebounded but was stopped again. The king spared no time punching and knocking Boyd around like a pinball in a machine. Yet he kept rebounding.

"It doesn't matter how angry you get; I'll keep coming at you until you're down!" Boyd yelled, going for another strike. Starpson had had enough, and punched Boyd into the ground underneath him. Though he rebounded, the mech had already jumped up. It started coming down quickly, right where Boyd was coming from. Boyd couldn't react in time, and the mech's foot came down. Boyd disappeared under it.

The king took multiple heavy breaths before saying to the drone, "You see, everyone? Our power is too great for anyone who stands in our way. Let this show that even the strongest opponent cannot best King Starpson!"

The cheers of the sub-humans watching could be heard near the palace, and Rachel as the host also cheered for what had just happened.

Chapter 51: The End of an Era! Psyborg Vs. The King Ends!

"I can't do this!" a kid in a white gi said. It was Boyd. At eleven years old, he was taking his physical assessment to reach the second belt, that being yellow. He had been doing good so far, but he was having trouble pulling off the final move, where he had to crouch onto the ground with two fists, and then do a corkscrew jump as he raised both fists into the air. He had already tried it twice in the assessment and had fallen both times.

"Yes you can, Boyd! Don't let a couple of setbacks get to you. Give it one last try!" Mr. Shin said, cheering him on from the sidelines.

Boyd, deciding to trust his instructor, quickly came up with an idea to pull it off. He tried it again, this time bringing both fists out for better balance, nailing the move, and making a graceful landing. The assessors were impressed, and gave Boyd his yellow belt.

"I did it!"

Boyd woke up, quickly realizing it was just a dream. What wasn't a dream was his current position, being stuck under the mech's foot. He could barely move or breathe, but he knew now that he had to give it one last push.

For my friends...for humanity!

***

With Boyd finally gone, the king could deal with the pest inside of the mech before he got into anything too serious.

He started messing with the controls when he noticed the ground begin to shake. It couldn't have been his impact; that had already happened. He didn't get much time to think, though. The ground beneath one of the mech's feet started cracking, and the force slowly pushed the mech upward. The king tried to resist it, pushing back down, but it was no use. The mech was sent flying into the air as Boyd revealed himself, unharmed from the mech's landing. The king was dazed for a moment, then refocused.

"I must say, you've gone beyond all my expectations. Even still, you've only delayed the inevitable!" Starpson yelled as he started pressing some new buttons within the cockpit. The mech suddenly flipped upside down as the fists detached from the mech. They were rocketing toward Boyd, and fast. He couldn't dodge, and one of the hands grabbed him as they continued toward the ground. "We figured out propulsion technology far before you ever could. Let the thing that brought you power bring you down!"

Boyd tried escaping from the grip of the giant hand, but it was no use. His propulsions weren't strong enough to change the direction of the hand, and he didn't have enough room inside to loosen the grip. He knew there was only one thing he could do now. As he concentrated on his stress for a second, he let out a yell as he released it. The pinkish energy reverberated across the hand, stronger than ever.

It still wasn't enough. Boyd had noticed the grip had loosened, though, and the falling speed had stopped increasing. He made sure his legs were far enough out of the grip of the hand and pushed at the air hard. He managed to flip the hand over, so his legs were facing the ground. Boyd had noticed the pinkish energy was something he could feel being reflected, almost as if the energy was a part of him. He was only a few seconds from the ground, and with this time, he gathered up his remaining stress and released it again. The hand broke into pieces, and now Boyd could see the ground. As he landed, he kicked back off, also punching the air. The combined power of the boots and the gauntlets allowed Boyd to shoot up into the air almost instantaneously. Within a moment, he had already reached the cockpit of the mech, halfway up the palace.

"You talk too much," Boyd said as he let off his strongest punch. It easily broke through the heavily cracked glass, and the shards flew everywhere. Both Boyd and Starpson blocked their faces when this happened. The mech had flipped right-side-up as it landed on the palace lawn.

***

298

Joei continued to work through the internals, trying to find any vulnerability he could take advantage of. Then he found it. There was a large control chip that was in charge of sending signals to the mech's body parts. He'd recognized it based on previous projects he'd worked on.

If I could just separate it...

He reached out to grab the chip when multiple lasers activated, one of them slicing his hand off. Joei pulled his arm back and started maneuvering around them, careful not to lose another one of his limbs. Although he was singed a couple of times, he pushed through. Finally, he reached the chip and gave it a strong pull, and it separated from its mount, causing sparks to fly in his direction.

***

Starpson motioned the controls for the mech to stand up, but nothing happened. Suddenly, another alarm blared, notifying him of the damage Joei had done. He exploded.

"NO! I won't let it end like this!"

He quickly pushed a button as the seat around him formed a small, circular pod with a window for his face.

"I've set off a self-destruct program for thirty seconds just for cases like this. The resulting explosion will reach so far that even you can't escape it. Say goodbye to your life and your friends."

Starpson's pod lowered into the inside of the mech. The opening where the seat was quickly closed, and Boyd suddenly became worried. He started punching the mech's chest, trying to make his way in.

***

Joei noticed a timer inside the mech had started for thirty seconds. He wasn't sure what it meant, except that it was probably deadly. He headed over to try to stop it. A pod had lowered into the internals with a small window. He looked, seeing that the king was inside it.

"It's no use. That timer has a passcode that only I know. With twenty seconds left, I doubt you could do anything," Starpson said, grinning from inside his pod. Joei had no time to get information out of him; he had to try at least guessing even if the odds were heavily against him. A keypad was just below the timer, so guessing he did.

***

Boyd figured out fast that punching through the mech wasn't gonna work. Not only could he not get through it on time, but even if he did, it could set off the explosive. He had one idea, but it would be difficult to execute. He started by grabbing onto one of the arms of the mech. He pushed off it with both his boots and his gloves, keeping his hands around the mech. The force was more than enough to lift the mech off the ground. Within a few seconds, the mech had already reached the top of the palace. This would work, but there was one issue: Joei. He then remembered there was an opening on the bottom part of the mech, where he had thrown Joei. As the mech topped the roof of the palace, Boyd jumped down to the bottom part of the mech. He saw the door had already been opened.

"Joei, come on! I got an idea!"

Joei turned his head and saw Boyd's face popping out of the opening he had come through. The deactivation idea wasn't likely to work, so he trusted Boyd and dropped toward him. Boyd grabbed him as he came through.

"What's your plan?"

"I don't have time to explain. Just jump off me, and land into the trees below."

Joei had multiple questions, but no time to ask. He let go of Boyd and jumped. Boyd couldn't see if he had made it. He knew what he had to do now. He jumped to the top floor to get a better view of the mech. It had almost reached the top of the translucent dome, but had slowed before reaching it. Then it started falling. With a better view, Boyd jumped to the mech and grabbed hold of the arm again. He landed on the top floor as he quickly started trying to spin. The weight of the mech was nearly beyond his ability to hold, even with the propulsions.

As they moved with him, however, he slowly started rotating. One rotation. Two. They were going slow at first, but quickly they sped up. Within several rotations, he was making full circles in less than a second. The rotations around the floor had leveled the king's room, destroying furniture and blowing away books and paintings.

With this speed, and ten seconds left, Boyd aimed upward and let go. The mech flew toward the top of the translucent dome, phasing right through it, barely slowing. He saw the top part of the pod peek right through the opening Joei had gone through, revealing King Starpson. Unfortunately for him, the pod was unable to escape the opening. Boyd saw him yell *"Psyborg!"* as the mech exploded like a firework high in the air. The explosion was so destructive that much of the mech had disintegrated. Only some smaller pieces remained as they fell beyond the dome's range.

"So long, King Starpson."

Chapter 52: Another Issue! An Argument Against the Sub-humans!

Boyd felt like he would pass out, but he knew he couldn't yet. There were still a couple of things he had to do. He gathered his strength and jumped from the palace, planning to fall into a tree. He was about to land on one to slow his fall, then touched the top of it. He looked around and found Joei and Taizen sitting at the bottom of one of the trees, looking up.

"You did it, Boyd. I don't know what you did, but you did it," Joei said, impressed.

"No, Joei, *we* did it. We've finally conquered the king. I couldn't have done it without you guys."

"You did most of the work, Boyd. Give yourself the credit you deserve," Taizen said. Boyd was about to reply when the drone suddenly flew down to several feet above them.

"You think that just because you killed our king, you can do whatever you want now? This society was built on King

Starpson and his beliefs, and it'll remain that way as long as us Elders are around," Rachel said through the drone. Sub-humans started crowding around the outer gate, and the three could hear their cries of anger and revenge. "How about I open the gates and see if this crowd can handle you?"

Seconds later, the front gates opened, and sub-humans started pouring into the front of the palace garden. Quickly, Taizen and Joei backed away and started climbing a tree, but Boyd remained on the ground.

"Boyd, what are you doing? Get up here!" Joei urged.

"You think I'm afraid of a few hundred regular sub-humans after I just defeated their king in that giant mech, which was half the size of the palace!?" Boyd yelled, letting off a pink wave of energy. The sub-humans coming toward him fell as soon as the pink energy touched them. "How about you all hear me out for a bit?"

"Why should we? You killed our king!" a young sub-human from the crowd yelled.

"Because I don't intend on hurting any of you. I've heard the experiences the Elders went through, and I'd like to make amends between us and you sub-humans."

"And who told you about that? Taizen? He's a traitor! He could've easily fed you lies," Rachel said.

"So, it's not true that some alien species came here when the civilization was young and killed one of the children at the time, the king's own son Quinn?"

The crowd got quiet for a few seconds after that.

"So what? You humans drove us to this planet and caused that to happen!" a middle-aged sub-human in a business suit argued.

"Listen to yourself! You really think humans caused aliens to come to your world and murder one of your own kin? Think about how ridiculous that sounds. I understand the Elders were rejected by society, but this argument about Quinn is preposterous! I'm trying to be understanding here."

"Our king knew what was best for us. Despite that, you decided to come to our world and kill him! Isn't that reason enough for us to not trust you?" Rachel asked.

"Did he, though? Why don't you play back a certain line after I cracked the glass the first time during our fight?"

"Now why should I—"

Boyd pointed his fist at the drone. "Do it."

"Fine."

She scrolled through the footage the drone had recorded. She pulled up the moment and played it.

"You think you're so powerful now, don't you? Let this be known: NO one messes with me! Not you, not Taizen, not even sub-humans!" Starpson said in the footage.

"You can stop it now."

Rachel paused the footage and switched the view on the livestream back to Boyd.

"What does this prove? Going against our king's wishes would mean we weren't doing what was best for our society. Betrayal, essentially," Rachel said.

"Maybe you could interpret that as such, but how about you go back to the fight from last night? To what he said right before he sliced my right arm off and dropped me off the edge of the palace?"

Rachel didn't argue this time and went to that point in the previous livestream.

"This is about advancing our society, and killing off those who reject it. Hear this, citizens of Newtopia and all sub-humankind! Let this be a lesson to anyone who rejects us and what we believe in!" Starpson said in the footage. Rachel switched back to Boyd.

"Is this not the same thing? He wants what's best for us."

"Except listening to that first part, you can hear his true motives: all he wanted was to advance society. Life hardly mattered to him; it was all about vengeance. Advancing technology so even a small society such as your own could kill off the humans he hated. Don't believe me? How about you answer this: Was James a different person before Quinn died?"

"Now why—"

"Answer the question! This is important!"

She sighed. "I guess, yeah, but it's been so long since then. He was always a determined person, though I will admit he was a lot nicer before that happened...but that was just motivation for his goals! He was still looking out for us. The loss of his child was just a motivator for that."

"James wasn't an idiot. I've already explained to you why blaming Quinn's death on humans is nonsense. You all got your revenge on those aliens, no? That would've been when he could have let go of that anger. There's grief, of course, which is understandable, but it's clear he changed after that incident. It changed him as a person, and his hatred for humans clearly seemed to increase after that, seeing as he was angrier and more careless. His own wife has told me of the lack of care he had for her, being treated the same as her own fellow Elders. Don't you think that's kind of messed up for someone who should be so close to you? I have one last thing for you to look at. Go to the part right after the king lost control of his mech."

Rachel obliged again without hesitation.

"I've set off a self-destruct program for thirty seconds just for cases like this. The resulting explosion will reach so far that even you can't escape it. Say goodbye to your life and your friends," Starpson said in the footage.

"Don't you see? He was willing to kill a good portion of sub-humans just to kill us off. If I hadn't thrown the mech outside the dome, a lot of you wouldn't be standing here right now," Boyd said. "Wouldn't you rather live a life in peace instead of one that's hatred-filled, where you're willing to sacrifice others for your own well-being?"

"Well...maybe. But it still stands that humans rejected us! They didn't want to hear or see what we had to offer, and we were rejected by society as a whole! What makes you think you could change anything?"

"I...can't guarantee anything. No one can. But one sub-human wanted to trust me and see what I had to offer," Boyd said, looking up in the tree. Taizen jumped down beside Boyd.

"Taizen here may be considered a traitor to you all, but he was the only one that was willing to trust me, despite everything. Our experiences together, and our newfound friendship, should be more than enough proof to show you peace between our two kinds is possible. It may not be easy, but trust between us could lead to a fantastic new world for us both to live in. I've already said I don't want to hurt any of you. Would someone who wants to kill you all say that?"

"Someone who wants to gain our trust just so we can be wiped out?"

"With my power, it would already be easy to do that. I wouldn't need to gain your trust to do that, yet here I am, wanting to gain the trust of each and every one of you sub-humans, and make peace with you all. Like I said, it may not be easy, but isn't it worth a try just so you can finally show off the great technologies you've created over the decades, and gain favor with humans? It would be a much better world than one run by hatred and vengeance, one run with little flexibility in beliefs."

The whole crowd of sub-humans stood there, silent for a minute. Then Rachel spoke up.

"Look, I don't know if what you say is even possible, but after hearing this, I'd like you to come into the palace. We've got a meeting room for us Elders. Let's all discuss this more in private. As for the rest of you sub-humans, get outta here. We're gonna have a talk with these three, so don't touch them."

The crowd of sub-humans grumbled and spoke among themselves as they left through the front gates. Some didn't seem happy about the situation. Boyd knew he hadn't won their trust, but had at least made progress with his argument. Now he had to fully win the Elders over.

Chapter 53: Meeting with the Elders! Can Peace Be Achieved?

The meeting room looked like the kind found in an office building, albeit futuristic. The center of the room had a long, rectangular table and eleven chairs that surrounded it. There was also a holographic screen that took up the center of the right wall. Rachel was already sitting in one of the chairs, waiting for them.

"You guys are gonna stay standing. The other Elders will be here momentarily."

Sure enough, a few seconds later, the rest of the Elders walked in through the door and took their seats.

"You want us to meet with these maniacs after what they did to the king? Are you insane?" Marty asked, looking toward Rachel.

"I don't know, but they would've killed us already if they were going to do harm to us. Considering their proposition of peace between us and humans, we can at least hear them out and decide what to do based on that."

"And why should we listen to them?"

"Well, they kind of got rid of our leader, so we don't have much of a choice, do we?"

Marty got quiet after that.

"All right, then. If you want peace between our two kinds, what exactly do you propose in order to pull off such a feat?" Claire asked.

"I haven't thought about it much, honestly. I was mostly focused on overthrowing the king. I think the best way to go about it, though, is for you all to make peace with us. That's a great first step. From there, we can show humans the peace we've built with each other. They'll see that we can coexist in peace. I would be an ambassador of sorts," Boyd said.

Claire thought for a moment. "Huh…is it that simple, though? This is the same society that shunned us for our ideas and intelligence. What makes you think a single friendship would change any of that?"

"Well, did any of you have friends other than yourselves during college?"

The whole group of Elders shook their heads slowly.

"Then I think that proves my point. If some guy like me can show other humans that we can be friends, then that shows them that you guys aren't insane and have great ideas to show off."

"There's another issue, though. Our civilization already sent that ship to invade Earth. Since that's happened, humans have no reason to trust us. We've already gone in too deep," Marty said.

"Is that true, though? If you attempt to make a peace treaty to show you truly want peace, they're likely to oblige. Your society has a military advantage over humans. Not in size, of course, but in technology. Previous major conflicts have shown that some countries do strive for peace. If you surrender and propose a treaty, the country that you invaded, the United States, would be likely to accept such a proposal, especially since your strength with soldiers, combined with machinery, isn't something they'd wanna mess with," Joei said, inserting himself into the conversation.

"Hm...you make a point, but I don't know. It's difficult to risk everything we've got, what we've been building up for all of our lives, just for a chance at peace." The rest of the Elders nodded.

"Joei has a point, though. Plus, wouldn't you like those who rejected you to finally accept you?" Boyd said.

Marty sighed. "It'd be nice. You know, what you said back there wasn't completely wrong. Starpson wasn't tyrannical before all those events happened. Something changed, and we've ignored it for so long. If I'm being honest with you, though, I still don't fully trust you. You can't guarantee your plan will work, so even if we do go along with this, you'll have to make it work. Otherwise, sub-humans and humans aren't gonna have a future together." The other Elders in the room slowly nodded.

"So then, are we gonna do this?"

"Depends. If you can lay out a simple plan on what we're gonna do, maybe so."

"Well, I've already discussed some of the stuff. All of you Elders, along with us, would fly over to Earth, where I would be the ambassador for sub-humans. I would discuss how I've made peace with you guys, and you Elders would make a call to stop the invasion and propose a peace treaty. You'd probably have to get in cahoots with people such as the president to make such a thing work, but once you did, the feud would finally be over. I can't guarantee everyone will accept you, but my friendship and your peace treaty will certainly help with that, even if it does take time," Boyd explained.

Marty sat there for a minute, thinking. "Well...with the situation we're in, I guess that's as good a plan as we're gonna get, isn't it? I'll follow you along with this plan, but you'd better succeed." He stood up and held his hand out to Boyd. The two shook hands, and the rest of the Elders followed suit, each agreeing to follow Boyd's plan. Some seemed more confident than others, but they all appeared uncertain.

"It probably won't be easy. Stuff like this isn't gonna be, but just know that I'm gonna try my hardest to help make it happen," Boyd said, standing up. The rest followed suit and started heading out the door.

"We head for Earth within a few hours!" Marty yelled. The rest of the Elders reacted in various ways as they left the meeting room.

Chapter 54: Returning to Earth! Prepare as Ambassador!

Boyd stood in front of the ship they had traveled to Mars on. It felt strange seeing it again, as he hadn't been sure he would be coming back alive. The ten Elders had gotten ready, and were already loading the ship with supplies. Captain Zaizo was reinstated, although he was none too happy about it. The Elders wanted to mentally prepare for the trip. They were leaving the planet to the captains, and they weren't sure about how well that would go.

"Don't expect me to be 'buddy buddy' with you all of a sudden just because they're asking me to take this trip. Even if you actually manage to unite our two species, it's not gonna make me forget what you did to me," Zaizo said as he was passing by Boyd. Boyd didn't care, though. He was more worried about getting his speech ready for his role as ambassador.

"Don't dwell on the speech too much, Boyd. You've already come this far, and you've got two weeks to get it ready. You'll have plenty of time to write something good," Taizen said, trying to comfort Boyd.

"Thanks, Taizen."

The three stepped onto the ship. They went to the observation deck, where the Elders had already been seated on the top part, taking up the available seats.

"Looks like you three gotta hang on to something. Serves you right," Zaizo said, smirking as he turned his head back to focus on the ship. "I'm ready to start the launch sequence when you all are."

"Go on," Marty said. Boyd, Joei, and Taizen all hung onto the nearest wall.

"All right, we take off in one minute."

Zaizo initiated the launch. They all prepared as the timer went down. The three held on as tight as they could as the timer approached zero, starting the launch. They were flattened into the back wall as the ship launched into space. Once they were in space, they fell to the floor.

"You all are now free to leave your seats, except for you three, of course," Zaizo said, laughing at his own remark.

They were dazed as they stood up. The Elders got out of their seats, and they all settled in for the two-week journey.

***

A week had passed, and the entire crew was sleeping, save for Zaizo, who was manning the ship. Then he noticed a call from Mars, and knew he had to find an Elder to take it. As he exited the control room, he noticed Marty was walking down the hallway and gave the communicator to him.

"M-my Elder! Things are becoming dire here," Arpmin said over the call. The Elders had been worried a call like this would come.

"What's going on?" Marty asked.

"We have many residents attempting to break down the palace gate! They seem unhappy about your decision to form peace with the humans."

"We don't know what's gonna happen yet with that. Threaten arrests for those citizens, and if they don't listen, you may stun them and arrest each one that disobeys."

"A-are you sure? There's a few hundred out there, and not a lot of officers to handle them."

"Then get the troops involved if you need to. Have them stun and arrest citizens if that happens."

"Okay, My Elder. I'll do my best," Arpmin said as he ended the call. Marty put his hand to his face. Sammy had heard the commotion and woken up, finding Marty just outside his room.

"What's going on?" she asked.

"Issues with the citizens having conflicting opinions o-ver this peace stuff. There's apparently a few hundred outside the palace gate trying to get in," Marty said, giving an angry grunt.

Sammy sighed. "Look, Marty, none of us are sure about this, but I for one would prefer this route over trying to hold onto anger and getting revenge. If it's possible for them to accept us again, then it's worth a shot. We'll get through this like we always have."

"But that's the thing, Sammy! *Will* we get through this? We're being forced to trust some human who wants us to live in peace, yet he killed James! Sure, James wanted to fight him, but my point stands. Boyd came onto our planet and killed our ruler! Yet he wants to try to have peace with us?"

"We invaded Earth, so he had a reason to do so."

"Now you're acting like you're on *his* side!"

"Well, I never truly supported James' actions after he changed like he did. I thought he would lead us to a better society, but Boyd showed me—no, showed *us*—that that wasn't the case. I felt like I had to play along and hope he would be able to advance us, but I think I prefer Boyd's solution. If peace with humans is possible, I wouldn't mind having it."

"Have you seriously forgotten what they did to us, Sammy? What makes you think anything's gonna change?"

"It's been fifty years, Marty. Fifty years of building a society, fifty years of following James along with his plans, and fifty years of wanting retribution. It's time to change how we look at the situation and apply it. I'm upset James couldn't change along with us, but he was the one who caused everything, so who knows if he ever would've changed. I'm just glad we've been given an opportunity to look at things differently, and I suggest you try changing your perspective as well."

Sammy walked back to her room. Marty stood there for a while, in thought.

***

Boyd's hand shook as he finished the final paragraph of his ambassador speech. He had gotten up early that morning to finish it, as today, they were arriving on Earth. He'd already read over the rest of it to make sure it looked good and had found clothes in the supplies area that were clean. He went into the control room, where everyone else was preparing for the landing.

"We land on Earth in an hour," Zaizo said. Joei and Taizen ran over to check on Boyd.

"Are you doing all right?" Joei asked.

"Yeah, I'm just unsure if my speech will leave an impact on humankind. I really want this peace plan to work out, and that heavily relies on me."

"Like I said before, Boyd, you've come so far. You just gotta finish this final step off strong," Taizen said.

"Well, thanks for that, Taizen."

Boyd walked toward the Elders. "Do you guys have a plan on what we're doing once we land?"

"Yes. As soon as we start to land, all of us Elders are going to shout into the ship's mic that we are stopping the invasion and retreating. You'll then be the one to leave the ship and say that 'we come in peace' and then make your speech. Rachel will use her drone, combined with Ted's hacking skills, to allow the entire local area to watch the speech. The rest will be determined on what happens after that," Sammy said.

"Well, that's good to hear. I'll get prepared for that then, I guess."

Just focus, Boyd. Focus on not messing this up!

***

The hour passed quickly, and the ship was already landing. Luckily, they managed to arrive quickly enough to not attract any attention that would cause them to be shot at upon landing. Captain Zaizo had looked for New York with the locator as they reached the exosphere of the Earth. The Elders had huddled up close to the speaker, waiting for the right time.

"We're coming up on New York. It seems like the remaining sub-humans scared off any efforts to clean up the area, so it's just a fight between human soldiers and sub-humans," Zaizo said. The ship was quickly approaching the landing area, and they slowed their descent as they reached it. "Alright, Elders, go ahead and say it!"

The ten of them took a deep breath and yelled together, "We are retreating! We are stopping the invasion!"

Chapter 55: The Speech That Brings Peace! A Talk with the President!

The ship slowly landed as Boyd stood behind the entrance. In seconds, he would be exiting the ship and giving his speech. Sweat beaded down his face as he gulped at the thought and gripped his megaphone tightly.

The hatch began to open, rising. The platform at the end turned downward to touch the ground. Anyone outside the ship could now see him. There seemed to still be an active battle going on, with more sub-humans than human soldiers. The fighting ceased as the ship landed, however, and all eyes were on Boyd. Rachel's drone flew out and hovered right in front of him. He took a deep breath as he lifted the megaphone.

"I know what you're all thinking. 'Did they just say retreat?' Yes, they did. You see, the sub-humans have had a change of heart. My name is John Boyd, and I was the warrior who put a stop to the leader of the sub-humans. I wanted to show them that peace was possible with humans, and through my friend Taizen, I did," Boyd said.

Taizen walked out to where he was and stood beside him. Boyd was a bit shocked, but continued, improvising.

"This is Taizen, who I met on this very ship. We shared the common belief of disliking the sub-human invasion, and together, me, Taizen, and a smart guy named Joei took down their leader. You see, things weren't as simple as them coming to Earth and invading it. There's a deeper story to it. Twelve humans once lived here, much like you and I, but the main difference was their intelligence. This trait put them way beyond what humans could achieve technologically, and they all had ideas they wanted to share with the world. Unfortunately, their ideas were too far ahead of their time for people, and they were shunned for them. They were banished from the university they were attending, and with no one wanting to hear them out, they stole a rocket, went to Mars, and started a civilization. To sum it up, their time on that planet changed them into a different species entirely, and they became sub-humans, as they call themselves. Though I don't condone their actions with the invasion and their grudge against humanity, it is understandable to a degree. I managed to talk with these leaders, and they decided they didn't want to live the way they were anymore. There was a leader among these leaders who held an intense grudge against humanity and caused the whole society to adopt his intense feelings. Had I not taken him down, it's unlikely any of this would be happening right now. Now, to the point: These leaders would like to propose a peace treaty, in which they agree to cease all hostile action against humanity if the president of the United States should accept this treaty.

They would also want to share their technological achievements with humanity and allow humanity to share their own culture with sub-humans. As someone who has gotten to talk to them, I strongly suggest you pass this peace treaty, as they, as well as I, would like to see our two kinds come together in peace."

It had ended up shorter than Boyd had wanted, but the task was done. The sub-humans and the human soldiers simply stared at the two for several seconds before a sub-human yelled, "Who do you think you are to try to tell us what to do?"

"Allies of the Elders themselves, that's who," Sammy said. She had walked out beside Boyd, and the rest of the Elders followed suit. In a few seconds, all ten stood beside Boyd and Taizen. The sub-human soldiers couldn't believe it.

"Y-yes, my Elder! My sincerest apologies for any doubt I had!"

The sub-human made a small bow toward Sammy.

"How about you sub-humans come into the ship and cease your fighting?"

"Yes, My Elder!"

The rest of the sub-humans gathered into a group and headed toward the ship. The human soldiers looked confused at what was going on. Boyd decided to leave the ship and talk to one of these soldiers.

"So, uh, you guys wouldn't happen to know how to get in contact with the president himself, would you?"

***

"I'm surprised how fast they admitted us," Marty said. The whole group of Elders, as well as Boyd, were walking down the hallway that led to the president's office. Taizen, Joei, and the rest of the sub-humans had stayed behind on the ship, while Boyd and the Elders were flown to the White House. The president had heard about the Elders promising to cease the invasion upon their arrival and wanted to meet with them.

"Well, you guys *are* the leaders of sub-humankind, so it's not that much of a surprise, considering you all declared your intentions of peace," Joei said. "We were probably urgent cases, since it involves a war, not to mention otherworldly beings, technically."

With that, they reached the end of the hallway, where the security guards at the door outside the office admitted them. Inside, the president awaited them, sitting at a fancy, brown wooden desk full of papers and books. He sat in front of a large window, and on each side of him were two tall shelves. Eleven chairs were crammed into the office, seemingly for their visit, making the whole room feel a bit cramped.

"Man, you have NO idea how glad I am for you guys to be here. I literally thought I was gonna have to go to war with you guys and stuff, and I was like 'dude! I don't wanna do this!'" the president said, chuckling a bit to himself.

"Uh, how old are you, exactly?" Marty asked.

"Thirty-six!" the president responded, laughing. "The previous president, before he was president, saw potential in me as a vice-president, and had me join his campaign. I was planning on going into a much smaller government position, but I couldn't say no to such a big opportunity. Unfortunately, he passed away over a year ago, and I had to take over as president. It's such a stressful job at times, believe me."

"So uh, can you introduce yourself, President Clark?" Boyd asked.

"Oh, of course. My name is George A. Clark, but you guys can call me Clark. Sorry for the strange informal language; I just never get to talk like that around anyone else with all the serious matters I have to deal with," Clark said, shaking each of the Elder's hands and Boyd's. "Anyway, let's get to the matter at hand."

"Of course. In brief terms, we're the leaders of the sub-humans. We want to apologize on behalf for what we've done, and have chosen to cease all fighting. We would like to propose a peace treaty that stops our fighting and allows us to not only make peace with humanity, but also to share our technological advancements with you, too. In exchange, you could share your culture with us and help us populate and terraform Mars," Sammy said.

"Right, right...you guys are like aliens, right? That's super cool. Plus, you guys claim to be smart? Extra cool, too. Sorry,

sorry, I almost geeked out there. I was a big fan of aliens and sci-fi stuff as a kid, still am to some degree. Anyway, let's discuss this peace treaty. The United States would definitely appreciate that you sub-human leaders make peace with us, so I don't think that'll be an issue. I'm very sorry to hear about the rejection you all faced during your university years. Personally, I think your intelligence will in fact be seen as cool now, so I wouldn't worry about that anymore. Just to be sure, the peace treaty involves the sub-humans ending their war with humans, making peace with humans, sharing their technological advances with humans, and humans sharing their culture with sub-humans and helping to populate and terraform Mars. Did I hear that right?"

"Yes, those are the terms."

"Okay, would you mind if I add something to this peace treaty?"

"Sure, I guess. What is it?" Marty asked, skeptical.

"Trust me, it would help you guys. I think we need to add one of those equality terms, where humans can't treat you guys differently due to your race, or in this case, species. It seems obvious, though this is the first time humanity is making any sort of agreement with an alien species, so I do feel it would be helpful to add this in. Of course, I'll also see if we can get an amendment proposed as well to truly set it national law. I will also hold meetings with the leaders of other countries to forge the path toward peace with the planet."

325

"Hmm, that sounds pretty good, actually."

The rest of the Elders nodded at that.

"Well, then, it's settled. You guys agree?"

"Yes!" all the Elders shouted, smiling.

"Well, then, I'll get an official document created with these terms and try to get an amendment passed with the equality thing. I'm happy that our two civilizations can come together in peace."

The whole room of Elders, plus Boyd, cheered in celebration.

"We did it...you guys have finally made peace," Boyd said before cheering some more.

"Yeah, we did! I don't know where we'd be without you, Boyd. Sacrifices had to be made, but this is probably the best solution we could've been given," Sammy said. "Let's give three cheers for Boyd!" The Elders cheered, picking up Boyd and lifting him up into the air.

"Now let's go back to the ship and pick up Boyd's friends!" Marty said, leading the group while they were still carrying Boyd.

Chapter 56: Peace Achieved! Sub-humans and Humans Unite!

Boyd was surprised by how things turned out. After all, he was only a normal person just a few months ago.

But now, a month had passed since the president approved the peace treaty, and he was shocked at how much had happened since then. Reconstruction of the two major cities affected, Atlanta and New York, had begun a few weeks back, and progress seemed to be coming along nicely. After all, Marty had offered to help with rebuilding, and also gave suggestions on how to incorporate some of their more advanced technology.

The Elders, of course, were very happy to finally be at peace after so much time had passed, and the overall reception of the sub-humans was positive. Things weren't perfect, of course, as some sub-humans were very resistant to the change, but overall, it was working out quite well. The Elders didn't want to abandon everything they had done on Mars, but at the same time, they wanted to spend some time on Earth to become invested in the culture and make their contributions to human society. They knew they couldn't all stay, though, as chaos would ensue with their society if none of them went back after a bit. Claire decided to volunteer and take up the role and become Queen Starpson.

"I just feel like I don't have as much to offer as you guys do. Being the ex-wife of the previous king, I think I need to be the one to go lead them," Claire said when she made the decision. The other nine Elders saw her off, as did Boyd, as she left on the mothership and went back to Mars. "I'll try my hardest to convince the sub-humans back on Mars that peace is what's best for our society, and pave the way for humans to begin to come to Mars."

She had done a good job so far. Boyd had heard from tellings of the Elders that things were stable and that she planned on sending multiple ships to Earth, since many sub-humans were interested in visiting the place. Humans had also wanted to visit Mars, but both the Elders and Clark decided that development with that would need to go slowly.

"We need time to make the whole process of heading to Mars and planning a trip there as safe as possible. You can't be like the Psyborg and head straight there hoping you'll survive," President Clark had said in a public hearing about the topic.

Things had changed with Boyd, too, as well as his family and friends. His parents had gotten worried about what had happened to him, but he managed to get in contact with them and assure them he was all right. He eventually met with them to explain what had happened.

"I'm proud of ya for stepping out of your comfort zone, Johnny boy. You may have been satisfied with a regular life, but seeing you do something like this is incredible," his dad said.

"Uh, thanks, Dad. I just did what I thought was the right thing to do."

His other friends, Nift and Max, had managed to evacuate, but were too busy to respond to Boyd at the time. Boyd hadn't forgotten about them, however, and had decided to contact them after he had gotten settled on Earth. He was glad to hear they were okay, and even hung out with the two without Joei and Taizen so they could catch up with each other. They both had to temporarily move in with their parents since their places had been destroyed. Nift wanted to move back to Atlanta once it was reconstructed, but Max had decided he would find a new home for himself, though he wasn't sure where yet.

"I'm not as attached to the city as you guys are, and I want to try and find a place that will work for me, since Atlanta isn't going to be active for a while," Max said. As for his new friends, Taizen decided he wanted to live on Earth, and Joei wanted a better space to work on his projects. President Clark wanted to compensate them for all the work the three had done and decided to buy any house they wanted, and gave them a check for ten million dollars to help with living expenses.

"You're joking, right?" Boyd had asked.

"Nope. It may be a lot, but you guys saved Earth from being invaded and potentially wiped out. Not to mention, you also managed to make peace with that same civilization that was trying to do so. I think you guys deserve it."

329

They agreed but still thanked Clark profusely for the gift. Boyd's only preference was to live in Atlanta, so he could still work at the same job once the shop opened back up. Joei and Taizen agreed with that. Even though Pang had moved to a temporary location in another city, he planned to reopen the local shop once the building had been repaired.

"I'm proud of you, Boyd, and feel bad for not believing in you before. Maybe we can serve some sub-human cuisine at the shop soon in honor of the peace treaty," Pang said when Boyd had come to visit the temporary location.

"I get it, Mr. Pang. It's hard to believe in such absurd things until they happen, so I don't blame you. Also, that's very kind of you."

Regarding the house, the three decided to go with a house with the largest garage they could find, so Joei could work on his projects. It also had a basement area, which combined with the garage, was larger than what Joei had worked in previously. He planned on finding ways to make himself stronger so he could stand up for himself if trouble ever came. They had almost finished moving in, but there were still a few more boxes to unpack.

That was the least of Boyd's worries, however. They had to fly out to Washington, D.C., as Boyd was chosen to receive the Medal of Freedom by President Clark himself. He was to receive the medal at noon, and it was already ten. Luckily, they had all gotten up early in their hotel room, so they were all getting ready. Boyd was the most nervous, as he needed to make a small speech for the occasion. He was already fully dressed and sitting on his bed. He just needed to write the speech before they left. Even though it was only a paragraph he had to write, he struggled getting the first sentence down on paper. Joei saw Boyd struggling and walked over.

"Don't stress it, Boyd. Look at what you've done already, making peace with both parties. There's not that much at stake here; just write down what you wanna say. I think the audience, and Clark, will be content with that," Joei said, putting an arm around Boyd.

"That sounds like a good idea. Thanks, Joei."

"No problem. You've got this."

Boyd thought for a few moments before knowing exactly what he wanted to say.

***

The crowd was giant, with the entire building being packed. Hundreds of fancy chairs lined both the bottom and second floors of the building. Luckily, the Elders, plus Boyd's friends, Joei and Taizen, were given front-row seats, appointed by President Clark himself, so they could see the event clearly. Boyd's other friends, Nift and Max, were also toward the front of the crowd, sitting alongside Boyd's parents. Even Mr. Pang had come to see the ceremony, sitting beside Nift and Max as well. They could all barely contain their excitement, as the event was about to start.

The president walked over to the mic and started the event.

"Ladies and gentlemen, I'm quite glad to see all of you here today. Welcome! As you should all know by now, John Boyd, who also goes by Boyd as well as his warrior name, 'Psyborg,' was the one who fought off the sub-humans who invaded our planet, then went all the way to Mars and even defeated their oppressive leader. He then came back to Earth and convinced their leaders to make peace with a treaty, unit-ing the two races. Needless to say, Boyd was a clear candidate for this award, as it is the highest honor I can bestow upon a citizen. Boyd, come on and get up here!" Clark said, waving his hands toward him.

Boyd stood up, speech in hand, and walked to the mic. The crowd's applause went wild, with some cheering happen-ing as well, especially from the Elders and Boyd's friends. "Boyd, for your outstanding action against the sub-humans, defending against them, taking their corrupt leader down, and even making peace with them, I present to you the Medal of Freedom, the highest award I can bestow upon you."

The crowd went wild, cheering everywhere and clap-ping. After a bit, they stopped to let Boyd speak.

"Thank you, everyone. I'm very happy, and honored, to accept this award from the president himself. I want to make it clear that it was a great shame to have to take down their leader. That sub-human meant a lot to other sub-humans, and although he was evil when I met him, he was not always that way. He used to be a determined young man who was both very intelligent and kind to his accomplices. Unfortunate circumstances changed him for the worse, and if it were possible, I would have wanted him to be a part of the peace between humans and sub-humans. Anyway, I have some people I'd like to thank for helping me get this far. Firstly, I want to thank the one that allowed me to get as far as I did due to the technology he provided me, Joei. I also want to thank Taizen, my sub-human friend, who showed me the ins and outs of his society and helped me take down their corrupt king. Finally, I want to thank each of the Elders, the leaders of sub-human society. They are Marty, Claire, Sammy, Pierce, Howard, Blake, Rachel, Beth, Stewart, and Ted. They all agreed to make peace with humans, even though they didn't have to. Let's give three cheers to all of them!" Boyd said.

The crowd cheered harder than before, and the applause continued as the President placed the Medal of Freedom around Boyd's neck.

"Three cheers to Boyd as well!" Clark said, smiling. The loud cheering and applause continued for Boyd, and he simply grinned at it all.

Acknowledgements

Writing this book was a blast, but there are several people who have allowed me to get this far and publish this book, so I want to thank them all here.

Firstly, I want to thank God again, for being there when I was uncertain on decisions and helping me to move forward with it one way or another.

I want to thank Mrs. Branden as well, my former college professor, for helping me out with the book early into its writing. Not only was she there to praise the book and encourage me to keep writing it, but she even helped edit parts of the book.

I also want to thank my mom and dad for encouraging me throughout the entire writing process. It was nice having people to send new chapters to after I had completed them, just to get initial feedback on them.

Thank you to Colin, a very good friend of mine, who I initially pitched the synopsis of this book to several years ago, when it was just a basic idea, and telling me to move forward with it. It may have taken me a bit to act on that, but it's awesome to have support from you.

Thanks to Nita, a fellow author, who came during a time when I was slow to making progress on the book, and showing me all of the post-writing processes I needed to go through in order to get my book published. She's the reason this book is out as soon as it is.

Thank you to my editor Laura Kenney, who did a fantastic job with editing the book and helping to clean it up. Your work has not gone unappreciated.

Lastly, I want to thank YOU the reader, for taking time out of your life to read through this book. I hope you enjoyed it!

ABOUT THE AUTHOR

 **A.J. TRIMBLE** has had a love for story-telling from a young age, writing stories since he was ten years old. He also wrote multiple short stories during his middle school years. He chose to pursue writing as a career during his high school years, starting with Psyborg, which he began writing in 2021.

He does more than writing, though. He also is a YouTuber and a mechanic of sorts. Even outside of that, he's had a love for video games from a very young age, and is a fan of older music, often either playing his drum set to a tune or listening to it.